Beside the Sickle Moon

A PALESTINIAN STORY

Thaer Husien

Daraja Press

Published by Daraja Press
https://darajapress.com

© 2024 Thaer Husien

ISBN: 978-1-998309-29-0

Library and Archives Canada Cataloguing in Publication

Title: Beside the sickle moon : a Palestinian story / Thaer Husien.
Names: Husien, Thaer, author.
Identifiers: Canadiana 20240460413 | ISBN 9781998309290 (softcover)
Subjects: LCGFT: Novels.
Classification: LCC PS3608.U77 B47 2024 | DDC 813/.6—dc23

This novel is one of defiance, speaking to Palestinian resistance, friendship, and community with searing honesty and penetrating depth. Husien has constructed a protagonist who reflects on the importance of disobedience and refusal in the face of annihilation. What I love most about this book is its confrontation of loneliness and futility and the desire to charge towards a future anyway.

– **Noor Hindi**, author of *Dear God, Dear Bones, Dear Yellow*

In his auspicious first novel, *Beside the Sickle Moon*, Thaer Husien dares to dream a complicated dream about what is to come. For Palestinians, the dystopian form is not a prophecy of a feared future, but a description of the present. Inviting us into the daily decisions that Palestinians like Laeth and Aylul must make about their individual and collective existences in their increasingly colonized town, Husien does more than humanize his people. He implicates us all, inviting us to avoid his nightmare – yet all too realistic – prophecy.

– **Philip Metres**, author of *Fugitive/Refuge*

Perhaps the most remarkable feat of this near-future literary novel is that Thaer Husien wrote it while parrying, as only a Palestinian could, his own people's extermination. As Israel's genocidal campaign continues to ravage Gaza, Husien pits pen against sword to imagine a land still inhabited by its indigenous Palestinians, even as it remains scarred by our singularly dark present. That the Palestinians in Husien's telling remain front-and-center – full of complicated interior lives – makes *Beside the Sickle Moon* something more than a literary achievement. It is, like Palestine itself, a kind of yearning.

– **Samer Badawi**, journalist with bylines in *+972 Magazine*, *Al Jazeera*, *The Nation*

To my ancestors
For Palestine

Acknowledgments

At the time of this writing, the majority of western outlets have estimated for several months straight that approximately 40,000 Palestinian martyrs have ascended in the current Gaza genocide while The Lancet and anyone with bloodshot eyes knows the figure nears 200,000 in just ten months. I often wonder if those in death camps poxed around Palestine are counted now, later, or ever. As for the ongoing Nakba in the so-called West Bank, the Zionist entity continues to mutate settlements like cancer on indigenous land. This is to the armed freedom fighters resisting colonial revisionism, the life givers, caretakers, healthcare workers, civil defense forces, journalists, teachers, cooks, artists, people, kids; to the millions of hearts and hands I call relatives from the river to the sea, I won't dare ask forgiveness. To my fellow diaspora: may we absolve ourselves in the eventual, literal understanding when they say it is a jihad until victory or martyrdom in all of its spectrum light.

I give my undying love and gratitude for their support to my mother and heart, Abeer. My father and spine, Anas; my sisters and steel nerves, Suehad and Jeanine, and to my teta and best friend in the whole wide world, Basema. Thank you dearly to my editor and guide from rookie to debut, Firoze Manji and the team at Daraja Press. And to every past, present, and future ally made along the way that I wish I could list for as many pages as this story needed: here's to you for being the better bones of belief.

SIDE **A**

1

hear the rhythmic pin-drop of muffled revenge from tunnels being dug twenty meters beneath my feet. The scrapped remains of Hamas stain their hands umber with dirt, gripping jackhammers tight under artificial light. They breathe through kufiyah swathed across their perspiring faces. The acrid nostalgia of what should have been keeps their muscles from failing. But the earlier expressions walking into my convenience store told me all that I really needed to know about their true disposition: they're sick of this shit. I am, too, only it isn't losing the struggle for Palestine that has me tapping my Converse shoes against the concrete floor. Their superior, Mo'taz, is half an hour into slow-counting money he owes while Aylul waits in the truck outside.

"Have I ever told you The Tale of the Ox and Donkey, Laeth?" His baleful eyes look up at me. They're strained red, glowing in dark sockets concave from lack of sleep and cheap cocaine. Mo'taz kicks his boots up on the register, knocking over a Kent Cigarettes hologram ad flickering neon blue. I wait for the stout man to regain his composure, wondering how many of his friends he's seen die.

"Once or twice – hey, listen..." I'm in no mood for the same old story. Given the chance, we'll be here for hours. I've got little patience for more disjointed stories while he scratches lice out of his mustache. It'll end with us bleeding out on the floor, and I just mopped. "I've gotta head out. As always, *ma'lim*, it's good doing business." It takes a second yank to get the wad of cash out of his thick-ringed fingers. Without a glance, I make my way to the front door between porcelain-tiled aisles of gumdrops and ketchup-flavored chips, cardboard toilet paper, and hanging bananas; women's perfume imported thirty years ago mingling with pita bread and canvas sacks of sunflower seeds.

"I must say, with the hero of Jericho dead – *Allah Yarhamu* – it's a shame to see his daughter living out her days with such little purpose." Mo'taz pauses to clear the tar from his throat. "She ignores an offer for leadership, then counters with discounted space for digging operations? It's an insult! A scandal! Khalid's sacrifice sinks further in vain each day as she pretends this lazy charity is enough for the Cause. Willfully deaf to the *Hadith*, living with a man she isn't married to!" He tugs at his paisley button-up, sweat flying off tungsten prayer beads entangled in his chest hair.

Whatever he's on seems to be fading fast. "Enough." I turn, aiming the onyx muzzle of my Taurus .22 at his head. I barely knew my uncle when he was alive, but I'll be damned if I let this zealot speak ill of his legacy. I like to think that in the time it took for the blood to drain from his face, Mo'taz acknowledges that the mistake he made is thinking power exempted him from entropy. In that space, there's no time to consider that I've never once pulled the trigger.

"Aylul's charity wasn't cheap rent: that was me. It's been six months without a thank you; you're welcome. It's my pleasure – really – where would we be if we forgot the hospitality of our ancestors? But no, MoMo, their gift was letting you live even though you're spreading that trite shit all over Ramallah." I take a few steps forward to highlight the five inches I have on Mo'taz and aim at his heart. "From now on, you'll take whatever Aylul gives you as benevolence. Nod if you understand."

Mo'taz complies, sweat dripping down his neck. I take a beat to close my eyes and bury the adrenaline. When he averts his gaze from the gun to me, I wink and turn the weapon over to reveal no mag and an empty chamber.

"*Ya hayawan!*" he shrieks, scrambling for something to throw. "You can't treat a captain of Al Qassam this way!" A can of Pringles launches, my wavy brown mane softening a blow to the head. "If this was ten years ago –!"

"You'd be three years away from becoming what you once were instead of seven into thinking you still are." I walk behind the counter and reach over his head for a pack of cigarettes, tear the aluminum, and pop one between my lips. Not a tremor. Mo'taz is a lot of things ugly, but a coward isn't one of them. Meandering my way back to the front aisles, I recall something as I push through the glass door. "Tell your guys not to shit in the bathroom this time, it still doesn't flush."

Living in a village turned two-star town all my life hasn't stopped the weekend summer skyline from making me feel invincible. There's a whiff of cardamom in the dusty breeze as I crunch along the gravel lot to a beat-off tune with the mating calls of sunbirds hidden in wilted palm trees. Delivery drones hum and buzz along their routes overhead against a backdrop of missile-thin clouds. I straighten out my leather jacket, excited for a night of possibilities.

Just five kilometers from Ramallah's southern checkpoint, Ayn Yassin is one of the last bastions of agriculture near the city. If it wasn't for the lazy river bleeding nutrients right along the spine, everyone's persimmon orchards wouldn't stand a chance on the otherwise rugged land. With the ozone nothing more than a childhood memory, it was only a matter of time before it dried up like the Dead Sea. Maybe another decade or two, it doesn't matter. Too many people started throwing trash in the water ever since some fool with a loud mouth mentioned how it might reach the Zionists upstream.

I look back at my father's shop as Mo'taz turns off the OPEN sign. Aylul's been pushing for a paint job, but I like the contrast between our limestone store and the vogue glass condo nestled on top. There's a trend nowadays to decorate homes with SnapSmart tech that tailor-fits iron bar *girih* against stone, but I see them as self-made prisons. It would be an insult to my parents after all their hard work renovating the space before they left for the States. It's been a couple of years, but it's still hard to imagine they trusted me with the shop after I declined their offer to live in Dearborn, which reminds me I should call. The truck's horn slaps me out of the memory.

"If you're done staring at the clouds, we've got places to be more colorful than this." Aylul leans over the passenger seat, a knockoff Armani suit fit for a funeral snagging on the driver's side window. They burst out laughing at my seizure, cranking the volume on the stereo to hide behind synchronized guitar riffs.

The noise upsets a street dog passing through, its chestnut coat spiking before it barks in my direction. I ignore the offense, jogging instead to greet my femme fatale. Gray sleet stardust painted on metal curvature meant to resist nature's might stands on twenty-inch black aluminum legs, each autonomous from the other. Shadow-tinted LEDs gaze unblinkingly at twilight, eager to witness land ravished. Opening the door, I lean on the side step and swing into the red-cushioned bliss of my Dodge Warlock.

"Where to?" I dial the music down and ask again.

Aylul sinks into their chair, tugging at a loose afro curl before popping the overhead mirror to apply caramel blush. "Cid wants to grab lumpia from that new restaurant before your big night."

It takes forty minutes longer than it should to get out of Ayn Yassin thanks to the new checkpoint; Israeli militants in scarab scale armor and automatic weapons lazily litter around a wooden cross lever, stopping cars to chat amongst each other. Whether you cuss or plea, it makes no difference unless someone leans too far out of their window. Such an offense gets you dragged out of your vehicle and into detainment. The occupiers ask whoever was with them to move the car or push it in a ditch. Aylul doesn't say a word until we get through, and even then, it's only to ask why I sprayed so much cologne.

It's not long before we reach the dune edge of Ayn Yassin. Here on Muzayin Street, mechanic shops line both sides of the median for the last kilometer stretch to Ramallah. Rusted tin and stone garages all advertise the same variation of chrome rims next to handwritten cardboard signs promising a better deal than the other guy. One of the greater mysteries of the universe is how they manage to stay alive clustered together like this. Muscle memory takes me left while I try to figure it out, easing the breaks and shifting to park in front of a scrapyard.

Cid Silang pushes through the front door of the forward-facing shed, white-toothed grin reaching past his aviators. He does a little jig, brown locks dancing in the wind, dusting off his Tommy Bahama shirt on his way to the truck with a shimmy. Aylul laughs, but I sense something forced in it.

"Diwa's hanging back; she's got a client in an hour." Cid's accent flows into Arabic like baritone silk when he enters. "Ya'll going to the protest later?"

"Haven't heard much about it," I reply, then ask, "Where?"

"Southern checkpoint at sunset," Aylul says shrugging at my raised eyebrow. "Mo'taz told me about it. Loads of media are coming; it's a good marketing opportunity for Fatah to peddle a unified front. All it took were outposts popping up and now they want to pretend Ayn Yassin matters –"

While Aylul and Cid talk politics, I focus on pin-drop pianos scaling through bass bubbles and synth waves, tip-tapping my finger along to off-rhythm thoughts of torn banners and tear gas burning the sky. I'm scared, but something inside me breathes a second wind: purpose. Now I'm scared shitless. Goosebumps raise the hairs on my arms. I try to suffocate grandiose notions of stopping rising tides by raising the volume.

Driving into Ramallah feels like leaving the past and entering the present of a different reality. Visiting the city so often never stops me from staring at the monument that greets those coming from the southern road. An onyx pillar etched with the silhouette of faceless crouching bodies erects skyward, a robed man chiseled from stone stands atop them, presenting the sun for all to witness. Cid notices me ogling the statue and chuckles before returning to a harmonized hum with the radio.

I direct us to cut through the area of the new-age metropolis in order to get to Little Manila quicker. You can hear Western currency breathing through the mortar and pipes in this borough: Roman pillars, even sidewalks, glass skyscrapers, and a Wendy's finer than most sit-down restaurants in Ayn Yassin. Here, you can visit national museums and nightclubs on the same block, shop at H&M or Zara, and find the USAID mansion next to karaoke bars, Turkish baths, and Thai food joints. Drones traffic fifty feet above us to lights and intersections different from our own. Self-driving vehicles honk their horns at my truck's manual errors as they pass. Hologram models catwalk between buildings, showcasing this season's latest lines of jewelry and fashion. Three-dimensional LEDs twirl spits of lamb dripping off awnings to form the perfect shawarma. The Abdel Nasser Mosque stands purposefully at the center, its Islamic spire grasping crescent tips toward heaven. The *adhan* blares through the loudspeakers, barely a muffle over the hustle and grind. It is gentrification at its finest, and like the deprived asshole I am, I love being here.

You know you're in Little Manila once you feel the violent rumble of cobblestone streets. The houses here are built on top of one another without regulation, mismatched puzzle pieces of anything that could be nailed or soldered together. As we hobble along, my destination comes into view: a steep hill outlined with contrasting buildings of bright blue, orange, and yellow. The three of us stop at a hole-in-the-wall Cid found online claiming to have the best beef lumpia in the city. Half a dozen picnic tables in the back facing an empty lot make up the dining area, all but two filled with American immigrants called expats sharing their roughin' it stories. From the sound of it, they're scholars varying from recent grads to retired professors, ruminating on a better life when they could flush mountains of paper down the toilet. All have VitaStim gills protruding from their wrists.

Years ago, when global climate reached a point of no return we all saw coming, reserves in countries along the equator hit an all-time low. To combat this, the United Nations pushed big tech corporations for a humanitarian solution. They discovered a method to capture moisture in the air to maintain constant hydration powered by the user's heart. While ingenious in theory, the faulty prototypes were tested on the poor while refined models were bedazzled for public consumption. The water conductors need to be replaced every six to twelve months depending on the make and brand; otherwise, the generators leak toxins into the bloodstream. For most here, it's more affordable to scrape thirty shekels for a day's worth of bottled water than five thousand upfront for a year's endless supply.

The expats' voices are louder than the overhead sound system straining a Beatles cover band. A man with a widow's peak thinner than my patience is haggling down a waitress to be his maid. She just arrived from the Philippines, she explains; *and doesn't know better than to set a fair price,* I think, while she goes over her list of services. I peek up from my fried roll at Aylul when one of the younger girls with a diamond Stim expresses how backward a country must be for not legalizing gay marriage.

"What would a Band-Aid on an artery wound know of complicated delights when they can't even honor basic human rights?" Aylul interrupts. The voices die down. An accented "Strawberry Fields Forever" crackles overhead; a meek apology follows from the table like a wisp. Aylul rolls their eyes and crumples an aluminum wrapper. "We're heading out."

I glance at Cid to gauge a reaction, but he's too busy staring down the expats behind me, so I stuff the last roll in my mouth and get up to leave.

With as much as two "I don't care's" to go off, I don't know where else to go but the Olive Tree. Blasting the air conditioner to cool some heads, I take us the long way up narrow streets that wind around the *jabal*. There's a bazaar strip between limestone high rises; women in lilac hijabs haggling prices beside dismembered mannequins. Laughter spills out of barbershops the size of my kitchen. *Ka'ik* stands reused from library shelves filled with sesame bread, rawboned fish on melting ice by the side of the road, and my personal favorite: five-table, no frills, card-dealing hookah lounges. I imagine it's Palestine that comes to mind whenever someone takes up arms against Israel, but it never settled well with me to have our poorest form be our highest aspiration. There's an irony that places like these aren't wholly defined by gentrification and survival, an essence that can't be found in the upscale parts of the city where Palestinian Authority execs languish.

Back in the chrome metropolis, I parallel park outside a monolith of tinted glass windows outlined in gold. Back in 2048, while Zionists celebrated a hundred years, the wealthiest moguls in Palestine built The Royale as a message of fortitude to their people. At the time, unemployment was at a dismal 51%, and land was being swallowed faster than Sheikh Omar knew how to guzzle profit. Most of us thought the end had finally come. So the linchpins reckoned if people saw a hotel that rivaled Burj Khalifa, confidence in foreign investment, and therefore improved quality of life, would soar. Never once crossed their minds that, lies or not, half a billion looked better in our stomachs. Now that the future's here, The Royale's lasting impression is one of backroom pipeline deals between the King of Jordan and the Knesset further dividing Palestine like their forefathers before them.

The three of us walk through sliding glass doors and frayed pixel walls past an unmanned front desk, our footsteps echoing down marble corridors branching off into empty rooms. We reach the far wall, which transforms into a digital night sky where a sapling blooms into olive tree branches with keys dangling amid the leaves. A dozen doves encircle above like a halo made of starlight, birds pulsing white in the growing expanse until the entire wall before us is a blank slate. From the middle a crack appears, widening until the elevator warmly greets us with an automated hello as we step inside. With the rest of the floors the same as the first, going halfway to the 36th floor is the only option the program grants us. I voice confirmation and in seconds, the doors reopen.

Metallic purple curtains fold back to unveil our regular watering hole. When the Olive Tree first opened, only the finest in Ramallah could catch reservations if they planned days in advance. Palm trees rose as high as the mosaic dome ceiling, the floor beneath an interactive display of guests' footprints on white sand beaches.

Back then, one could grab a fifty-shekel cocktail of fireworks in a martini glass while performance troupes and local pop stars dazzled the crowds on the magnet stage floating in the center. Now black holes dot the sands, palms wilted brown by gravity and negligence. Cracks web across the sapphire tile overhead, the stage replaced by a touchscreen jukebox off in the corner by the bar. Low-rank Fatah militant grunts clutter around half a dozen tables, chain-smoking cigarettes between passing puffs of double apple hookah clouds. They hoot and groan like rabid dogs at each play of hand, much to the annoyance of a black-clad waitress just trying to hear an order.

"We get the table, you grab the drinks," Aylul says, already heading for the balcony.

I'm about to mention that this is the fifth time I've paid when I notice their eyes darting around, presumably searching for any sign of Leila. We part ways crossing the opposite side of the room, broken digitized footsteps treading sand with an old Fairuz love ballad melancholic in the airwaves. I nod to the tuxedo bartender, new on the scene – Malik, I think – but the amateur bodybuilder stays fixated on a video reflected in his contact lenses, hands rubbing his shaved head.

"Hey, is Leila working?" I ask, leaning over the counter.

"Tonight," he replies vaguely. "Goddamn Fatah," he mutters more to himself, "cannibals the second TFO shows up. If they'd put half that energy into the Cause instead of running when the Yahud show up..." Malik's voice trails off when flames bloom in his iris. He blinks twice to cut the feed.

I avert my gaze away from the luminescent shelves of liquor so I can push the taboo topic. "I take it you wave the white flag?"

Affiliating yourself with The Forgotten Ones, a social movement resurging among younger Palestinians, is a quick way to get your ass kicked anywhere outside a college campus. Coining the derogatory term that their critics slung at them, the grassroots NGO advocates for a peaceful transition to Israel's one-state conquest where most Palestinians hear whimpers of surrender.

"Nah," he glances around like he's nervous to lose his job. "I'm no normalizer; just sayin' we're livin' in stone bubbles, but they're still beggin' for '67 borders? C'mon, bro."

"Hmm," is all that's required for his shoulders to slack, "What were you watching? Last week's shit show in Huwara?"

"Ayn Yassin," the bass in his voice threatens to crack the glass he's shining, "bastards never stood a chance."

My heart drops through the earth. "The protest isn't until sunset."

Malik shrugs me away to hear an order. "Dunno what to tell ya," he says eventually. "Looks like the party started early. Now, what can I get ya to drink?"

I break away from the bar and cross the cracked beach fast. Pushing through the glass doors to the balcony, a sense of vertigo lifts my nausea horizontally, adjusting to the glass floor half a kilometer off the street. Cid and Aylul lean over the railing due south where soft plumes of smoke rise just before the ridge. They turn as I approach, fists at their sides saying more than words can. Silence clouds my hometown at this distance except for the whoosh of the wild wind blowing. The gun stashed in my glove compartment comes to mind as I watch smoke rise.

"Let's go," is all I say to get us moving.

Testing the redline, I push the truck's engine to shave half the time getting home, its four-wheel drive ravenously chewing through dirt roads and tight turns. We're not far from the checkpoint when we hit a fifty-car backup. Aylul instructs me to pull off to the shoulder to park. As the others climb out, I open the glove compartment and grab the pistol, wedging it behind my waistline. Once I open the door, a cacophony of wild arguments and shapeless screaming overwhelms the senses. The familiar *pop, pop, pop* of teargas canisters reverberate as streams of choking white clouds arc over and into the crowd. Those with something to prove grab the piping hot metal with the shirts off their backs, tossing them away from the others. Few attach the canisters bursting with steam to mechanized slingshots; lasers detect the distance between them and IOF fifty meters back before sending it to return address. Protesters in the rear wave Palestinian flags while some Lebanese, South African, Irish, Yemeni, and even Israeli flags rise above their heads, shoulder to shoulder. Men, women, but mostly children raise their fists as people in Hamas green and Fatah yellow roll tires to the frontlines chanting, *"Bil roh, bil dem, nafdiqa ya Falastin!" With soul, with blood, we will defend you, Palestine!* It takes several repetitions, but soon they are one voice.

We three stand arms-crossed on the outskirts of the crowd. We've been here countless times before, now watching for catalysts: an occupying prom king raising his gun too high, hive mind reactive sways, a Palestinian stepping too far over the tire line. If this were fifteen years ago, I'd be wrapped in a *kufiyah* taking a sledge hammer to bus stops for ammunition too. But watching rubble crumble under a sonic shield's pressure does the same to the soul over a lifetime; really puts things into perspective. It doesn't matter how deeply one believes. All three hundred here have at some point felt the stolen strength of Goliath. For some, it burns a new dimension to their fury. Others alchemize despair into suicidal bravery. For most of the five thousand behind the checkpoints in Ayn Yassin, it's praying for good health and good luck.

"Move!" English assaults us from behind. A forgettable man hidden by a trucker hat leans out of a slow-moving news van late to the development. He pushes Cid to the side as he gets out of the vehicle to set up a trifold camera bigger than my torso. The rooftop satellites hum as journalists jump out in scarab armor the same as the IOF's. The only difference is a sticker that says PRESS on their chests. A hooded person unpacks a dozen dragonfly drones from Styrofoam briefcases to record from up high while a few flutters and sift through the crowd with prerecorded questions to interview protesters.

A commotion stirs at the nucleus of the masses, limbs tangling into themselves before a bubble ripples from the core. In a tightly knit circle, university students clad in white push their way into expanding far enough for some white-clad boy to raise a ladder. Halfway to the top, one of his ilk hands him a blank banner twice their size to swirl above his head. The kid barely manages a hello to the soldiers behind beige-plated Humvees. For a moment, the tear gas stops and the smell of burning rubber overwhelms the pepper mist. An all-encompassing tide of color demanding justice ebbs back and rushes forward against the receding white circle, their voices lost to a higher purpose. Swarms of platinum-plated dragonflies hurricane above the fray, blocking the sun in a whirl.

"Bil roh, bil dem, nafdiqa ya Falastin!"

Cid and Aylul look over their shoulders at me. We recognize the penumbral moment for what it is. Being the largest, Cid takes mid-point and together we link arms before walking into the maelstrom of twisted faces. Humidity rises the deeper we push, limbs catching limbs like bramble. I can barely see the boy waving the white flag just ten meters away, brow arced, teeth bared in a scream swallowed by screams. Someone punches a girl in White square in the teeth, knocking her bloody to her knees. Another protester shoves her back, and with that, the link's broken and the crowd comes pouring through. An older gentleman pleads with the boy on top of the ladder to come down, but before he can, a protester kicks the ladder out from under him. He falls sideways, briefly suspended in the air, grasping out for a sun eclipsed by a hundred unblinking eyes before gravity claims him to the crowd below.

Keeping my knees bent to sway with each lean and shove, I crane my neck to check in on the Israeli line. I have to blink twice to make sure I'm seeing things right, but sure enough, they're laughing. Some double over, leaning on their partner for support. As if the theatrics weren't enough salt on the wound, none have their weapons ready. Cid tugs at our laced arms, leaning into my ear.

"On me," he shouts, "Aylul wants to get the kid."

Of all the unexpected things to happen at these protests, Aylul guiding us to rescue a normalizer isn't something I would have wagered. To them, the only thing worse than Western colonizers called Zionists are Palestinians uncommitted to the Cause. It's difficult to breathe as we force our way through with our shoulders and elbows to where the boy was last seen. A woman in a suit grapples with a schoolboy who accidentally elbows Cid in the jaw. He barely flinches but spits blood back on the kid's shirt continuing through the crowd. The toxic black smoke of burning tires grows strong enough to blur my vision. Luckily, my stomach's had a lifetime ingesting this shit not to go sideways on me now.

Aylul stops to pull us close. The boy who was once on top of the ladder is sprawled on the ground inches from our feet, eyes obscured by bulbous bloody puffs of broken sockets. I think he's dead until someone steps on his chest, causing him to convulse and wheeze. Aylul scrambles on all fours to lift him up. Cid bends over to help. I clasp my fists together and use my forearms as a barrier against the thrashing protesters. I'm not even sure if they know why they're here anymore. Do they know this is Ayn Yassin?

From the corner of my eyes, I notice a man standing still amid a crashing wave of bodies. He's facing me, and for a moment, I think he's staring back until I realize he's looking through me to where the IOF soldiers observe the fighting.

He looks like many of the other outskirt men in attendance here: a tired, sweat-bleached *taqiyah* stretching over a wrinkled head, *dishdasha* draped over bones. There's something uncanny: his beard isn't moving with the motion of his body. In an instant, a flailing arm from a protester goes through the hairs like gliding over water. Pixelated ripples of artificial light reverberate across the mask, breaking the illusion just long enough to witness the lie in sapphire eyes, shrapnel scars like acne from temple to cheek. The image adjusts and snaps into place.

Then I'm positive he locks eyes with me and winks before lifting a modded Desert Eagle with both hands to shoot. The concussive snap deafens those in the immediate vicinity. Many drop to their stomachs as panic tangles outward through the masses. What was once a school of fish is now a scattered outbreak of people not knowing what they're escaping.

Cid and Aylul get back on their feet with the beaten boy hanging between their lopsided shoulders. I vaguely hear them yell my name over the chaos, but there's a *pop, pop, pop, pop* that grabs my attention more. Occupiers with guns raised hip level taking tighter formations. One of their own is on the ground, blood pooling the dirt into clumps of mud. Another soldier slides to their knees, lifting him up in their arms. That's when I see a hole fit for three fingers where his eye used to be. A teargas canister activates not far from where we stand, searing my eyes to water. Bile burns my throat. I swallow the sensation, looking back for the shooter one last time in vain. So I move to relieve Aylul of their burden. The boy's shirt is in tatters, damp with blood, smells like he pissed himself.

"We've gotta go," I shout just as the *pop* of tear gas turns into the *crack, crack, crack* of live gunfire aimed skyward, ricocheting off the dragonflies back into the crowd. I toss Aylul my keys to the truck and haul the boy with Cid in a weighted sprint. He's heavier than I thought and after a dozen clumsy steps, Cid pushes me away to fireman-carry the boy over his shoulders. I run ahead as an escort, shielding them from protesters as best I can. We're nearly out when a barrel-chested man bulldozes me out of his way, knocking the wind out of me as I fall to my back.

Panic to regain my breath turns to fear of being trampled, but I'm immobilized as my lungs gasp for air. I somehow manage to roll on my stomach so I don't get kicked in the face, but my vision's a saturated pulse of disfigured legs running in opposite directions. I spit congealed dust, chewing and coughing the grit from my mouth. When a semblance of balance returns, the face of a woman in white sharpens into view; black tangled hair covering half of her face, mouth slightly open as if there's a word on the tip of her lips. No light in the dark of her eyes, downcast and unblinking. I follow her line of sight to a hand over a cauterized tunnel clean through her chest. It's tough not to puke. I scream instead. Not this shit again.

A hand grabs me by the wrist and yanks. If they catch me now, they'll use me as a scapegoat. I'll spend the rest of my days in a cage that isn't open air like this. With my free hand, I reach behind me, grip the acrylic handle of my .22, rip it free, and aim at the silhouette. I squeeze the trigger and nothing happens. How could I forget? The blurred figure disarms the gun from my hand with a slap as I scurry back with my legs when Aylul comes into focus.

"You forgot the bullets." They're covered in splatters of dried blood dust like we've been at this a while. They reach out a hand to help me up as if I didn't nearly end their life. "It's fine, hey –" they kneel beside me, face to face, and clasp my shoulder, "I'm fine. But we have to run. Now."

The agency in Aylul's voice anchors me away from the guilt enough to grab their hand and stand on my feet. They press the pistol back into my palm and smile, of all things. I'm shaking but manage to stow it as I gain my bearings. Over half the crowd has vanished, running in every direction away from Ayn Yassin. The news cameras in the sky shield those who remain from an all-out massacre. IOF begins making arrests, tossing hexagonal grenades that expand on impact like five-meter boiling warts radiating cerulean light. The crowd-controlling ultrasonic domes are enough to immobilize a baker's dozen. Ayn Yassin's screams hush under the muffling savagery. I leave the dead woman, taking Aylul's hand home back to the truck. Cid's already in the backseat with the boy from earlier, who's laid horizontal, head on his lap.

"What's your name, kid?"

The boy in tainted white manages to rasp, "Jabriel."

"He'll live," Cid says to us, "but that might change if we don't get him to a hospital soon."

Aylul nods, whipping the truck around to peel off sand back toward Ramallah. In the rearview mirror, Cid's looking down at the boy whispering something I can't quite hear, but it sounds like the scathing words of a worried father. In the growing distance, black smoke and white gasses obscure Ayn Yassin from sight.

Aylul and I wait in the truck outside an elementary school turned hospital while Cid admits the boy into the emergency room. Nothing's playing on the radio, but Aylul's tapping their finger on the steering wheel to a beat of their own in the silence. Staring out the window at the overcast sky, all I see is the girl's bloodless face; the tunnel in her chest. I'm sure she died before having the right to any last thoughts. Something about that bugs me more than her murder. The pungent acidity of burnt flesh can't escape me, even now in the truck rich with sweat on leather.

Rolling down the window, I lean my head out for fresh air. Closing my eyes can't shake the image. I try to focus on the muffled honks and bustling humanity behind us, looking again to the sky for answers that will never come. The blue hidden behind nimbus clouds reminds me of the masked shooter; his true face revealed for only a second, maybe two, but it was long enough to brand the image to mind. There's vague familiarity, but maybe I'm grasping at straws. As with every protest, I'm inching closer down a rabbit hole of self-loathing. Why do we romanticize resisting futility? Stop, stop. I focus on the metronome *tap, tap, tap, tap* of Aylul's finger for a boxed breathing exercise, then sit up straight in my seat.

"I swear," Aylul gets ahead of me, "if you apologize one more time, we'll both have pointed a gun at each other. I'm more inclined to celebrate."

"Celebrate?"

"Might have been empty, but that was the first time you've pulled the trigger, no?" They turn their body to face me, eyes still straining to recover from the tear gas. Bits of rubble entangle their curls, and their blazer is a soot-stained relic, but they smile with the warmth of sincerity.

"Yeah," I say, swallowing disgust.

Before more is said, the door behind me opens. Cid climbs into the truck with a snort, slamming it shut. I turn between seats to scold him, but his face stops me cold. A thick brow furls inward, fluctuating muscles clenching along his jawline.

"Let's swing by the garage," he says. "I need to see Diwa."

We ride back to Ayn Yassin with the radio off and enough on our minds to keep our mouths shut. Despite Aylul's call for celebration, I feel like we should be making our wills. I don't like being forced to confront the fact that I have no one to leave my things to outside of whoever's in this truck. My mind wanders to Sundus, shades of children with my last name double helixing around her. Which side would they be on when they had the strength to stand?

Soon as I exit the truck outside Cid's garage an orange tabby trots toward me from the front gate. I whistle a hello, scooping the cat to cradle him in my arms for scratches. Aylul comes around my side at a distance. Usually the type for animals, they're cautious not to get hair on their clothes.

"Toho always seems to know where the trouble's at." Diwa Silang leans arms crossed against the frame, a contagious dimpled smile bringing out the same in us.

Aylul runs up for a hug, getting swung around like a carousel. "Is it inside?" they ask once on two feet again.

"Top shelf in the bedroom closet," she confirms. "Just got a few more lines to finish up and I'll join ya."

They head inside, and I faintly hear the hum of his Diwa's tattoo gun go back to work not long after. Cid pops a rubber band between his teeth, tying his hair up in a bun, giving me time to pet Toho some more. Keeping with tradition, he offers me coffee or tea.

"Got any wine?" I counter.

Cid wags a finger and starts walking around the shop, gesturing for me to follow. "We celebrate with whiskey in this house, *pare*!" He looks over a broad shoulder at me, a coy twinkle in his eyes. "And I have just the thing."

We make our way behind the garage across the backyard, soles grinding on a desolate plot of totaled cars waiting for Cid to need something specific for a job or hurt bad enough to sell for scrap. Diwa's gun start back up inside the garage as we head to the side shed, the walls between us muffling an excited pitch of gossip.

"Just gotta find it. Take a load off," Cid says, entering his workshop, nodding over to a couch nestled between stacks of spare parts. He turns on the holovision with a command, and two news anchors start arguing on mute in three dimensions. "I know you've got a fetish for products made in hell, so I shipped in somethin' special from home."

I throw myself at the loveseat, peeling attention away from the Technicolor drones fluttering in light. Cid disappears behind the makeshift bar, popping back up a moment later with a liter in one hand and shot glasses in the other. "Evan Williams, brother: smoothest bourbon the States have to offer, I guarantee it."

An hour later, there are knocks at the door, and my legs are feeling heavy. Diwa shoulder charges it seconds later.

"Is this what I can look forward to five years from now?" They make it a point to widen their eyes at the empty tub of *ful* beside me.

I rise from my seat to hug Diwa. She laughs into my shoulder, leading me into a clumsy dance of sorts, and kisses my cheek after a twirl.

"Good news!" She sings, thermochromic lily shimmering burnt orange on her neck. "The ink we ordered arrived just in time, and count yourself—" Diwa asks her husband in English for a translation "—lucky that I liked ya enough to clear my schedule."

"Actually," Aylul interjects. "Laeth reserved a table at the Olive Tree tonight."

"Isn't Leila working?" Diwa asks, shooting me a glare.

"It's okay, I –" they start.

"Are your Forgotten friends gonna be there too, Laeth?" Cid antagonizes over the two.

Not willing to hear what's coming, I lead Diwa by the shoulder to form a circle with the group. "New plan: I get this back piece while ya'll get a pizza. Maybe beat your demons once and for all..." I see temptation's pull tug two pairs of eyes to the VR suits.

"What about everyone waiting?" Aylul grabs my hand, leaning in doe-eyed.

"Fuck 'em," is all I need to say for them to gallop away.

We're a few hours into the session when Diwa informs me it's almost over. I'm laid flat on the cushioned table beneath a car lift, mumbling acknowledgment, too numb-comfortable. My mind's a fuzzy peach under the overhead light, rousing only when several of the blades gash deeply into flesh. I look back and Diwa shakes her beaded dreads at me, mock apology pouting her lips.

"Squid ink." She gently pushes my head back down and presses on. "No easy task taming liquid shadow." Her phone on the tray beside us plays a pensive oud from its speaker, both of us focusing on separate things in silence. After a time, she pats my ribs and asks me to check it out in the three-way mirror.

Moving makes my head hurt, but after a groan or two, I manage to shuffle barefoot across the concrete floor. I turn this way and that to fully capture my first addition. The artwork is in constant, predetermined motion like black dye in water. My dried blood smears across an arrowhead line traveling in a fluid circle from one shoulder blade to the other, cut horizontally through the diameter; axes Z, Y, X marked clockwise in spectral font.

"It's just as I imagined."

"And...what is it again?" Diwa asks.

"A tale as old as time."

After a quick introduction to the monomyth, we make our way back to the shed after wrapping me up in saran wrap, raw back throbbing in pain to the beat of a new step. I open the door, turning to see Aylul snore-drooling against Cid's armpit with Toho curled up on their lap. Cid's face is half covered by a light-pulsing headset, neck craned back over the couch as he snores evenly. Diwa coos when she sees this and takes an antique camera out for a picture, the flash illuminating dust and smoke. We give each other a smile, agreeing with a closed-eye nod that it's time for bed.

It doesn't take long to wake them up, give thanks a dozen times while we cross through the property, and climb back in the truck. Aylul remembers something they left inside when I turn the ignition, running out the door before I get a word in. They return by the time I find my movie scores playlist and settle on something with violins.

"Ready?" I ask, noting the small box on their lap.

"Let's go home."

A few minutes after we leave, Aylul straightens in their seat and nudges my hand with the box. I pull off to the shoulder, sand pluming around the vehicle.

"What's this?"

"Surviving twenty-seven years in this place deserves something." Aylul hands me the gift wrapped in white.

I lose myself to being a kid again, tearing it all off in one swipe only to see a magazine full of bullets when I lift the top. "Aylul, I haven't made a decision and I –"

"– Don't have to say another word." They reach into the glove compartment, take out my handgun, and feed it the mag. "Now you've got a little bite for all that shit you talk."

I receive the black steel from their outstretched hands, feeling the difference in weight. "Thank you," is all I say before storing it in the middle compartment. They squeeze my arm warmly, then turn to face the window as I shift to drive.

My eyes glaze over as I watch yellow dotted lines get swallowed by headlights on the midnight freeway. Distant billboards looping video advertisements for things I'll never need pollute the sky. I turn left off the road toward Ayn Yassin when I'm assaulted by headlights facing my direction. Aylul yelps as I slam on the breaks. We lurch forward against the dash, and they frantically scan every which way. On either side of the street in front of us are two Humvees; between them, a wooden lever roadblock is firmly planted with sandbags. None of this was here when we left. Shit.

One of the doors opens. Aylul's hand slowly move toward the center compartment. I reach their fingers and lace them with mine just as there's a knock at my window. An IOF grunt wielding a rifle meets my gaze from behind a camouflage mask. I roll down the window just a knuckle.

"Identification," a feminine voice speaks broken Arabic like chewing teeth.

To avoid drawing this out, I use my free hand to dig my card from denim pockets and hand it over. When she reaches for it I notice the lack of gills from a VitaStim on her wrist. Interesting; usually, all Zionists had them implanted when they were forced into service as an incentive to stay. It's hard to breathe steadily, even when the soldier heads back to check my information. Aylul takes the time to curse their ancestors for existing. We wait far too long for the hundred pounds of propaganda and body armor to saunter back from her fortress. She yawns as she approaches, stretching her limbs out in a proud display of boredom.

"Happy birthday," is all she says, tossing my card through the slit before walking away.

"Wait!" I roll the window down further.

The figure turns, eyes glaring. "We have the right to know what's going on here," I say.

The soldier laughs, flashing the light on their gun at a sign that was hidden in darkness.

"What does it say?" Aylul seethes.

"The Ministry of Defense is proud to announce the future construction of the luxury hotel..." I read slowly, eyes scanning and burning through Hebrew for a date. When I find it, my heart sinks: only a month away.

Aylul has been here once before and requires no further explanation. "What'll they call it?"

The truck's still moving when Aylul hops out, storming toward the store as if magnetized by self-fulfilling prophecies. I park as quickly as I can, grab the keys, and trot after them. An owl hoots on a night too cold for September given the new season rotations. Something shiny gleans off the moon around the corner and I crane my neck, surprised to see Mo'taz's Lada still here. Aylul's raising their voice inside, triggering memories of the first time they came to live with us almost a decade ago. Who knew two liberal arts degrees with different methods to the Palestinian condition would short-fuse like a shoe bomb. Goddamn, it's cold. I rub my hands together and push a shoulder through the front door.

"You're taking me to see your boss tonight." Aylul grabs Mo'taz by the collar, causing his five gangly pawns to step closer.

The man's drenched in sweat after digging tunnels for hours, jawline flexing like a threat. But he knows the family name they carry, so instead, he raises a hand for his men to back off. "As I said..." He takes a slow step back, allowing Aylul the opportunity to let go, and they do. "It doesn't matter who you are, you cannot just summon him on a whim. There must be time to secure a location, make sure the Shin Bet rats aren't on our tail – *ya rub*, Aylul – think."

I realize with disgust that I'm impressed with his composure for a man who seems on the cusp of withdrawal. "Think," he says, making a show of running his hands through thinning curls. His eyes roll back closed. He follows this by sucking air between pursed lips in a type of shrill ohm between a few Allahu Akbar's, peripheral lackeys showing their support with somber nods.

The room goes silent enough for me to hear the bug zapper sizzle as each member of Hamas joins their leader in meditation. Aylul doesn't move an inch, their face a mask of ambiguity. Part of me wants to laugh. I move from my spot at the door to stand behind Aylul at the cash register while keeping an eye on Mo'taz.

The former commando stays locked in his breathing exercise until the men steal glances of confusion.

"Tomorrow will do," Aylul concedes to time. Straightening their blazer, they take a step forward, reaching a hand out.

Mo'taz flutters his eyes open to assess a new environment, gesturing for a handshake only to pull back right as their fingertips meet. "Ah – before that – there is one last matter to resolve," he feigns a tone of apology. "Now that the *Yahud* have unhinged their jaws for Ayn Yassin, they will be patrolling her borders. Invisible men, sonic turrets, canine drones – those abominations of *Allah* – with teeth as big as my head!" Mo'taz smacks his lips at the Hot Pockets behind the register. "This is no time to be traveling the roads, you see."

"No fucking way." It's me who breaks the peace. "The downstairs bathroom doesn't flush *because* of the last time you guys stayed here. Did you honestly believe I wouldn't notice six cartons of cigarettes missing from inventory?"

Mo'taz looks at me as if he just noticed I was with them in the shop. Thumbing a bead at his neck, there are no obstacles of etiquette in the way of his disdain. "Laeth Muhammad Awad," he grumbles. "Your father would be ashamed of what has become of his son if he wasn't a *sharmoot* himself."

Decades of urban warfare pack one hell of a punch.

"*Hajj!*" Aylul snaps.

"I will not respect a man who held a gun to my head!" Mo'taz cries, arms waving separately from his body.

Aylul whips around to face me with open-mouthed dismay. I start explaining myself, but the realization that I've lost this battle comes quickly. Plus, there's a big boy in the back that I don't want to be angry with me.

"You'll sleep in the storage room and leave come sunrise," I say, raising a finger, "but disrespecting my father just cost everyone their bathroom privileges." A broken band of objections erupts, and I'm pretty sure there are tears held back. Good.

"Help yourselves to whatever food and soda you need, but hoarding water won't be tolerated." Aylul repeats over them until they're quiet then glides intimately close to Mo'taz, grabbing his hand to shake. "Tell your boss I'll see him tomorrow."

We guide our guests to the storage room shelved with enough junk food and lukewarm energy drinks to last until the end of *Nakba*. Not much is said while the men find some comfortable way to sleep with their backs against the wall, peeking between boxes to get a glimpse of future boons. Having them sleep just under my stash of water jugs makes me nervous, but there's not much that can be done. We cross through the room twice over to account for all members present before reaching the metal latched door leading to our apartment upstairs. I'm about to shut the lights, but getting one last look at them shifting on the floor sets me over the edge.

"Upstairs bathroom's first on your right," I say with my finger over the switch.

Mo'taz stands to peek over at me from his claimed corner, leathery face placid enough to be mistaken for gratitude if not for the curtsey that follows. I roll my eyes and cut the power as soon as Aylul's through the door.

The imminent erasure of Ayn Yassin dawns on me as the latch clicks into place. It comes in silence, as nausea does in waves of momentous momentum; gravitational shifts of people, places, and things in kaleidoscope vision. Slightly dizzy, I lean an arm on the door leading outside, synapses infinite, brow sweat, lungs humid heavy; one, two, two, two, three; in and out, and difficult to close my eyes. Breathe. Pause. Ignore. Where's Sundus? Haven't spoken in a few days. With a flick of the wrist, I activate the cylinder glass bracelet; my phone glows amber, encircling wide-berth fingertips hastily flickering through hologram contacts. Forehead on forearm, I ignore missed calls from forgettable names, find hers, look up, and see a divot in the drywall.

"Remember when that happened?" Aylul glows under the overhead fluorescent upstairs. They stand tall, their observant gaze piercing without judgment.

My throat's too dry to speak at first. The shredding plastic crunch of candy wrappers starts gradually like a symphony from the storage room. "What's the plan?"

"It was autumn," they say. "The morning Tulkarm was ruined. We were waiting for your mom to finish the *manakish*. You knew *za'tar* is my favorite, so we waited. Only... we started arguing after I heard you tell *'amto* that at least it meant no one there had to pretend anymore. I recall the sentiment being: it's better to be dead than a zombie." They don't stop. "At least the dead don't have to fight for a place that died long before them. At least occupation means the ones who are left don't have to be ashamed of moving on with their lives. At least, at least, at least…"

I can't maintain eye contact with them. "Laeth," Aylul gently says my name and waits for me to see them again.

"We were late for class, coming down the stairs. You quoted someone – I forget who – something like, 'Cowards look at the swords of their ancestors as relics of the past,' right?"

Aylul tilts their head, the collar of their shirt shifts to reveal the scar on their neck. "And you said?"

"Better to forget the dead than join them."

I imagine 'Amo Khalid from a time before he commanded the Jericho Brigades and sacrificed himself for the safe passage of refugees. Back when he was still a lieutenant and had time to care about applying half a pound of gel to slick back his hair, pointed goatee combed like a wave under his chin. Back when he was a man who laughed at his own jokes and wanted to see South Africa and Berlin. I wonder if he saw anything beyond this place after the IOF took Aylul the night before the battle as revenge for rallying so many to the Cause. "You pushed me on the way out," I say, picking at the indent in the drywall. "What's the plan?"

"Embrace our birthright, Laeth: uphold the *thawabit*. Resist colonization like the indigenous of Turtle Island so long as one of us lives. The hotel's just another beginning, you know this. After the enemy baits their most indebted citizens into footholds – old men, young women, and families – they'll need work and schools for their children. Only after we fight back against our occupiers will their armies come to swallow us whole; no – not swallow," they correct the common saying, "absorb. Assimilate. And the world will champion them as shields against terrorism. Because, of course, what monster would harm an innocent child?"

Plans within plans; how many has Aylul made over the years without me knowing? One age-old question elbows its way through the maelstrom: had 'Amo Khalid groomed them for succession? "If resistance only serves to feed the paradigm, why give them the necessary ingredient? Why not something other than horror?"

Another unfamiliar thing happens in the way Aylul shifts from one foot to the other, brow unfurrowing into an upward slant, body sighing inward. "After all we've been through you're still asking the wrong questions." Without another word, they turn to the door to our flat and slam it shut behind them.

I wake up gasping for air in the backseat of my truck. The morning sun radiates through the open windows, dangling feet burning out the passenger's side. My back's sore between seats; Diwa's heavy-handed mistake itches something fierce between my shoulders. Rubbing the sleep from my eyes, I use sweat like gel to push hair back from my forehead. Roasting coffee fills the space between me and Ibrahim's pop-up cart across the street; that's definitely the move. Told myself last night I'd pull up to the side door of the shop and keep an eye out for any late-night wanderers in Mo'taz's group, but the empty pint of vodka on the floor makes me suspicious of myself. I slink up to the driver's seat, breathing deep for some type of mental balance. Unsuccessful, I push open the door into a brand new day.

Scorching as it is, there's a line of five waiting for their Dixie cups of coffee by the time I reach Ibrahim. He's too busy spitting injustices through his ten remaining teeth to notice my arrival, waving three-fingered hands lost from diabetes toward the new checkpoint. His customers nod along, grumbles of discontent rising with the cicadas. Ibrahim uses a spatula in a wok to sift sand around a large copper ibrik, stabbing for emphasis, burying it closer to the single burner fire.

"Morning, handsome," comes a sweet voice from the front. Hunched over a walking stick, my neighbor Teta hobbles over with an open arm.

I meet her halfway for an embrace. Afraid she'll catch a whiff of booze, I plant kisses on each wrinkled cheek away from her nose. She still furrows her unibrow at me when we part. "You look as lovely as ever, *Hajja*." I make a move to distract, eyeing her earth-toned *'abaya* up and down, "It's no wonder Ibrahim lets you skip the line every day."

Teta waves a hand over her heart, feigning flattery. "Saw you sleeping in your truck," she leans in, getting straight to the point. "As if we don't have enough to worry about with the Zionists unhinging their jaws, you're picking fights at home? *Ya Rub, habibi,* if that isn't the region in a nutshell. You're lucky she's still around, you know."

"I know," I say sincerely. Looking back at the shop, I notice Mo'taz and Aylul's cars are nowhere to be seen. "Anyone ever tell you you're too perceptive for a farmer?"

"Aren't you supposed to be too educated for classism or does that still go hand-in-hand?" Teta murmurs disappointment when I don't take the bait and changes the subject. "Town's been buzzing since the red sun rose, kid. Those checkpoints kicked a nest of wasps without stingers and queens without brains; takes me back to Jericho before it fell..." she trails off.

I recall the stories Teta told Aylul and me growing up about the siege. All I could do was stand there, thinking of how I couldn't find a way to comfort an old lady reliving her neighbors being dragged behind Humvees. Memory twitches her free hand to a pulsing loose grip, and I'm back in the same useless state. This happens whenever she gets worked up. It's an irremovable stain in the DNA reminding her that the only defense against rail guns and exosuits as she fled the ruins of her home was its rubble.

"Any word from Ramallah?" I ask to bring her back.

"None yet," she says faintly, then with more bite, "those Forgotten Ones draped that white flag of theirs over city hall before Sheikh Omar had the chance to wipe his chin from whatever Zionist bed he slept in last night."

I laugh through my nose. "That's the P.A. for you." With a swivel of my wrist, orange light projects the time in my eye: 09:38. Didn't think Aylul would be gone so early. Worry swells into a knot in my chest. I consider calling, but who knows what I'd be interrupting? I glance down the road, hoping to catch a glimpse of their car – nothing but mirages.

"Those normalizers wouldn't have the strength to wave that flag if they saw what I've seen," Teta spits foam.

"Remind me again, Laeth," Ibrahim's voice calls out, "you take your coffee *wasat*?"

I confirm with a hand over my heart, bowing my head, ignoring what should be known after all these years. Barely listening to the old man preach about the importance of fighting a battle he'll never be part of, my eyes wander over to Teta's half-acre farm. Surrounded by high-rise slums, perfect rows of stubby dry bark trees bloom bright orange fruit like low-hanging balloons. Her nieces and nephews walk between them, snipping branches, not taking the luxury to examine for bruises or rot, and carefully placing them in baskets. Ibrahim shoves a Dixie cup in my hand without stopping his spiel. I flinch when a bit spills over; the molten lava cardamom on my skin makes my eyes water.

"Laeth?"

I recognize my ex's voice instantly. Now I'm all too aware of how I smell after a night in the truck. Sundus stands at the opposite end of the cart, waving a hand at her side. The sun gleams off her VitaStim. She wears a denim jacket littered with multicolored pins of books and bands clinking together as a gust of sand parts her bangs. I can't resist smiling at her memory as I say hello.

"Long time," I try to sound casual. "How's the family?"

Sundus side eyes me as Ibrahim hands her a cup. Double, no sugar; the bastard didn't even have to ask. "Is a week a long time now?" she chides, "c'mon, weirdo." Digging around in her pockets, she slaps a few shekels down on the cart. "I've been looking for you. Time we catch up."

Considering the mess I made, I'm amazed Sundus is climbing the stairs behind me to the rooftop. The door swings open to a radiating wave of morning sun. We make our way over to a plastic coffee table between lawn chairs and plop down in our seats as silently as we came. Nerves get to me, so I light a cigarette. Didn't realize I'd have to figure out so soon what to say after declining her proposal. What's left to say? Sorry six months wasn't long enough to know forever when it only took our friends one or two?

"Crazy, what's happening out there," she says.

Never thought imminent colonization could be so effective as filler conversation. I stand to lean on the guardrail, gazing out over Ayn Yassin without responding. Delivery drones flitter underneath a cloudless sky between mismatched ivory brown and gray buildings reflecting the ground they're built on. Donkeys pull carts of produce down the streets leading toward Ramallah, kids chasing behind them with hoots and howls on hoverboards too broken to levitate for long. One wouldn't think we were surrounded by enemy forces; just another day in the neighborhood if you don't look to the horizon. In the distance, men like ants scale city hall to take the white flag down. I wonder if it'd matter to the Israelis if they chose to keep it up. I let my vision blur, searching for anything but what's in front of or behind me.

Sundus takes a deep drag. "My father said he's meeting with the other P.A. execs to negotiate a response. Fingers crossed, they'll mediate Fatah and Hamas merging for a unified front."

"Think they'll come to an agreement right after or long after we're occupied?" The words come out harsher than intended, and I turn to apologize.

Veins protrude from the dusk of her temples like belated warning signs. "And what'll you do, Laeth? Wave a white flag in front of the store while they gun down Ibrahim? Offer surrender as they salt Teta's farm? Say, 'Please, don't,' when they take me back to their barracks? At least we haven't given up. Some of us still care about doing the right thing."

"Some things are more important than the right thing," I shoot back.

Sundus grabs her purse from the floor, retrieves her keys, and stands tall. "I know you've been hanging with TFO sympathizers lately, but it amazes me you share the same blood as Khalid Khater. Choosing the coward's way out is becoming a habit." She chews the inside of her cheek, arms-length apart from me as the sunbirds sing.

"I didn't technically say no." Once upon a time I was naïve to think that after five years at university I'd know the right words to say when necessity hit. The thing is, lessons from Jung and Marx only helped me understand my deepest flaws, not withstand them. I lift my gaze from the ground in time to see her jaw drop.

"What else would you call it when someone tells you 'I've never considered that before' after you propose?"

"Look," I try not to match her tone, "we were coming down after a night out; my brain was Swiss fucking cheese. The last thing I expected—"

"-Then why haven't you called all week? Better yet, why haven't you answered mine?"

She's got me there. I'm not sure what to say, mainly because I don't want to lie to her. Is that possible when I don't know the truth? "I'm sorry," I say, but a rush pulls me deeper. "I mean, if six months is long enough to know who you want to be with for life, I'm sure you've moved on by now. Is he handsome?"

She flings the metal latch to rip the door open. "Fuck me for trying to help you believe in the future." Sundus pauses with her back turned to me, shakes her head, and descends the staircase.

The door shuts as I will it to open again; simultaneously convincing myself she's better off without me. I know it's only true because I want it to be. When I hear her car peel off the gravel lot, I figure the money I'm making off Mo'taz can afford a day off. I leave the sign shut as I make my way down to the cellar.

It's high noon by the time I've smoked an entire pack in self-pity. Told myself I came up here for some self-reflection, but all I've done is watch customers walk up to the store and throw their hands up in defeat. I think some of them can see the top of my head. Times like these, I wish I hadn't talked so much shit about deleting my social media accounts for some distraction. Instead, here I sit like some sort of serial killer staring at children playing in Darwish Park. For the second time some kid goes down the slide too fast and tumbles on the rocky ground below. He holds his knee; vague echoes of crying barely reach my ears. His parents rush to his side but don't pick him up, talking him through the ordeal. I look away between dunes at the jagged Ramallah skyline, wondering what plans a council full of generational denial are being devised. Then a car door slams shut, with footsteps coming up toward me not far behind.

"You look like shit," Aylul says, tousling my hair on their way to the empty chair.

I sit up straight, watching them look at their hand with disgust and wipe it on their trousers. They pop my last cigarette between their lips and loosen their tie for respite.

"Sundus stopped by."

Aylul grunts. "Sucks."

"Sucks," I agree, knowing they know it was my fault it ended any other way. "Why didn't you wake me, I would've gone with you. Sundus said something about negotiations?"

"Got the call at 5 AM, and you're a bit of a bitch to deal with that early," they laugh dryly, "and I'm not sure either will ever trust the P.A."

Aylul has a point. Not that the Palestinian Authority ever deserved trust from any of us. "Did you meet with Al-Qassam?"

"Ugh," they respond flatly, afro bobbing from side to side. "By the time Mo'taz and I got to some sketchy factory in Ramallah, they left on a tip Mossad was closing in. Met a merc that freelances for Fatah though, Uri—"

"A Russian?" I exclaim. Over a century of soft power only now to have direct skin in the game?

"Neturei Karta," there's excitement in Aylul's voice. "I—"

"Wait, what? An Israeli?"

"Except they're not really? Stop interrupting," they lean in, arm over thigh, taking off their shades to reveal an adrenaline rush. "Uri said Wissam Tayyib wants me in Fatah's fold, said there's a new project in the works they want me to join."

I must've had fuck that written all over my face because they raised a hand to stop me. "We scratch his back, he gives us a team to deal with what's happening here."

Why would Aylul align themselves with puppets of the enemy they resist? Too many questions come to mind. Gibberish sputters out of my mouth trying to ask any of them. I stop trying to know what I want to say and let them continue. "I know your feelings toward the Cause, cousin, but the time for philosophy is over. They're here, now, and they're going to turn Ayn Yassin into one of their sterilized settlements unless people stop *Waiting for Godot*. Jordan, Egypt, the Gulf; they've all turned their backs. Hell, Wissam is only willing to part with four people –"

"*Four* people?" I exclaim. "What can you do with four people against legions?"

"They'll take your dad's store without consequence," they press, "our home. Bulldoze it for shits and giggles to plant their flag and use it as a post to..." Their eyes lose some luster and they grip the scar just above their collar.

I cup their cheeks for a guided breathing exercise we picked up once at a mandatory therapy seminar our university held after Tulkarm was nearly cleansed off the map. It's quiet enough to notice the absence of chirping in the sky. Their grip loosens after a few iterations. "Do you get it, Laeth? You may not be killed, but they will take your life."

Aylul reaches into their satchel and sets my pistol on the table. I consider the metal shadow outlined in sunlight while my heart breaks further. The window to mention the option falling from city hall closed for now, I clasp their hands in mine.

"How can I help?" I ask.

Aylul doesn't smile, and that's the reassurance I need.

ع

Aylul and I head downstairs to our apartment on the second floor, footsteps echoing off white tile hallways with waiting room paintings. Part of me feels bad that we never properly decorated the space my dad built, but I never saw a point in spending what little cash I had on potpourri. Hell, we didn't even bother putting a holovision in the family room. At least we kept it clean; "guest-ready," as mom used to put it. Aylul walks ahead past the small kitchen corner down the hall to their room, saying they need fifteen minutes before closing the door behind them. I don't have to smell my armpits to know I'll require more than that and head to my bedroom across from theirs.

"Change your sheets while you're in there," Aylul calls back.

A waft of old incense escapes as I enter my bedroom, floating light orbs aglow from the last time I slept here days ago. It reminds me that I have to refill the utility meter soon and take a mental note with a sigh. Money's never been tighter. Guilt from taking the day off starts weighing me down, but it wouldn't have made much of a difference, really. I look around the barren walls of my bedroom. All that's here is my twin bed and a cedar desk I never use to study anymore. Political Science lost its flavor when everyone in power kept playing a fifty-year game of musical chairs. Aylul's right though, I should really change my sheets. After two months without a wash, the food and sweat stains are starting to make a pattern of their own.

"Let's go with a classic today," I say, "LoFi Beats to Study and Relax to."

Xylophone beeps confirm my request followed by a sudden burst of synth-wave violins at a volume that scares the shit out of me. I grab a towel off the floor and throw it over my shoulder as I head for the attached bathroom but catch a glance at a framed photo on my dresser. In it, my mother is dressed in a thobe stitched with cascading geometric red, black, and orange patterns with a matching hijab. She's smiling outside the second store we used to own near Jericho before it fell. I can count on one hand how many times I've seen her so happy. More than the wedding we were headed to, I remember this as the day they decided to sell the land to Bedouins. I can't recall who the wedding was for, but I'll never forget how often they reminded me in whispers not to tell a soul about their plans to leave. I should call soon. One unreturned call is enough to worry her and I've been missing since things with Sundus went south.

Once I'm clean, I meander through the hallway in nothing but underwear, brushing my teeth as I pop my head in through a crack in Aylul's doorway. They're wearing a white hijab and *dishdasha*, facing east toward the window, seated on their knees, bowing in prayer. A framed charcoal sketch portrait of their father watches over them. I can hear the faint poetic whisper of *Surah al-Fatiha* and close my eyes, hoping to absorb some semblance of faith like osmosis. They recite:

In the name of God, the Entirely Merciful, the Especially Merciful.

All praise is due to Allah, Lord of the Worlds

The Entirely Merciful, the Especially Merciful,

Sovereign of the Day of Recompense.

It is You we worship and You we ask for help.

Guide us to the straight path—

The path of those upon whom You have bestowed favor,

not of those who have earned Your anger or of those who are astray.

"Where to?" Aylul calls out once they're done. "Cid and I were thinking somewhere in Al Bireh; treat ourselves a little."

I'm about to suggest the Olive Tree for the hundredth time when I remember their fight with Leila. Two peas in a goddamn pod, them and I. When we pick him up, Cid makes no grand entrance as he walks out his front door. He climbs into the truck, granting us a faint "Hey" before turning toward the window. Now I see Aylul's reason for wanting to splurge on something extra. The man looks like he hasn't slept all night. I make a few attempts at conversation but take the hint after enough one-word answers. It never seems to take as long to leave Ayn Yassin as it does returning home. After twenty minutes of a one-sided conversation with the GPS, I'm parallel parked in front of a lovely brick teahouse covered in grapevines.

"Oh shit," Aylul exclaims. Their bracelet hums to life with a magenta glow, circling their fingertips as they tap away at invisible buttons, text scrolling through their left eye contact lens.

"What is it?" Cid asks.

There's a long pause while Aylul is lost in conversation beyond us. The sun is beginning to dip below the horizon, bathing the truck in a deep orange light. "It's Uri. He told me to look out for an unknown number – burner phone and all – but I wasn't expecting it so soon..." They're lost in thought, fingers still.

I notice I'm holding my breath. "Well?"

"Midnight: 31.867018, 35.188319."

"Coordinates," Cid says.

Aylul looks at me, but I'm lost wondering how the hell the mercenary plans on visiting my shop without getting himself and the rest of us killed.

"The tunnels," I say when the pieces click into place.

Aylul nods. "Mo'taz mentioned we weren't the only ones in Ayn Yassin."

"I'm coming." Cid leans in between the seats. Aylul opens their mouth to object, but he raises a hand to stop them. "Either you take me with you, or there'll be a knock on the door. If being a mechanic was enough, I would've stayed in Ramallah." He nods with determination pushing through bloodshot exhaustion.

Cid and I wait outside the teahouse on a hill while Aylul finishes their cigarette. Lost in the weight of what's to come, we forget to go inside long after cherry meets filter. Between brick and limestone buildings, the sky makes me sick with vertigo. With too much hanging over our heads, it only takes a few nods to each other for the three of us to climb back into the truck. The smaller the teahouse gets in the rearview mirror, the more I regret not encouraging the others to go inside.

As we turn into a long line of cars forming at the northern checkpoint, floodlights saturate the afternoon sky like pearly gates of heaven. The trash all around us shimmers as the only evidence of the protest. I spot something metallic on the ground beside the truck and open my door to pick it up. It's a teargas canister, bent down the middle cylinder. It's as big as my forearm; the heat from being fired has eroded most of the blue lettering, except for a Made in the USA print at the bottom. Cid asks what I've found, but I toss it out the window instead of facing the lecture sure to follow. Aylul punches my thigh for littering.

It takes an hour and I'm low on petrol when we reach the front of the line. A lanky boy no older than eighteen decked out in double-plated scale armor too big to fit properly saunters up to the driver-side window, knocking on the glass inches away from Aylul's face. They take their time acknowledging his presence, rolling it down just a knuckle. The boy's already agitated.

"All way," he speaks broken Arabic behind a mesh scarf hiding the bottom half of his face.

"Why?" they ask.

"All way or I break!"

Whether the boy soldier meant Aylul or the window, enough had broken for one day. "Just do it," I command.

When they do, the boy turns on the flashlight attached to his rifle and points it into the car for inspection. I've lost count of how many times I've had a gun pointed at me, but it's not something I can ever get used to. I glance at his hand when he angles himself toward Cid and his sleeve pushes up. No Stim on this guy either. The lack of trigger safety makes me want to laugh and cry at the same time. Less than an inch to squeeze and we'd all be dead for no good reason, and this kid barely needs one.

"I see you before," the boy says to Cid. "Do not move." The soldier leans his chin on the radio attached to his vest and speaks Hebrew too quickly for me to translate.

"What's this about?" Cid speaks only in English, a tactic used in tight spots.

"Do not move!" the boy screams, raising his weapon to head level.

"I'm just reaching for my passport," Cid shouts back. Too late: by now there are four other IOF soldiers swarming the car. Before my friend has the chance to say another word, they all have their guns raised, commanding us to unlock the doors. One of the soldiers says they too saw him at the protest earlier.

Aylul keeps their hands on the steering wheel, staring straight ahead as if death wasn't staring right back. Their shoulders slack, head poised high with a serenity that makes me wonder if they are even here in the present with me. Amid a torrent of demands from broken accents, it's Cid's voice that snaps them out of it.

"Do it."

"No," they respond. Their fingers inch slowly toward the glove compartment, but I press a knee against their intention to grab the pistol.

"I'll be back before breakfast," he says calmly in an attempt to reassure us.

"Or in a cell on the other side of the Wall," Aylul quips back. The voices outside are getting louder.

"I love you too, but shut up and unlock the doors."

Another second too long, and I was sure they were going to break the glass and force their way in, but Aylul concedes to circumstance and does the work for them. The back doors whip open, and in seconds, my friend is ripped out of the car. The soldiers throw him on the hood to detain his hands. There's some yelling from people in the cars behind us to let him go, but they're less than gnats to the soldiers as they push and tug Cid back to their tents for questioning. It wouldn't be the first time, but the more this happens, the more I wonder if his small bribes will work.

Aylul and I wait as the line into Ayn Yassin grows like a serpent. The soldiers at the gate ignore honking horns, but it's back to silence in the truck. Neither of us is in the mood to complain, not with everything that's happened today and the rest of tonight pressing down on our nerves. I think about the first time I met Cid over a decade ago at a rally to stop the demolition of some village I can't remember the name of near the Jordanian border. Seeing Filipinos on the frontlines was common back when #BeforeItsTooLate was trending among the community. Scores came from all over to defend their Arab cousins from the erasure they knew all too well, despite their second-class status among many.

The reason Cid stood out wasn't because he stood taller than the rest or the Tommy Bahama shirt but it was when I heard him say, "If only we knew how to fight." Ten minutes later I found him struggling on the floor with IOF, trying to wrestle a weapon away. I remember thinking how gloriously stupid this guy was as I kicked my steel-toed boot across the settler's jaw. Cid invited me over for beef tapsilog. The rest is history. Come to think of it, Diwa was there too. I tap a bead on my wrist, flicking through contacts scrolling through my contact lens.

"It'd be better if we tell her in person," Aylul says. They're looking dead ahead at the gates with a white-knuckled grip on the steering wheel. Over the years, Aylul's mastered composure, but I don't need wet cheeks to know when they're crying.

"Fair enough." I double-tap the bead to close out of the menu. I can usually read Aylul better than myself sometimes, but reaching out is still a struggle; getting closer will only serve to make things worse. Instead, I lean my head against the window and watch clouds lit up by distant lights travel far from this cursed place. The wooden lever lifts up thirty minutes later.

When we reach the garage, Diwa is already sitting outside on the stoop smoking a cigarette, the butterfly on her neck pulsating amber light in the dark. She crosses the gravel lot over to us before I'm even out the door, leaning inside and reeking of booze.

"I thought you guys were done using my husband as a shield."

Aylul leans across my lap to look her straight in the eye. "Diwa—"

"I don't wanna hear it." Her Arabic slips the more worked up she gets. "You're getting him out of there now. I don't care how, but he's not sleeping in a cell because you were too chicken shit to act."

Her words embarrass me. Of course it's not fair; the only thing we could've done is land in jail with him, but she makes a good point. I'd need five hands to count the number of times Cid stepped up for us to get out of trouble, and it's starting to feel like being out of options was just an excuse. Then again, I know that's the privilege of having time to think speaking for me. "There's nothing we can do for him tonight," I say, "but tomorrow I'll talk to Sundus' father, I promise."

There's a fire in Diwa's eyes that compliments the red emanating from her tattoo, but it's soon put out by tears. "I know it's not your fault," she says unevenly, "but it's your responsibility."

I nod, "Let's go inside—"

"No." Diwa puts a hand up. "I'll be fine. Just...figure it out and call me in the morning." With one last look at Aylul, she turns away and heads inside.

Again, there's silence in the truck while we make the short trip back to the shop. I'm not in the mood to let music guide my thoughts, so I keep the radio on static and try to imitate the blank canvas noise over my torrential anxiety. Hell if I know whether Sundus' dad knows about the breakup, but the man's always hated me for not taking an active administrative role in Palestinian affairs. It wouldn't be the first time asking him for a similar favor, but perhaps now I'll be in his debt.

"I know it's been a long one already," Aylul says beside me, "but there's still Uri to think about."

"Trust me," I snort. "I'm more worried about what's coming than what's already happened."

When Aylul parks the truck outside the shop, I grab my pistol from the glove compartment and head in with Aylul not far behind. I don't bother with the overhead lights, making a beeline through neon ad holograms straight for the basement. It's a large room, one I had thought to renovate into an arcade for some extra side cash when Dad first signed the store over to me, but it wasn't long after that Aylul approached me with Mo'taz's proposition. Now it was nothing but an empty warehouse with a walk-in freezer in the far corner. Soon as I open the door, dust clouds sting my eyes. Sneezing as I hold the door, Aylul props it open with a jackhammer from inside.

"Now what?" I stare at the human-sized hole in the center of the freezer, a tunnel without end or light. In about an hour, one of the most powerful men in Palestine would emerge from its depths. What will he ask us to do? Will he even ask?

"I need some coffee," Aylul says casually. They turn from me, heading back up the stairs but pause at the top to ask if I want any.

"I think I'm gonna throw up," I call back to them.

"You're not the only one," they surprise me by saying.

It's a minute past midnight on fold-out chairs outside the walk-in when I faintly hear the sound. At first I think it's my imagination playing tricks on me to fill in the silence, but then I hear the dull rhythmic sound of footsteps. Aylul lifts their head then stands, straightening out their clothes and patting out their hair. I'm not sure what to do with my hands, sweat sticks to my seat.

"Let me do the talking," Aylul whispers as the footsteps grow louder. "And be on your best behavior."

I'm tongue-tied from trying not to think about all the things that could go wrong. For all my bluster, Aylul should know better than to think I'd risk challenging Uri. With Mossad probably searching for him, I get the sense there's a satellite somewhere in space targeting us from above, waiting for the right moment to drop a bomb. The soft steps become ringing clinks as make their way up the ladder.

I stare unblinking at the black void inside the freezer, resisting the urge to scream when Mo'taz's gangly face pops out of it. In any other scenario I would have laughed at the dwarfish man pulling himself out of the hole with his grunts and moans. He pats the dust from his brown suit, moving out of the way for another man to make his entrance. He has gilled wrists blending with skin like sand, sideburns resting on his shoulders as black as the hole he spawns from. When he stands, he's a head taller than me, equipped with the same armor issued to the IOF with the desert camouflage plates painted over black. Even with three-inch armor, I can sense the muscle beneath it. He scans his surroundings as he steps out of the freezer, hand hovering over a hand cannon the size of my forearm at his waist. Seeing the two resistance fighters side by side helps me believe there might be unity in the fields again. Maybe there is hope for joint negotiations after all. Aylul moves to greet the man I can only guess is Uri.

"Apologies for being late," he says behind a face mask.

Mo'taz slaps the mercenary's back in good nature as if they are old friends, but Uri doesn't move an inch. "Had to take this one to HQ to meet the boss."

"You mean the one that's too shy to meet me?" Aylul quips, but drops it when all Mo'taz does is shrug, turning to Uri instead. "Please tell me yours isn't as nervous on a first date."

"After our conversation the other day, I expected you to know we wield the tools we must," the hired gun says evenly. "I prefer you not refer to Wissam Tayyib as 'my boss.' He is a client."

Aylul ponders this for a moment before gesturing back to me. "This is my paternal cousin Laeth; he owns this shop. Laeth, Uri."

"Hello." I reach out a hand that he does not take.

"The unbeliever. Yes, I've heard of you."

Unbeliever? Before I shoot Aylul a critical look, Uri continues: "Come. We can discuss matters of business on our way through those dreadful tunnels. We're running out of time."

Aylul steps forward. "Actually, it's just me who'll be joining you. Laeth has other matters to take care of."

I purse my lips feeling awkward. Why don't they want me there?

Uri chuckles without slowing his pace. "Come, son of Muhammad: it is time to weigh the worth of a man with the luxury to choose his own path."

Standing in front of the human-sized hole has me shivering despite the fridge being disconnected. Adrenaline keeps my body alert, but after the day I've had, the gears in my head slow. Maybe it's a good thing. Having time to process that we're striking deals with some of Israel's most wanted would only keep me here longer. The rest of the group's already climbing down the ladder. It doesn't settle well with me that we're going into this blind, and for what? A small crew who can't change the tides with Fatah, so they swear allegiance to someone as wet behind the ears as Aylul? My heart aches watching the tops of their head get swallowed by shadow. I take one last look around the basement with half-empty shelves searching for a reason to stay. For all of my privileges, I can't. Turning my back to the hole in the ground, I swing one leg over the other, descending into the underground.

I lose sense of form going down the ladder, creaking with every heavy foot. Mo'taz's ragged breathing below is a comfort in the void. Sweat drips from forehead to nose, but I barely notice the agitation in my haste to find the bottom. It's taking longer to climb twenty meters than I expected, but the soft amber glow of some distant lantern acts as a warm welcome before the end. Hopping off the ladder, I take in my environment while everyone pats dust off their clothes.

Despite allowing Hamas to dig these tunnels, this is my first time down here. It's bigger than I thought, spanning a few meters wide with cement walls and overhead lights on a dome ceiling guiding the way forward. Uri checks back that we've all made it before taking the lead with Mo'taz in tow and Aylul at the precious center of our single-file line. Aside from Mo'taz clearing the tar from his throat, no one makes a peep. I zone out watching Aylul's afro bobbing to the beat of their step when I think again of satellites watching us from space. This would be the perfect time to attack; no need for dropping bombs when all it'd take is a fart for the rock tunnels to collapse all around us. It's not long before the line stops and I pivot to see a one-track railway with two large mining carts waiting for us single file in front of Uri. An unmistakable buzz reaches me in the absence of shuffling feet.

"What is that?" I ask for fear of being caved in.

"Anti-radar tech nailed into the rock," Uri says, "the vibrations throw off their sonar seismographs. Mo'taz." Uri beckons the captain over. "You and Laeth take the rear while I speak with Aylul."

Surprisingly, the captain doesn't complain about the order, but what I'm more curious about is why they want to separate me from Aylul. There's nothing left to say when my cousin steps forward to climb into the front cart. Aylul looks back in my direction, but it's too dim in the tunnel to read their expression. All I can do now is trust whatever words of poison Uri intends to pass won't make it into their bloodstream.

"*Yallah, ya amira,*" Mo'taz says impatiently from our cart. He nods to Uri, who's typing something on the monitor connected to combustion engines.

As soon as I swing into the cart, the one in front hums to life like a swarm of hornets echoing through the chamber, taking off with impressive speed. A breath later, ours revs up and snaps like a bullet, making the already uncomfortable ride unbearable with how much the iron casket shakes. Before I know it we're riding through the tunnels with enough speed to turn the lanterns into amber shooting stars. Mo'taz shuffles around for a more comfortable position, kicking my shin in the process.

"Where are we headed?" I ask him over the whirling wind.

He grins, gold tooth shining in the makeshift underworld we've found ourselves in. "I've never seen you so nervous."

"Mo'taz." Much as I'd like to reach into my arsenal of insults, I'm in his world now. I bite my lip enough to cause me more pain than what comes next. "I'm sorry for pointing a gun at you." The falsehood almost feels real exiting my mouth. "But if there's anything you know about the shit we go through, it's how much I care for Aylul." Half-truths are easier than lies. I can tell he buys it when his shoulders slack. "What do you all want from us?"

The captain reaches into his back pocket to retrieve a crumpled box of cigarettes, popping a bent one between his lips. He pauses a moment, then extends the offer to me. This alone cuts a bit of the edge from my nerves, so I grab a cigarette from the box. We take a minute to duck our heads between our legs as low and far away from the punishing wind to get the lighters working.

"You know," he starts, "it is often said the Cause is less about preserving faith and more about reclaiming land."

"Well, I never took you for someone I'd find at Friday prayer," I retort.

"You wouldn't," Mo'taz admits, "though my father used to drill me with *Qira'at* lessons until my head felt like bleeding. After years of practice, when I could recite every *Surah* from memory, he gifted me with a trip to Al-Aqsa. *Ya rub*, Laeth, you wouldn't believe how beautiful." The captain looks to take another drag but drops his hand before it makes its journey. "I was overcome by the sheer magnitude of where I stood. Pillars reaching toward the sun, *girih* etched into every corner like hallways to heaven. I remember staring at the golden chandeliers larger than ten men and felt as though I were king – *me* – a nothing from Al Khalil." This time the soldier inhales his cigarette until it burns past the filter. "We didn't know it at the time, of course, but we would be some of the last Palestinians to ever see the holy site again. An honor wasted on someone like me."

I'm so accustomed to Mo'taz peacocking in front of his herd that self-deprecation isn't expected. "It was written for you to be among the lucky few," I mutter the ideology and receive a grunt in return.

"For most of our people, victory lies in the heart of *Al Quds*." Mo'taz meets my gaze with steel resolve. "I fight for peasants to feel like kings once more; for generations of possibilities not confined to ghettos erected by wardens of the same past."

His speech is enough to inspire, but I'm irritated he didn't answer my question about what we're doing squished together in a cast iron soup bowl hurtling toward the unknown. Leaving well enough alone, I lean my head back off the cart and stare at the lanterns streaking past us. The brakes screech to a halt long after I'm finished with my second smoke. The two in front are already walking, so I hop out of mine to make a beeline for Aylul.

"You good?"

They nod, a gravity pulling their lips.

"Up and out from here," Uri interrupts.

As we make the climb, I mention the supposed business he would share in due time, but the respect of a response never arrives. Once we find ourselves at the uppermost limit, Uri slams on the dark ceiling until it gives way to a trapdoor.

Pushing topside, we find ourselves crammed into a makeshift outhouse without any actual plumbing, yet it still smells like shit. We push out the front door, quick to be baptized in much worse filling the damp September air. We are situated outside a cramped alleyway between two high-rise slums just outside Ayn Yassin a block beyond the checkpoint. Sewage overflows the gutters to seep into the gravel trail beneath our feet. Uri motions us to hurry, pulling down the toilet bowl trapdoor before locking the entrance behind him.

Small shops without rhyme or reason for what merchandise they carry litter this residential neighborhood without a name. Butcher shops sell more toys than meat; pharmacies beg for backroom deals from bathtub mixologists; there are more orphanages than apartments. With Nablus overrun, internally displaced people from Qalqilya migrated here to make new lives for themselves but thought better than claiming some newfound identity that would just be stolen again. It's a place close to my backyard that I choose to pretend doesn't exist since every poor soul I see could be me. We cross the threshold from alley to street, moving against the current of migrant workers heading toward Ayn Yassin's checkpoint. All seems to flow like water until Mo'taz stops dead in his tracks, causing me to smash against him.

"What?" I ask when he doesn't move. Following his line of sight, I notice a small crowd gathered around a shop with HoloVisions lining the front window. They broadcast live news in Hebrew since all foreign media is forbidden on these desecrated lands. The Zionist anchor flies in a helicopter well out of range of a giant plume of dust rising from the west. Every witness here knows it's a bomb without needing our oppressors to inform us over a microphone. The slow-rolling text on the news ticker at the bottom of the screen reads War on Terror: Last Hamas Encampment Destroyed. There's more to it, but before I can continue reading, Mo'taz makes a break for the store. I look back to catch Aylul hot on his heels, but Uri doesn't move an inch.

"There's no time to waste; we must make our rendezvous," he tries, but no one's listening.

It's not often I pity my own people, but watching the former captain tremble at the news hits me somewhere squishy. Hamas was Mo'taz's family; his forever-purpose entwined with faith in God and country, and he just watched what's left of it become a footnote in history. A century of resilience not even allowed a whimpering end. Of course, he could find other members scattered throughout the country, but with their headquarters reduced to rubble, al-Qassam is no better equipped to fight the Israeli colony than a middle school street gang. The crowd that formed around the screens already disperses with nothing but a few "What a shame," whispers on their lips before moving on with their day.

"It was you, wasn't it?" Mo'taz turns on Uri, pointing a gun between his eyes. "This is no coincidence!"

Uri doesn't flinch. "They were only supposed to take Ibn Walid. I didn't know this would happen-"

"Who did this?" Mo'taz cocks his weapon.

"You can either shoot me or follow me to see for yourself. Just know that without me with you, there is no escape." Uri points to our left in the distance where a security drone is heading our way. "There isn't time to—"

A gunshot makes people and sunbirds scatter. Next I know Mo'taz is on the ground in a nearby alley with Uri on top of him. Aylul makes a break in the direction of the rendezvous point, leaving me flaccid as the drone nears. The mercenary uses his fists like mallets, beating the former captain's face until he goes limp. Uri stands, shaking the blood from his knuckles as he turns to me.

"What are you waiting for? Let's get the fuck out of here."

When we near the van an elderly man dressed in a white *dishdasha* pops out of the driver's side door. The lift in his hollow eyes tells me he's surprised to see so many of us, but he doesn't ask questions – even when Uri catches up with Mo'taz unconscious in his arms. The captain groans unintelligibly but otherwise stays put. Uri and the driver argue in hushed tones, but the man concedes to time and opens the back doors. After a few tries, we manage to squeeze in, crouched from each side, splaying Mo'taz between us. Tires peel off the gravel shoulder with Arabic love ballads crackling over the radio at a volume too loud to think.

"Why didn't you leave him?" I ask Uri. "He'll kill you for turning Hamas over to the Zionists."

"I work for the P.A.," he speaks to half the question.

I mutter, "Same thing."

Uri can't argue that.

The van stops about a half hour later. When the driver opens the back doors for us, I realize we're in the east side slums of Ramallah. Uri and I sling Mo'taz over our shoulders to follow the old man's direction. We pass through a courtyard where children play football and cuss at us for interrupting their game, making no mention of the bloodied man over our shoulders. With enough effort to soak my shirt through, we climb three flights of stone steps up the side of a brick-and-mortar apartment complex. Dust cakes my body from head to toe. There better be a shower wherever we're going. The old man unlocks a gated door on the far side of the outdoor hallway.

"*Itfathalu,*" he croaks, welcoming us with a sweeping arm.

Uri and I head in first and find a couch in the open room to throw Mo'taz onto. Stretching my back out straight to scan the apartment, it looks like we're the first visitors in years. The floor is littered with cigarette cartons and take-out

Styrofoam boxes, wilted irises on a coffee table, and black mold oozes through the floral wallpaper, tainting the air. There's a foldable TV blinking static on the wall opposite the couch, something I haven't seen since I was a kid. Crossing the room with Aylul, we peek into two bedrooms with nothing but mattresses on the floor as we make our way to the kitchen. After searching through a series of empty cupboards, we find some mugs to fill from the tap.

"Mr. Tayyib will be with you shortly," our driver says from the door, then closes it behind him.

Uri fills a mug and walks over to Mo'taz, carefully lifting his head to take a few sips then says, "If you'll excuse me." He grumbles over to a bedroom and slams the door shut behind him.

Aylul grabs my hand to lead me to the bedroom opposite Uri's, closing the door behind us. They look up at me expectedly, but now that I have them alone, my tongue is tied with too many thoughts.

"Why do you want us to work with these people?" I blurt out in frustration.

Aylul sighs as if they predicted something disappointing and turns to me, arms crossed over their chest. "Work with what you've got, right? Didn't think you'd be here. Wasn't expecting all of…" they flutter their hands in the air, "this to happen."

"You told me to trust you wouldn't fall for Hamas's schemes, but you will for the Authority? And to think, your father—"

Aylul saunters over and punches me square in the jaw, knocking me back to stumble into the wall. A pulsing pain from where the fist makes contact rattles my teeth, blotting orange dots searing my vision. "My dad was a good man who died in vain because he was affiliated with weak people," they quip. "They're not one and the same, Laeth; don't use that ignorant shit against me. The man was ordered to hold his position long after the evacuations for the sake of a false image," their voice cracks, "but that doesn't mean he didn't fight for our liberation, and I'll carry that goddamn banner for as long as I live."

"Look around you, Aylul, there isn't a chance in hell because we already live in it."

Their glare carries malice. "Where's the man who has protested our oppression since he was old enough to carry a stick like a sword?"

"He got tired of shooting arrows at flying fortresses."

Aylul steps close to lay a hand over my heart. "Not believing makes you incapable of accomplishing. So long as you only protect me and not the people, you're only giving the mistakes of our forefathers new skin to walk in."

Before I get my piece back into the age-old argument, there's a knock at the front door. At first I think it might be Uri returning from a smoke, but then there's a second knock followed by a deep, familiar voice that wakes me up more than Aylul's right hook. I turn to them with so many questions left unasked, but when a third knock comes, Aylul wipes already drying tears from their eyes and leaves to answer the door. Standing five feet tall in a silk black trench coat is Wissam Tayyib, vice chairman of the Palestinian Authority and Sundus' father. The bulbous man takes off his bowler hat, holding it to his heart with a small bow and grin that splits his twirling mustache.

"May I come in?" he asks, pushing past us to get inside. "It would not do well to have prying eyes see me here." Taking off his coat, he holds it up with both hands, expecting one of us to take it.

He's the only man I know who has gold Stim implants in both wrists, a superfluous show of his station in life that totally disregards the religion he supposedly follows. I almost smile at what's left of Aylul's dignity when they slap it out of his hand, letting it fall on the dirty floor. "People have died for lesser offenses," he says passively, almost as if bored with their outburst. "But I understand you're stressed after—"

"Murderer," they seethe.

"Child, please. Do not lecture me on morality," he warns. "Fifteen hundred prisoners were released today in exchange for a zombified faction long since dead. Everything I do, I do in the name of *Allah* and, by extension, our dear Palestine. It has been that way since before your mother was old enough to ingest you in whatever backwater shed she came from."

He must really think we're stupid enough not to see the political motivation behind having a rival faction removed from the board, but dealing with Wissam Tayyib is in a far different league than Mo'taz. There is actual, physical force behind him. It would come as no surprise if the safe house was swarmed with personal guards in the event we attempted something unsavory. Aylul knows better than to press their luck and takes a step back. Smug satisfaction fidgets at the corner of his lips. Makes me want to smack him harder than the time he offered me fifty thousand shekels to stop seeing his daughter.

"Laeth?" He looks as if he's just noticing me. "I'm surprised to see you here. Sundus hasn't left her room in two days and hasn't told me why. Any ideas?"

The rhetorical question makes me want to gouge those beady black eyes from their sockets. "None," I say to wipe the look from his face.

Uri waltzes out of his room pouring a bottle of rum into the Stim hole in his wrist. When he notices Wissam in front of me, his face blanches.

"Is that any way to greet an old friend?" Sundus' father clicks his tongue as if he were scolding a child. "I never understood why you wanted to save those degenerates."

Uri pushes Mo'taz aside to make room on the futon and takes a seat. "Knafeh tastes sweeter when there's unity."

"Enough of this," Aylul interrupts the reunion. "We've risked a lot just getting here. It's time to hold up your end."

Wissam glares, clearly unhappy being told what to do. Like a light switch, his double chins slack, and the porcelain smile of diplomats smears across his face. "You have all done a great service for the Cause on this glorious day," he says robotically. "Plans have changed, however. I was listening to Israeli airwaves on the car ride over; a security drone seems to have identified one among your group. By the description, it was you." He points an accusatory finger at me, but it's Aylul who winces. "So there is a decision we need to make first."

The air hangs heavy in the room. None of us needs an explanation. If the IOF has identified me, my capture is inevitable. They'll make me talk, one way or another. Everyone here knows it. There's no shame in the fact, despite what people say. What can man do without basic human rights and a car battery shooting twelve hundred volts through him in a concrete room where no one can hear him scream? When it does not matter even if they did?

"I'm no collaborator," I say, wounded by the accusation.

"So say we all before the gulag," Uri chides in from the couch.

If Wissam could ever get his hands dirty, he'd put a bullet through my head now to tie up loose ends. He has too much to lose on someone he doesn't even like.

"He's my responsibility," Aylul breaks through the junction. "And part of me by extension. You will not harm him."

One demand was enough to test his patience, but after two, Wissam reaches for the pistol at his waist. In a flash, Uri bolts from his seat and grabs the vice chairman's wrist.

"I wouldn't. The boy's marked. The colonizers will burn any who stand between their prey; maybe even you. Take us to the safe house in Nablus," he continues quickly. "We can plan for Ayn Yassin in the time it takes for the dogs to lose our trail." Uri releases his grip. "Of course, the choice is yours to make."

Conceding control to Wissam seems to relax him. "You will stay with us?"

"Double the pay and I'm yours."

"And we have a friend sitting in a cell who needs to be freed, Cid Silang." I add to the list.

"I'll make the call from the car," he says to me. "And half for touching me," the businessman counters. When Uri nods, Wissam claps his hands together at a deal struck and moves for the front door. "It will be a long trip to Nablus. Leave your phones and let's go. The more time we waste, the longer our enemy has to shut down Ramallah." Without any regard for us, he throws on his trench coat and heads outside.

"Surprised he didn't ask about him." Uri nudges Mo'taz with a foot then looks at Aylul. "He will hunt us if he remains. I'll leave it in your hands; just don't expect me to call you 'Boss.'" He claps Aylul on the shoulder, giving me a pitiful look before joining Wissam in the courtyard. Mo'taz begins to stir, eyes and lips a puffy purplish-red obstructing any comprehensible expression.

"What *are* we going to do with him?" I ask Aylul.

"Leave him here, he can find his way to a hospital," they say coldly. "You'll never get back to Ayn Yassin with him in a taxi."

I nod along until what they're saying registers. "Wait, Ayn Yassin? I'm coming with you." They're not meeting my eyes, so I grab their chin and tilt it up for them to meet my gaze. "I'm coming too."

"No," they say pressing their bracelet into my palm. "This isn't your path, Laeth. It never was."

"So your answer is to abandon me halfway on it?" I plead.

"They will try to convert you before killing you. Let them. We'll see each other again, cousin. Just do me a favor, if you see Leila…" They stop, shaking their head before kissing my forehead long enough for a goodbye. "I love you," Aylul says for the first time. They turn to leave the apartment, keeping the front door open on their way out.

I watch them go, lost in confusion until Wissam's car peels off the courtyard. Making a break for the guardrail outside, I lean over to yell at them to come back, but only catch a glimpse of a black SUV turning onto the road. It's hard to breathe. My chest feels gravity's pull; my shoes don't fit right, my eyes liquid burn. Defense mechanisms derived from watching childhood friends spend lifetimes in jail for the crime of their birth can't salve the splinters pulling, cracking, breaking into smaller pieces the further from my reach Aylul spirits away. Their name becomes salted taboo in a mind that can't process the abandonment. Their absence reminds me I stand sixty kilometers away from a sea I've never seen. Can't help but shake the railing. I want to tear it from the concrete floor. I pull, leaning with all my weight, but bang with my fists instead when nothing budges. Dead skin knuckles rip into white flakes until bludgeoned red smatters on iron.

By now the dissonance of an entire people struggling to put food on the table fills the autumn breeze. Vendors yell *"ka'ik!"* or *"thurmus!"* in desperation, kids with backpacks laugh in the courtyard heading off for school, honking zealots and morons in bumper-to-bumper traffic, tea kettle whistles of grandmothers preparing their morning dose of gossip and cigarettes out on their balconies. And then there's me, easy to disregard inside the moving parts of a society gnawing and gnashing for the equilibrium of a normalcy undefined. It's only when I'm squatting down low to catch my breath with my hands hanging out across the overhead rail that I hear Mo'taz shuffle behind me.

"She betrayed you too," he mutters through a fat lip.

I stand off balance and turn to tell him how wrong he is, but lose all steam when I see his condition. Beyond the broken nose and right eye swelling shut, Mo'taz holds himself slumped inward against the doorway like a wounded pup. He's exposed, vulnerable to a gust of wind in the new world he's woken up to. His mouth wrinkles deepen with nothing sarcastic to say. He can barely make eye contact with the one good eye, preferring to gaze skyward as if begging questions from God.

"We should get you to a hospital," I finally say.

Mo'taz stares at the sun without blinking for so long that I wonder if he's blind by the time he sees me. Then he turns to limp down the hallway toward the staircase leading down into the courtyard. I call his name, but he doesn't stop to look back. I could catch up to him with a few great strides but don't make the move. I watch him from the guardrail while he slowly makes his way past the courtyard, through the alley, and turns out of sight into the moving city.

Eventually it dawns on me that I can't stay here any longer. I'm starting to get weird looks from the elderly folk trying to enjoy their morning without some haggard stranger staring through them. Really, I'm just wishing someone would invite me over so I don't jump over the ledge. Someone to tell me it'll be okay without asking what happened. But neither comes to pass. Soul and body distinctly apart, I trudge the same path as Mo'taz and stand on the side of the road until a taxi stops in front of me.

"Ayn Yassin," I mumble when I get inside.

A hotdog-necked man with glasses turns between the front seats to look me up and down as if to say, "What the hell?" Instead, he tells me that prices have jumped since the bombing: twenty shekels for the time it takes to get in and out of the checkpoint.

I gawk at the driver, who seems to know how ridiculous it sounds by the way he shrugs. It isn't a price most people can pay on a daily routine. Traffic in and out of town is going to bottleneck to an eventual drip. So it's begun. I numbly confirm so he can start driving and lean my head against the window, my eyes glazing over as people, places, and things become formless shapes passing me by.

The bumper-to-bumper line into town extends over a kilometer away from the wooden lever. Aside from failed attempts at making small talk about what a shame it is to lose Hamas, the man wishes to sit in silence for the hour it takes to reach the front. I'm too tired to worry if I was somehow identified during the robbery and if, at any moment, IOF soldiers could swarm the car. Frankly, I don't care. If the future doesn't exist, what good's the present? When a boy soldier knocks on my window, I flick my ID card at him through the slit, letting it fall on the ground. He picks it up and cusses before traipsing off to the outpost.

I wait for judgment with an immature excitement that surprises me, but not as much as when the boy returns to grant us safe passage not five minutes later.

When we turn onto the gravel lot in front of the store, dread claws at the back of my head. I've done nothing but lose ten years' worth of progress since I was last here. As I exit the car the smell of burnt cardamom coffee fills my nostrils. I can hear the dull echo of Ibrahim lamenting the end from across the street. My truck shines in the sun where I last parked it, a vague reminder that not all is lost. I should get in touch with Diwa and ask if Cid's been released yet. Maybe contact Sundus, if she's willing to speak to me. But all of that can wait until after I get some sleep. A headache starts to spider web pulse against my temples. I should eat something first.

Patting my metallic steed on the way over to the shop entrance, I fumble for the right key as sunbirds sing in the palm trees. I shoulder the door open with a grunt, walk through, and get slammed against the wall with the force of a hurricane. Before I can even open my eyes, a cold barrel presses against my temple. I gasp when I see the cold blue eyes staring back at me with shrapnel scars from cheek to tear duct. The attacker's face is fully exposed unlike the time I saw him shoot an IOF soldier at the protest rally. Side-swept salt-and-pepper hair, clean-shaven jawline opening with a sick grin to reveal straight white teeth when he sees familiarity in my reaction.

"Do you know who I am?" he asks in perfect Arabic.

Of course I know who he is. His face was plastered on billboards outside the territories for years throughout my childhood. For a time, you couldn't watch the news without hearing his name. How could I not recognize the face of the man praised as the Hero of Israel? The same man who infiltrated Hamas in Gaza and killed one of his own in cold blood outside of Ayn Yassin?

"Meir Cohen."

His face splits euphorically when I say his name. "We have much to discuss."

It's strange, really. After everything that's happened in just the span of a day, I can't seem to give a shit that my life is ending. There's no courage in this, but fear's hard to come by when you're born into endings. There's an old cliché that right before you die, your life plays back like a record for you to admire or regret everything that's come to pass, but as Meir Cohen's elbow digs deeper into my trachea, I don't find this to be the case. There's only pain and the desire for it to be over already. Part of me wants to struggle against his grip; maybe dig a finger into the hole of his simply made Stim, but there's also a gun against my head. Any Palestinian would feel at home in this disposition, I'm sure of it. It's a feeling closer to home than the land we've retained. I'd wager every shekel that any of them would use these last moments to spit in his porcelain face, but instead, I laugh.

"What's so funny?" He leans back to give me room to talk.

"It's just," I say in a coughing fit, "at first glance, you could pull off Aryan descent."

Meir Cohen, the Butcher of Gaza, starts chuckling in a gradual fit of laughter as he backs away. Massaging my throat, I'm stunned by his reaction but soon join in the hysteria. As he's doubled over, I notice a crowbar leaning against the wall just out of reach. There's a chance I could move quick enough to grab it and bash the son of a bitch over the head. Smash his skull in until he's only recognizable enough to showcase in front of my brothers and sisters in Ayn Yassin. I'd be revered as a national hero. My name would echo from Ramallah to Nablus until it reached Aylul's ears. Maybe then they'd think twice before presuming my path and abandoning me at this dead end. But I don't do that; I just keep laughing with the enemy until things wind down to silence in a dark room.

"Why did you kill that man?" is all I can think to ask.

Cohen holsters his weapon, intrigue dancing in those stalwart eyes. "They used to call me Caesar, but if I had half that man's political prowess, I wouldn't have been demoted to overseeing this absolute shit-bore." He complains as if expecting me to sympathize with him. When I cross my arms dissatisfied with his answer, he clicks his tongue, disappointed. "Can you think of no reason?"

I can think of many. "You needed the world to see a justification for the occupation."

Meir groans as if I'd said the stupidest thing he's ever heard. "Twelve million Uyghurs lost to concentration camps and you still think the world gives a damn about your long-winded plight, good man?" He sighs when I don't reply and heads for the back door. "Think about it. And consider the possibility that I see what you don't: some role for you to play in this yet. All that's left is convincing you it's real."

"Wait," I reach out to grab his wrist, wanting to ask more, but regret the moment I do. In one fluid motion, he twists my arm and flips me on my back, knocking the wind out of me.

Meir stands over my body waiting for me to catch my breath like a disappointed parent. He grabs my hand to pull me back to my feet and pats the dust off my jacket. "Every drone in the system is an eye, and there are a hundred thousand in the city alone. It took one frame to find you, and three to erase any evidence of our first date." He puckers his lips and winks, turning for the door again. "Now if you'll excuse me, the chef is cooking falafel for breakfast, and I don't want to be one of the unlucky bastards left with the burnt ones at the bottom." The bell rings upon his exit.

My mind splinters trying to process what just happened. I tap a bead on my wrist and speed-dial Aylul, only to remember they left their phone with me when there's a buzz in my pocket. It's at this moment I realize just how alone I am. I have friends I can go to, sure, but we've all got problems, and burdening them with something they can't handle will only make me feel guilty for bringing it up. They probably wouldn't believe it anyway. I barely can. Staring at the back door, I wonder why Meir Cohen didn't kill me. Better yet: why didn't I kill him when I had the chance? The birth and death of the day staggers me to lean on the wall, exhausted from hunger and lack of sleep; I can hardly believe it is morning. Maybe I'm already dreaming. With nowhere else to go I grab a fistful of baharat seeds from a bag and head upstairs.

Home feels emptier than usual. Aylul's perfume still lingers in the air. I never really stopped to notice the blended notes of cedar, rose, and citrus, but now I do nothing but bask in their memory as if they were gone for good. I reckon I can go to their room and take the bottle, but when I cross the hallway and reach for the door handle, I stop. A sudden, irrational thought relating cause and effect tells me that if I enter their room now, they'll never come back. Better safe than sorry, I slam my bedroom door shut behind me. Tossing the seeds in the trash, I throw the weight of my body into bed and wiggle out of my clothes. The sheets reek of use. As soon as my head hits the pillow, my consciousness drifts from time and place into an oblivion cozier to me than this open-air prison has ever been.

By the time I wake the digital readout on my contact lens tells me the sun's setting. Not ready to open my eyes, I tap a bead on my wrist and open the home screen. Among a few unread messages, I see six missed calls from Cid and sigh with relief at the first good news in what feels like ages. I pull up his icon, a picture of him pretending to eat Diwa's head while she laughs, and call my friend.

"You okay?" is the first thing Cid asks when he picks up.

It's good to hear his voice. "Sorry, I was sleeping. Did you make it home in one piece?"

"More or less," he grumbles, "no bruises this time. I guess I have you to thank for that. Or was it Aylul? They haven't been picking up either."

My heart pangs at the sound of their name; I pause, not knowing what to say. Come to think of it, with Meir Cohen's attention on me, it's likely my phone's been tapped. Considering he was here before I arrived, the store's probably bugged too. "Pick me up around ten, let's go for a drive." We usually ask each other to go for a ride whenever it's time to vent about life's problems or silly things like spill on town gossip out of earshot. Luckily Cid seems to pick up that this is something more.

"I'll be there," he says before hanging up.

I open my eyes to sunset sepia spilling through the window into my room, but it lends no warmth. My stomach cramps from hunger, but I lose my appetite by the time I reach the kitchen. I lean against the counter, not knowing what to do with myself between now and the few hours before Cid picks me up. Unable to bear the silence, I decide to open the shop and head downstairs.

The fluorescent lights overhead flicker on as I walk the aisles counting inventory to get back in the flow of things. As expected, all that needs restocking are loaves of pita bread and cigarettes. I'll speak to Akel, the baker across the street, tomorrow morning about putting in another order. We went to secondary school together but ran with different crowds, never having much of a chance to speak. Back in the day, I thought of the people he ran with as sellouts to the country because I'd never see them at protests; how times have changed. A few years ago, he opened a bakery across the street but had difficulty making ends meet. He stopped by the shop one afternoon and we struck a deal that benefitted us both. He's a nice enough guy but we still don't talk often. I'm sure he saw enough hypocrisy when we started having mutual friends. I turn the open sign on and take my place at the cash register beside an old floating hologram of Fairuz coyly smiling against a microphone back in her golden years. My thoughts gravitate toward wondering what Aylul is doing, so I grab a remote to turn on the speakers and settle for Lahav Shani's piano melodies; they always hated when I played him.

Few customers pass through the shop in the first hour, most just happened to be walking by on their way home to pick up some last-minute things for dinner. Whenever a regular stops in, they lament the inevitable fall of Hamas or ask what's kept the store closed, or warn me not to fall into the same laziness my generation seems to be afflicted with. Some inquire about Aylul's whereabouts, and I'd lie, saying they were sick in bed or visiting friends in Ramallah. I should really get my story straight. Even the most menial details you'd never think anyone would care to remember are important enough to gossip about. When it's nearly time for Cid to arrive, Teta walks through the door, smiling big at the sight of me. It warms the heart. Never having the chance to meet my grandparents, she's the closest thing I've got. Now more than ever.

"You look as beautiful as ever, *hajja*."

She sweeps back her emerald hijab as if it was hair and bats her lashes at me. "It's so good to see you," she says as we kiss cheeks.

"What can I get for you?"

"Oh, just a half kilo of bread for today."

"None left, but I'm picking up from Akel in the morning if you wanna stop by then."

Her eyes go steel sideways, the playfulness in her demeanor gone. "You haven't heard? Akel gave the bakery to the Judeo-Nazis out of fear for retribution, the *khayan;* moved to Germany last night."

A failing business for the price of a passport anywhere of your choosing isn't a bad deal when it will just get bombed or taken anyway, so long as you can live with the fact that you've sold everyone else out. I don't say this, of course, but it does have me wondering when they'll be back to ask for Dad's store and the answer I'll give. He would never stand for it, but I could go to Europe and live the life of a free man. I'd fit right in too. After all, abandoning community for individuality is the price all Westerners pay for freedom. "Anyone else sell?"

Teta gives me an inquisitive look but doesn't answer, tossing a few candy bars for her grandchildren onto the counter. When I reach out to bag them, she grabs my hand suddenly with wide eyes watering. She's trembling and in that moment, I know she has read my mind. Instead of the anger most would meet me with, there's a depressed understanding of my consideration when she kisses my hands. She caresses my palm against her cheek, looking at me with eyes too old to beg. Here's a patriot who's never known the country they've fought for as a consequence of simply existing. From Gaza to Tulkarm and now Ayn Yassin, Teta's been a refugee in her own country since she was old enough to walk. Standing with her now feels like an unspoken acknowledgment of the futility against our occupiers, though she shakes her head after a moment passes. She pats my hand before letting go, turning to walk out the front door.

"You forgot your candy," I call back to Teta.

"Be back for it tomorrow. It's not good for someone my age to indulge in sweets so late at night: heart burn, ya know?" she croons, waving without turning back.

Cid lays on the horn of his Frankenstein sedan out front not long after Teta leaves, so I start closing up shop. Walking through aisles, turning off the lights, making sure the shutter gates lock tight. Meir's visit breeds paranoia, so I double then triple-check the store's security. A little truth inside my head tells me it doesn't matter, but I brush it aside for the sake of sanity. It's a chilly autumn night like they used to be back when seasons had a uniform identity. There's smoke rising in the distant east with the faint smell of burning tires threaded in gusts of wind. I don't concern myself with it as I walk to Cid's car. Put together with spare parts from his lot, the thing has no shame being six different colors. I nearly rip the door off just by pulling the handle.

"All those cars in the yard and you couldn't put together something better than this?"

"You of all people should understand the way of fragile things, *pare*," Cid chides from the driver's seat. He doesn't wait for me to respond before reaching over for a hug. He tries to pull away after a beat, but I bury my head in his shoulder. "Hey...what's wrong?" he asks.

That's all it takes for me to start crying. Not the single teardrop sniffling kind either. I'm weeping between broken gasps for air. Can't control my shaking, and the thought of how hard I'm crying makes me cry even harder. Cid doesn't say a word and just holds me tighter as if I might fade away. When I finally regain my senses I notice I've soaked his shirt through with snot. Being the guy he is, Cid ignores the mess, starting the car up with the deep rumble of mismatched parts coming together.

"See? You two are more alike than you think," he says, and it gets us laughing enough to move on.

"Diwa's not joining us?"

Cid scratches the back of his head with a shrug. "She was too embarrassed to come."

"I should be the one apologizing."

Cid looks over at me with one of his dimpled smiles. "We're family, Laeth. We do what we can for each other."

Cid winds through the narrow high-rise streets of Ayn Yassin on the way to our usual hangout spot. Not many people are out tonight thanks to the cold, so we speed through concrete slums and neon lights until they gradually thin to empty gravel dunes. Climbing up a hill, the car groans as if it'll give out any minute but somehow makes it to the top. Cid parks beside a red plush couch sitting on the edge of the cliff and brings blankets from the trunk. There's a hookah already set up from the last time we were here. I get our stash of tobacco from underneath a cushion. Cid throws tunes on from his car, raising the volume just enough to hear a jazz quartet play from where we're seated. I start the hookah up, double apple mist spilling from my mouth with a pleasant head buzz. We sit in comfortable silence as dusk gives way to winter night. The astral lights of a city alive grow steadily in number beneath our feet. When I pass the hose to Cid he takes a long drag, enveloping his entire face in a cloud of smoke.

"So, let's have it."

I take a deep breath for balance and recount everything that's happened over the past twenty-four hours. There are moments throughout the story that I find myself laughing incredulously at inappropriate times. At least I don't have to worry about whether Cid will believe me or not. Aside from the occasional exclamation, he stays quiet the entire time and well after I end on the part where Aylul abandons me and Mo'taz at the safe house.

"Makes sense," he finally says.

"What about anything I just said made sense to you?"

Cid stands to stretch, arms reaching up toward the stars. "Do you know why I stay here instead of hanging it up in the city?"

"The shawarma's better?"

He cringes at my timing. "Here's a purpose for me between what's happening and a balikbayan box; something bigger than surviving this boring dystopia." He grabs the hose back from me and takes a long pull, enveloping his face in smoke. "There's no greater purpose in life than lending a helping hand. Diwa showed me that. You know, I'm a master of machines." he jokes, "but don't get me wrong, it's not like I thought I'd be the hero of anyone's story. Even the old gods needed our prayers to keep the lights on though, so... Do you know why I stay?"

"For us?" My heart swells with love.

Cid shakes his head. "Because the *musakhan* is better." He passes the hose back as he sits on the couch, coughing at his own joke. "Take it from me, *pare*. You shame the plight of your ancestors by not believing in your future. You spent most of your life fighting against the occupation; protests, rallies – you've thrown rocks and Molotov cocktails – even let Hamas dig tunnels underneath the shop – right? But despite all that, brother, you won't know the first thing about what it means to be a true freedom fighter so long as you continue capitulating to normalize relations with the enemy entity. And that's why Aylul let you go."

He says it so casually it takes a second to register the combo. I flinch away from his touch, standing to face him. I want to tell him he can shove his nationalist ideologies up his ass; scream something naïve but true about a borderless world. That he shames himself for being a hypocrite who left his own country as a cause long lost to imagination. Anything to fight back. Doesn't matter if he's right; I'm sick of having to revolve my identity around an occupation. And maybe that's the problem. But right now, I'm frustrated and tongue-tied, so I kick over the hookah, and the glass base shatters. "Fuck you," I spit. Not knowing what else to do, I stomp away down the road we came. Cid calls for me, but I'm not listening.

It takes a couple of hours to get home. By the time I push into the shop, I've exhausted all arguments playing out in my mind. I take a Hot Pocket out of the freezer and throw it in the microwave, chewing on the plastic cheese and rubbery meat sixty infinite seconds later. I lean against the kitchen counter with eyes glazed over. A sudden urge to call my parents tugs at my heartstrings, but I don't want them to hear me play it like this. Something as simple as Mom saying hello would break me to healing, but I can't burden her with a decision they've already made. It's time to visit Aylul's room; superstition be damned.

It's immediately apparent just how much bigger it is than mine. Been a while since I've been here; privacy's always been important to Aylul. There's nothing hanging on the eggshell walls, no rug on the porcelain tile to warm the feet; just a queen-sized bed and cedar desk beside a window that looks out over dunes. I open the closet to look for their perfume, but it doesn't take me long to feel like some sort of pervert as I sift through their clothes.

Crossing over to their desk, I leaf through a sapphire-covered Quran laid half open and pick it up. Reading through the passage they had last left off, I try to find some deeper meaning to correlate their reasons for leaving me behind. Ever since first grade, I was taught *Qira'at* relentlessly the same way Mo'taz had, but looking at it now, nothing makes sense. As I move to put the book back the way I found it, I notice an empty glass frame where a picture of Aylul's father used to be. Gliding my thumb across the blank face, the simple truth dawns upon me: they were planning to desert me here from the get-go. In my squeezing grip, the frame cracks.

I set the broken pieces back down where I found them and hesitate a moment before pulling Sundus' contact information up in my lens feed. The phone rings several times before going to voicemail. I cut the connection without leaving a message. Damn Aylul; to hell with them all.

Days turn to months before I see them again, and when I do, my neighbor is Israeli.

SIDE B

"I don't like her." Teta's face scrunches like she's eaten a rotten apple, glaring at the white sedan parked in front of my shop. She turns away to thank Ibrahim for the coffee to sate the bad taste on her lips.

"You haven't even met her," the words drone out of my mouth from repetition over the past two years. Taking my turn in line, I nod to Ibrahim and toss him a shekel. "Why don't you come over some night, and I'll acquaint you two over some mint tea?" I ask Teta.

"Coming right up," the old man crones. "No sugar, yes?"

I sigh in disbelief. Just then a group of IOF soldiers march in uniform from across the street. Don't even need to look behind me to confirm; the tension in the air is enough to know, stiffening the group around me. Ignoring the moment I take the wrong order in hand and bless Ibrahim for his hands. While most around me glare in the soldiers' direction, Teta's eyes are still glued to the white sedan in front of my shop.

"I don't trust her," she says adamantly.

Were she to accept my offer meeting Leila, Teta would all but confirm her suspicions. I'm grateful she's as stubborn as a mule and leave the comment hanging.

"I've gotta go," I say, closing the distance between us to kiss my surrogate grandmother on her cheek. "Stop by later tonight, a shipment of olives from Nablus just arrived with your name on them." I thank Ibrahim once more, nodding to Teta with a smile to reassure her, and cross the street toward the car waiting for me. Such a short distance to cross, but each time I make it, the space between me and those staring at my back grows enough for oceans.

I throw the weight of my body into the passenger seat and stretch across the median to greet Leila with a kiss. A foreign waft of perfume tickles my nose as I trail my lips from mouth to cheek, and it gives me reason to pull away. I brush her caramel hair away from her brow to stare into chestnut eyes, searching for an answer.

"Jealousy doesn't suit you," Leila's anise-sweet voice carries annoyance with it, "especially when it's about men old enough to be my father."

I'm not convinced, but drop the matter entirely. It's too beautiful a morning to start by arguing about Meir Cohen. Maybe I'm the asshole if the bastard has no business buying my girlfriend perfume. I roll the tinted window down to let the autumn sun break the smoky interior when we're clear of Ibrahim's coffee stand. My nose barely registers the smell of burning tires and tear gas surrounding Ayn Yassin. Ever since Ma'al Luz began construction a couple of years back, the protests have only grown in ferocity – or rather, consistency is the more accurate term since we're still fighting empires with hopes and dreams. The fifty-story hotel exponentially expanded ever since the Knesset approved an amendment citing mandatory military service may be waived for five years' duty squatting in developing settlements. Those choosing the latter option are given government subsidized jobs based on the applicants' experience and how quickly the IOF can financially or forcefully coerce Palestinian landowners to give up their property. On our way to the southern checkpoint, I've never witnessed so much construction transforming my hometown. For every ten buildings passed, I notice an Israeli flag hanging outside storefront windows, doctors' offices, and single-family homes. Back when this first began, it baffled me why the settlers would paint such a target on themselves until Meir explained that it was a mandatory requirement.

"Never forget," he'd always say, "postulation is the beating heart of politics, and the show must go on."

Never thought it'd go on like this. The occupation of Ayn Yassin felt inevitable, but to think I'd be this alone. Leila stops at a red light. Outside my window, a black flag billows in the wind from a small corner bakery owned by one of Sundus' cousins – Rashid, I think. I'm amazed by his stupidity. Hope he kisses his children twice tonight because it'll be the last time they see their father.

It's been months since I've seen anyone dumb enough to fly that flag after this summer's mass exodus. Al Mubarizun, a group calling themselves the final resistance, had been growing in popularity after a third suicide bombing pushed their kill count to a hundred lives in just under a year. Led by Aylul and financially backed from the shadows by Sundus' father, they're a secular organization with only one prime directive: the liberation of Palestine. They made their start taking a leaf out of the Forgotten Ones' book, spreading flyers all over college campuses, making it clear a person's byproduct-affiliations do not matter. The duty to liberate Palestine from Zionist cleansing is one we all share. It is not our fate unless our consciousness accepts that imposed reality. "And we will only accept independence," the pamphlets read at the end.

It was a simple tactic, playing identity politics is hardly fresh or brilliant, but it worked unlike any rally Palestine has seen since the fourth intifada. A possibility to exceed it in the future exists. An organization of freedom fighters without dogma is exactly what the people of our generation needed to feel emboldened enough to heed a call to arms. Many skeptics of Al Mubarizun would say their rapid growth is attributed to the nearly thirty percent unemployment rate, and there's certainly some truth to that. However, the fact remains that the time of divine will empowering bravery is over.

"You gonna tell him or should I?" Leila says beside me.

"Why would either of us tell him anything?" I'm annoyed that we're talking about Meir again, but even more at Leila's eagerness toward our cause. "I'm sure he already knows." In a huff, Leila pulls off to the shoulder and parks the car.

"So that these embers don't ignite." She looks at me like I'm some kind of idiot. "Because our people will only burn themselves with that fire as our history's shown time and again. What's with you lately?" Leila's irritation recedes to genuine concern. She cups my cheek with a hand, making me look at her.

"You're right," I concede, "just tired of thinking about tomorrow." Of course, she doesn't know where I'm coming from because Meir sends me out into the field, not her. Leila handles things on base most days. Witnessing what happens on the front lines isn't anything she cares to see. No...no, that isn't fair. Considering her history, it's more like she decided she's seen enough.

Leila rubs a thumb against my brow, considering something for a moment before breaking into a smile. "I know just the thing," she says and pulls the car back onto the street. It's not long before we're in front of Ja'far, one of my favorite knafeh spots despite what everyone says about the slices in Nablus. Credit where credit's due, Leila knows how to lighten the mood. We walk into the white-tiled store as big as my living room to the sound of sizzling cheese, catching whiffs of baking phyllo dough and simple syrup. There's only one woman putting in an order at the register. After all, most people reserve knafeh for big occasions and certainly not for breakfast. Suckers, I say.

"Ah, if it isn't my favorite couple!" Ja'far raises a spatula in greeting from behind the line. "Coming in to finally give me a wedding invitation?"

The joke used to make me cringe, but getting harassed about marriage is a consequence we must accept for being so public with our relationship. It's been a year and a half, and neither of us has broached the subject – not once. "Two orders *na'ameh, ma'lim*," I say, not wanting to touch it now.

In no time, we're served two plastic plates with extra crushed pistachios on top, just the way we like it. We lean against an open windowed counter over-looking a row of storefronts all selling home furniture. I question why it's so commonplace for businesses to cluster together like this. My eyes glaze over as I stuff another piece in my mouth, losing all concept of my surroundings as I try to figure out the endless mystery. Simple syrup goodness drips from my lips. My mind shifts to the black flag in front of Rashid's store. I think of Aylul commanding Al Mubarizun and wonder where they are right now. I think of Cid just a few kilometers away but far out of reach. I think of Sundus and the permanent silence between us since she discovered my new side gig.

"Tomorrow won't get any better with you brooding over today," Leila says from beside me. I think she's been staring at me this whole time with the way concern still scrunches the bridge of her nose. "Do be careful, hm?"

"Aren't I always?" Hell, even I don't know the answer to that. Too many unknowns to account for, and I've never been at ease standing in the dark. "Meir's coming with me – hidden, but there – and I'll have all the support I need if there's another Bayt Thul on our hands."

Leila shudders at the mention of the Forgotten Ones' biggest failure to date and crosses her arms, shrinking inward. "We haven't visited the graves lately..."

I'm being too cold. I've gotten into the bad habit of not separating her from TFO's agenda. All she's ever done is try to help my stubborn ass get through this mess. I rub her shoulder and bring her close to me regardless of conservative onlookers from front and back.

"How about we visit them tonight? We can even stop at the Olive Tree on our way back; it's been a while since we've seen old faces."

She nods but leaves her slice half-eaten slice in the trash as we make our way out.

Sometimes we permit ourselves to wait in line at the checkpoint just like everybody else. Flashing the papers Meir gave us to expedite the process would undoubtedly lead to a brick through our windshield once our people were wise to our scheme. It takes half an hour to reach the wooden lever blocking the road. Leila digs through the glove compartment while I scroll through her playlist to find the right vibe. I let it ride on reggae until an IOF soldier knocks at the window, prompting the music off. The man at the window is a behemoth, towering over Leila's sedan as if he could flip it with one arm. I haven't seen this man before. He must be new, and with all fresh soldiers often comes a dangerous desire to prove oneself to their comrades by being a piece of shit like the rest.

"What do we have here?" His Arabic grates a trained ear, face half-masked by a tinted visor attached to his helmet. This man is prepared for battle.

Probably sensing the same thing I am, Leila practically shoves Meir's documents through the slit in the window. "Off to work," she says, "and good morning. How's your day so far?"

The titan ignores the question as he scans our paperwork. "A pathetic attempt at forgery," he sneers. "Do you have any idea the trouble you're in?"

I sigh at the predictability of the outcome and unlatch my seatbelt, ready to slowly exit the vehicle for a few rousing hours of detainment. Before I can push open the door, a familiar voice calls out.

"Horam, what do you think you're doing?" Lieutenant Haya strides forward with a formal grace in her second tongue. She doesn't wear body armor like most under her command. Her blonde locks freely bounce behind her gaunt as she keeps adjusting those ridiculous bifocal glasses. One would think she was headed to the library rather than leading the maintained occupation of Ayn Yassin after Meir relieved himself of charge. She doesn't stop until she's between our car and Horam.

He clasps his hands behind his back, snapping to attention. "Protecting our nation from any who would dare harm us, Sir."

"If that's the case, I insist you search the pantry since you won't find them here." Haya doesn't revert back to her native tongue. "And be a good dear, since you'll be there already, give it a good mop." She pulls our papers from his grip. Horam looks ready to pop a blood vessel but salutes his superior with an affirmative before stomping off.

"Thank you," Leila and I say when she hands back our documents with a satisfied smirk.

"Think nothing of it," she responds sincerely. "Plus, Meir would have my ass if I kept his favorites from him."

I find the term revolting, but Leila glows under the status recognition. Those at the checkpoints who have been around long enough have come to call us Meir's Favorites. Sometimes said in jest, but more often than not synonymous with dogs. Not like they have the wrong of it.

"Bring you back anything from HQ?" I say to bring matters to a close. Our run-in with Horam reminds me I want to get this day started so it can more quickly be over.

Lieutenant Haya perks up at the offer and clasps her hands together. "You know they keep the best halva for the enlisted officers."

I pop a cigarette in my mouth and make a mental note for the return journey as I light it. "On my head."

Haya slaps the roof of the car and barks at a soldier to raise the wooden lever for us.

The drive to headquarters is a thirty-minute drive south through uncontested Bedouin land, cracked and unfertile. Small clusters of sheared tents and salvaged metal litter each side of the freeway, only able to expand as far as a football kick. Some dwell between stacks of scrapped cars and others attempt to maintain tradition by herding anorexic goats. All sit at the foot of hills, white stone Zionist settlements ever watchful at the top glistening in the sun. Many Bedouins beg at the freeway intersections, holding out their hands without a word of plea. We ignore them all.

We're not far from the Jordan Valley as we approach TFO's newly assigned headquarters. Surrounded by high barbed wire fences, the compound facilitates barracks for our growing numbers as well as soldiers assigned to patrol the Allenby Bridge connecting the borders. Leila's recently been on about us moving in together at the compound, but I'm not abandoning my father's store. The soldiers guarding the entrance recognize our vehicle as it pulls up, raising the gates without making us go through the motions. We both wave at Private Sadiq as we cross the threshold, and the gates shut behind us.

We park in front of Meir's personal residence, a trailer straight out of an eighties flick barely holding its piss-colored walls together. The thing is dingy at best and furnished as though someone's blind great-grandmother had the final say. I'm sure Leila can recall the story, but all I remember is Meir claiming it's his good luck charm ever since he took refuge in it during his days in Gaza. I hate spending time here, but it's the only place Meir's willing to instruct the two of us since he believes every other building is bugged by his government. We're met with an unhelpful breeze in the scorching sun as we make our way to knock at the entrance. In front of us stands one of Israel's most treasured operatives, straightening his uniform and priming his hair before reaching out a hand to shake ours.

"Good to see you both," Meir says groggily. "Come, I've got coffee on the stove, and the bar is always open."

As we enter past him, a waft of must assaults my nose more than the burning tires of revolution ever could. It's any wonder what could be found in the fibers of the shag rug. I pour the three of us coffee from the ibrik and take my place at the half-moon table. I pick at the lid of my Styrofoam cup while a stillness lingers between us.

"Oh, stop it, you two." Leila flicks our foreheads with a level of familiarity I find interesting Meir accepts. "Believing the worst before the beginning only serves to invite your greatest fears. Right? Right?!" She holds each of our gazes in turn until we concede. "We're doing what's right here. If it were easy, the task wouldn't have fallen to us after all these years."

"To business then," Meir's usual gravitas returns. He unrolls a screen onto the table and taps a black device attached to his temple. A map of Huwara comes to view in front of us, and Meir tinkers with the settings a moment before tactical objectives highlight areas in the southern market district. He pinches his fingers and pulls, zooming in on a mosque located at the center of the bazaar.

People roam the streets laughing, bargaining, and shouting in real time thanks to extensive Zionist surveillance bots hidden in the sky. "As you know, our rally takes place in front of the Ibrahimi Mosque at 1500, before things are at their busiest. Laeth, I want your eyes scanning for any threat to Samira while she's speaking. Don't think if, but when."

I nod hearing the same things we've said a dozen times before. "Yeah, okay." I pull a cigarette and move to light it, but Meir snatches it out of my mouth.

"You know how much I hate these," he sounds surprised at my petulance but returns to the map, grazing a finger over the surrounding bazaar. "Signal those you trust to break off into two groups to patrol the outer edges for any signs of unrest. This is our first time in Nablus since Bayt Thul, and, well, 'fool me once,' as they say."

I know what's coming next as he fiddles with his laser pointer, glancing at Leila, who nods encouragement back.

"This would be easier if our acolytes had weapons," he says slowly. "If we *are* to learn from Bayt Thul, then we know one man with a pistol can't change the tides alone when the waves are hundreds of bloodthirsty people." Meir holds my gaze, but all I can wonder as I search his face is why he's waiting for my permission when he doesn't require it.

"Do I have to repeat myself?" This all but confirms that I still shouldn't trust him. "Do I have to spell out the irony of peacekeepers wielding guns? Having one is enough."

He rubs his temples. "Really, Laeth, you're an educated man. Think of how the scales tip without a way for your people to defend themselves."

The way he says *your people* set me on edge. It's as if he's forgotten the six souls we buried just last month. He probably doesn't remember being as drunk as he was at the ceremony. I swallowed the thought from furthering. "They'll continue defending themselves with the talking sticks."

Meir rolls up the screen on the table and tosses it to me. "Triple-check these plans you're so prepared for. Jerusalem and Ramallah were simple enough, but we need a foothold in Nablus. I don't need to explain the importance of tomorrow's success." He faces away to fix himself a heavy drink at the bar. "Leila, I've got this dreadful grant meeting, so I'll have to meet you in our office later. Keep the comm lines open, you're our bridge home."

She perks. "Aye, sir."

Meir nods, unfurling his brow to muster an encouraging smile. "We're on the brink of a new dawn. Don't forget why we do this. It's not for ourselves, but for the ones too dejected to voice their plea for war's end. We do this to leave the past behind so that we may finally find a future of coexistence as cousins, as family. There is no greater cause in these lands, from Golan to Gaza. Let us sow the seeds of peace so that our children's children may bask in its shade. Tomorrow's success will bring us one step closer to those better days. I know it."

Meir's fervor amuses me. What works on Leila won't on me. She thanks him and dismisses herself for work. "See you in Huwara," I say to Meir as I follow her out.

"Remain a moment," he commands.

Leila looks back, hesitating before closing the door behind her. I turn back to plop back where I sat. Meir slides me a whiskey glass filled with some pink concoction. Strange, he remembers I like my drinks fruity.

"Word finally came: Al Mubarizun scattered more than we previously thought, but we're certain now *they're* based somewhere in Jenin."

The mention of Aylul makes my palms itch. "And?"

"And that's it, for now. I'll divert them with my inside man if the need comes up." Meir pauses for a reaction. When I give him none, he clicks his tongue with dissatisfaction. "I would have you ride with me tomorrow," he starts. "It's been a while, no? Part of me feels as if... you're beginning to forget the lesson I taught you in Hebron."

My grip on the glass slightly slips from sweaty palms as I find the strength to look at him. "How could I?"

"A question I asked myself last time, yet here we are, and I sense a waning within you." He clinks our glasses together as he stands above me, guzzling his drink down to the last drop. "Meet me tomorrow bright and early. I would have you recollect your memory before the event horizon."

I f there's a hell, it dwells above. The sun singes my skin crisp in real time as Leila and I make our way through the Compound. Moments like these, I wish I would've taken Meir's offer to pay for VitaStim implants. I lick my tongue over chapped lips in hopes of some relief and figure it's better to deal with this than a mob outside my store when everyone in Ayn Yassin puts two-and-two together. We say our hellos to the smiling faces of soldiers and members of our organization alike, mingling as we zigzag our way between barracks and offices. Pressed against the eastern wall is a small collection of van merchants shouting and laughing between *"But for you, my friend?"* deals. I approach one of the few Arab traders selling persimmons, thumbing a few to inspect their ripeness.

"Haven't seen you here before," I ask without making eye contact. From the moment I pass through these walls, I'm always on the job. Few can say what that job is – least of all me – but security detail sums it up well enough.

"First time," he says offhandedly, disregarding me to charm Leila with honeyed words. He goes for the wrong thing and compliments her beauty, only to get an eye roll. The merchant turns to me as if to say, "Women, right?"

I point at the brass ibrik boiling coffee in a wok of sand behind him. "Two, please." Let us see the weight of his soul. The air thickens in the autumn heat as I watch him pour two double-stacked paper cups full with molten cardamom. He sets them in front of us and I slide a couple of shekels his way. Feeling his gaze upon me, I glare at the coffee as I blow at it to cool, raising it to my lips – no, not yet – and lower the cup, blowing once more. Should he undress, I'm sure I could see the man's heart beating out of his chest. I raise the cup again, ready this time, and tilt it back to slurp. Setting it back on the table, I close my eyes and smack my lips. Perfection. "Welcome to the Compound, brother."

The merchant pulls the *tuqia* off his head and shakes a clenched fist at me as Leila laughs. He introduces himself as Tariq Hamdaan, born in Al Quds. "But enough about the past, no? Why not buy a persimmon for you and your lady to sweeten the present?"

I give him a look to let him know his tricks won't work on me, but I buy the persimmons, so maybe they did. Leila and I agree that work can wait a few minutes and perch ourselves up on an unconstructed portion of the wall. Sitting under the infinite azure like this with the breeze in our hair taking hearty bites of honey-sweet fruit to quench our thirst heals a deep wound within me. The distant laughter of coexistence fills the air around us. Leila throws her pit into the expanse of dunes when she's done eating and leans her head on my shoulder. We sway our feet off the rock ledge until my right and her left entwine, and we swing together. She giggles. I allow myself to laugh too. At what, I don't know, but it feels nice. A few minutes pass, and we let a few more go.

Someone clears their throat behind us. "When they call you our leaders, it's not so you can blatantly ignore your responsibilities."

Leila's intern assistant, Abigail, is the one dripping venom. She couldn't look at us for a week when she walked in on us in Leila's office last month, and it seems the disapproval still lingers. "Good morning," I say.

"Mr. Awad," she says, using her customer service voice to let me know we're still not talking, "Amir and Moshe have been looking for you."

Hearing my assistants' names tethers me back to an unforgiving reality. Leila's already pulling apart our sweat-adhesive clothes like a zipper. She gifts me a kiss on the lips before jumping down to greet Abigail. "See you for lunch?" I ask.

"Can't," Leila calls back as they walk away, "but I'll be there tonight." They disappear behind the maze of structured tents before I can prolong their departure.

My appreciation for the view doesn't last long alone, so I concede to those waiting for me and hop off the ledge. I still take my time heading over to my office by saying hello and how are you to anyone who makes eye contact with me. This kind of living is fine enough but I'll never love anything more than the act of simply living. Whoever first decided that man had a duty to produce deserves a special place in hell. Finding myself in front of the entrance to my tent, I sigh before pushing through a flap to the sound of racked billiard balls. Our station isn't much bigger than an average living room, but I made the executive decision to push our desks to the corners and do away with everything else when

Moshe informed us his father was giving away his table. Amir didn't approve of the change at first, calling it irresponsible. Eventually, he conceded to Moshe's encouragement. Seeing the stiff bastard line up his shot as I walk in makes me feel nostalgic for something right in front of me.

"Y'know, Boss." Amir doesn't lose his concentration, breaking the balls with a loud clatter. He gets two stripes in and nods, satisfied. "They're going to start calling that part of the wall Makeout Point if you two keep at it much longer."

I appreciate him trying to speak to my love for American cinema, but cringe underneath. "Maybe then ya'll would have the balls to go somewhere public." Witty comebacks have never been my strong suit, but the mention of their little secret hits the right nerve. Moshe blushes through his fair features, shaking his head downcast.

Amir shoots daggers, bushy brows darkening sharp angles. "If someone hears you –"

"– They'll do what, exactly? Last I checked, it's legal in Israel." If Aylul were to hear me so casually affirm the colony's pinkwashed existence, they'd remind me what their right hook feels like. I think of them every time I let it slip. Amir sighs, and Moshe rubs one of his shoulders to calm him down. My petulant retort aside, it's a shame he has every right to be nervous. Best we move on before the mood sours. "What's on the agenda today?"

Credit where it's due, Amir shakes off any ill will quick and resumes his position as my right hand with dignified decorum. "At this point, we've checked every box in preparation for Huwara." He strides over to his desk opposite mine and rustles through some papers. "Except one, that is: we're still short on intel regarding Al Mubarizun. Ever since the last exodus, people have been afraid to even mention their name for fearing association much less willing to part with any rumors."

Moshe fusses with the buttons on his military uniform but eventually gets on with what I'm expecting next. "We thought, considering your history with certain people..."

I pop a cigarette between my lips and light it, policy be damned. In the past, whenever someone would mention using Cid to further the organization's agenda, I'd either pretend it wasn't possible or tell them to piss off. Then Bayt

Thul happened, and although no one's said it outright, there are many in the Compound who blame me for the deaths of our comrades. There's only one person within reach who may know what's going on, and the likelihood of him spitting in my face is about as high as the chance of me grabbing a second slice of knafeh tonight. But I can't let another Bayt Thul happen. My friends expect me to protect them and, by extension, their message. So I surprise them by finally saying, "Fine."

"Excellent!" The shrapnel scars littering Amir's face like acne dance when he grins. "Just give us a moment to get everything in order, and—"

"No." I raise a hand to stop him from going on. "I need you two here in case Samira needs anything."

"But, Sir—" Moshe moves to argue, but Amir grabs his wrist.

I smile for the sake of encouragement, but my heart takes a hit. I swear for twenty-five, he looks fifty – the curse of the modern Palestinian. I get off my desk, glancing around as if there may be something important to take with me. "You both know how to reach me if you need it." I think about what's coming for a moment. "But try not to."

I shield my eyes with a hand when I'm back outside; the morning's earlier bustle now calmed by everyone hard at work. Those who I do see are laser-focused on where they're going, hardly noticing me pass. No doubt everyone's nerves are on edge for tomorrow. For as long as it's been, Bayt Thul still humbles us. Most nights, I can still hear the crowd swallowing our straggling comrades' whole. A thousand angry voices drowned out any last words they may have had for someone to remember. I wind through tents and push through to the mess hall. Save for some of the cooks in the back prepping for lunch, the large room of picnic tables and vending machines is empty. I fist bump the chefs I know, taking in the smells of hard yogurt, lamb, and pine nuts cooking in the ovens. I better be back in time to score some *mansaf*. I reach the storage closet and rifle through some crates until I find what I need before heading out. Technically, the liquor is reserved for Zionist personnel only, and I could get written up if discovered, but no one in the kitchen would snitch on one of their own. I grab two bottles of bourbon and tip-toe back, holding the door so it doesn't slam on my way out.

"What's this?"

"Eh?!" I whip around to face my accuser to see Samira grinning up at me.

She wags her finger, curls and hoop earrings bouncing from side to side while she *tsk*s. "How many times does this make it this month, *yaa zift*?"

"More of a sin it's not five considering the surplus they've got here." I stand there dumbly, thumbing the labels of the bottles in my hand. "I'm going to see Cid."

The playfulness drains from her face as she fidgets with her nose ring. "Guess that means Moshe and Amir couldn't find any leads."

"It's fine. Not like I wasn't expecting this sooner or later."

"Can't blame you for trying to push later into never," she says gently. "Anything I can do?"

I swat away the offer. "Meet me and Leila at the Olive Tree after the rally?"

"I ask your team to do one simple thing...." She looks like she's going to chew Amir and Moshe out. "We need you here at 2100; Abigail should have informed Leila by now."

"For what?"

My sister dazzles me with a smile and a two-fingered peace sign as she leaves through the exit door. "Just don't be late!" It's about to close when she pops her head back in. "And wear something better than that," she says, eyeing my flannel and jeans, "*Allah yusaeidak*." She laughs at the look on my face and slips back out before I can defend myself.

I borrow Leila's car to bump along potholes, foregoing Fairuz love ballads on the radio as I make my way back to the outskirts of Ayn Yassin. Wish a checkpoint would obstruct me from getting to where I was going. I haven't spoken to Cid since our falling out, and I'm not looking forward to a reunion. Our friendship was born of the Cause, but it wasn't until Aylul left that it became the driving force of our bond. Maybe things would've ended differently if I hadn't waited to talk about my deal with Meir until he saw me leading a rally in Ramallah. Certainly wouldn't have led to a fist fight outside of Olive Tree when he called me out.

Unlike Ayn Yassin proper, the occupation hasn't changed Cid's neighborhood much since the last time I was here. Pondering the elusive business savvy behind people choosing to start their mechanic shops in an area where there are already a dozen leads me to Cid's garage before I have time to find the answers I've been looking for all my life. I turn the ignition, grab the bottle of bourbon from the passenger's seat, reach for the door handle, and stop. Maybe I should call first. I tap a bead on my wrist for my contact list and scroll down my implanted lenses until I reach his name. No, no – don't wanna give him time to back out. Plus, I'm already here. Let's just get this over with. I kick open the door and crunch along the gravel lot when I hear a cat's meow. Looking down, I'm greeted by the cutest tabby face there ever was. I coo at my old friend, scooping him in my arms for scratches until the front door unlatches.

"Toho always seems to know where the trouble's at." Diwa Silang leans against a pillar, arms crossed against her chest. If this was two years ago, she'd be running in for a hug. Now she stays planted, waiting to hear the reason why I've come after so long.

I set Toho down and lift the bottle as a sort of peace offering. "Thought we could catch up."

"How's the tattoo?" She ignores the offering. "Still itching after all this time?"

"Most days I forget it's even there," I reply honestly. Using my sleeve, I wipe sweat from my forehead. "Any chance Cid's inside?"

Diwa stares, the butterfly tattoo on her neck glowing from red to sunflower yellow. She rubs her thumbs, fussing with stray dreadlocks. "He's in the back," she starts slowly, "but let me get him. He doesn't like people in the shed anymore."

Stings I've been lumped in with "people" after all this time, but I get it. We're already further into this than I wagered. I watch Diwa hook around the shop and back to the shed before something comes over me. "I miss you," fumbles out of my mouth. The sound of footsteps ceases. Well, shit. No stopping now, I guess. "I never wanted it to be this way. I... I wish it wasn't. They don't have to be." I know I'm losing grip because I know it isn't true. Not when it comes to Palestine.

Diwa peeks back with sadness in her eyes. Her lips part slightly, then close, then open, then close. "I'll get Cid."

I lean against Leila's car, lost in non-thought under the beating sun. My mind tries to focus on anything to escape my feelings. Children's laughter as they play soccer on a dirt field behind the shops; the hearts and hands behind every power drill, tire change, and tool falling to the ground. No matter where the wind blows, the thinly veiled smell of petrol permeates the air. I would always get nauseous coming here on humid days with Aylul. Most days, I can't believe it's been so long since we've spoken. I know Cid has an open line to them, but that's because I also know why he doesn't allow people in the shed any more thanks to Meir's bribery. If Cid knew I was holding back the dogs from eating his handsome, dimpled face, would he think of me differently? Probably not. I hear the gravel crunch of footsteps approaching and look over to see my old friend. He's still the same beautiful man, but his dimples stay hidden. Like Diwa, he refuses to speak first.

"Think we can talk?" I raise the bottle sheepishly.

His eyes narrow between me and the bourbon. "Some fancy shit ya got there," he calls over. "I may be thirsty, but only fools drink from a poisoned well."

I want to roll my eyes, thinking maybe this was a waste of time, but then Cid says, "But talk."

I look around, and while there's no one immediately around us, that doesn't mean prying ears aren't present. "Can we go somewhere a little more private?"

He looks as if he's about to tell me to piss off, but Diwa tugs at his plain white tee. "Just don't bring one of your talking sticks."

It takes a moment to register that he's talking about the TFO tactic I adopted from being friends with him. "Noticed that, did you?"

"Yeah, real fucking cute, dude."

Thought he would've taken me inside the shop, but instead, we snake our way through the backyard opposite the shed. After all this time, the towers of stacked totaled cars seem to have only gotten taller. When we're surrounded by wreckage on all sides, the couple stops to face me.

"So talk," Diwa says to her husband, neck tattoo changing a reddish hue.

Feeling dumb with it in my hands, I set the bottle down between us. "I'm sure you're both aware we're having a rally in Huwara tomorrow." Ignore Cid's scoff. "Regardless of how you feel about us, I know you; I know you don't want innocent blood on your hands. After what Al Mubarizun did at Bayt Thul, I –"

"We didn't raise a goddamn finger against you!" Cid lashes out.

"We're only trying to end this mess for a future without violence."

Diwa clicks her tongue. "Yeah, that's all fine and dandy, but who benefits from that colonized future while you're scraping for basic human rights, Laeth?"

"You and your forgetful people may be aiding the enemy, but Aylul would never give orders to murder innocent Palestinians," Cid chimes in.

I think of my fallen comrades: Anas, Abeer, Jeanine, Suehad, and Basemah. Inciting the people to violence against us makes Aylul's hands just as dirty. That's what I want to say, but I can't lose this chance for an argument we've already had a dozen different ways in our past lives. "There won't be a future to arrive at if Palestine doesn't stop bleeding her children. Just..." Fuck this. "No news is bad news, the bad-bad kind of news. What's the plan?"

Cid shakes his head at me. There's enough hate in his eyes to let me know this conversation's over. "Nothing you should be worried about."

"What does that mean?"

Diwa wrings her hands between us. "Can you leave, please?" The sincerity in her voice throws my heart into a meat grinder. "You come here after – how long? – and you don't even ask how we're doing after all this time or even," her Arabic sputters in a flustered state, "or even have the balls to say Aylul's name, for fuck's sake!" She glares up at me.

I can't meet her gaze. "Cid, I –"

"– I know, man." His voice is softer than it has been. "But the fact that you still can't see means you had no business looking for anything around here."

I want to reach out; tell him to show me what I've been blind to despite living here all my life, fighting side by side with him at protests for nearly a decade while Palestine only grew smaller. I desperately want to believe; to have the same faith as those who believe in God. Such blind devotion is something I never turned my nose up at, but a quality I simply lacked. Cid knows it, and I know I can only live to honor the truths as I see them. So I leave the bottle on the ground and turn to walk back to the car when another urge hits me.

"Are they safe?"

Cid chews on his lip, then looks up at the sky to eventually point at the barely noticeable glean of a surveillance drone whizzing beneath the clouds. "Are any of us?"

Waiting at the checkpoint outside Ayn Yassin only gives me time to replay the scenario over in my head to look for something I could've done better. By the time I reach the front half an hour later, I've found many.

"Surprised to see you without your better half." Lieutenant Haya walks over and leans into my open window, craning her neck in search of something. "You forgot the halva."

"Shit, Haya. I'm sorry. It's been a long day."

She gives me a look, tapping one of the beads over the VitaStim implant on her wrist. "It's not even dinner time, there's still time for you yet."

"Heh" is all I can muster through rubbing my eyes.

"You good?" There's a concern in her voice. She presses the back of her hand against my forehead.

"I'm fine, thanks." I swat her hand away. "Haven't been sleeping well lately with Huwara coming up, is all. Shouldn't you be...I dunno, doing something more appropriate for a commissioned officer?"

Haya laughs, and I can't help but smile about that. "Being here is my favorite thing to do," she says. "You don't get to meet people the way you should when you're stuck in an office. It gives me a chance to show the locals we're not all assholes. After that – who knows? – but the start of something's always the hardest part."

My doubt gets the better of me. "You seriously telling me being nice is going to change anything in this mess?"

Haya shrugs off my skepticism. "Got you to turn that frown upside down, didn't I?" She slaps the hood of the car. "Good luck with the rest of the day, Laeth. I'll be expecting double halva tomorrow."

Not long after, I roll up to the front of the shop and park. I should really be back at the Compound, but the perk of having assistants means passing off the finer details onto them. Rather, I'm practicing my delegation. That's all it is. Plus, I haven't been to the store when it's open for well over a week now. I miss going at my own pace. When I walk through the front doors, the nostalgic waft of canvas-bagged sunflower seeds and pita bread mixed with the stale tobacco of someone smoking where they shouldn't hit me in all the right places. Teta's nephew Hassan is working the cash register, closing out some older man in a white *dishdasha*. When

Teta asked me to help him out last year, I was skeptical of letting another man handle my father's shop. After working at the organization so much, I couldn't deny the help if I wanted the store to survive. And Hassan's been doing a fine job. He has a charisma others gravitate to and an inherent honesty in his soul. Whenever I inquire about him at Ibrahim's coffee stand, everyone only has good things to say. It's nice seeing the floors mopped and the aisles stocked again. By the time I get behind the counter, he sends the customer off laughing with some joke about Sheikh Omar wiping his chin in an Israeli stall. He's definitely Teta's kin.

"*Assalamu 'alaikum, ma'lim*," Hassan greets me formally. "I wasn't expecting to see you today."

I shake the man's hand rough with callouses. "I've got some free time," I lie, "thought I'd take over and give you the day off." Despite treating me like a student would regard their teacher Hassan is ten years older than me.

He shuffles awkwardly, looking at his shoes. "Actually, Sir, I was wondering if I could have tomorrow off. See, there's this TFO rally, and I'd like to go with some friends to remind those khawana the faces they're betraying."

It takes every ounce of control I have not to stiffen. "That's alright," I say slowly. "This place would have closed permanently by now without you; what's one day?"

His face lights up like I've given him a gift on *Eid Al-Adha*. "Thank you!" He grabs my hand and shakes it aggressively. "God bless your kindness, if there were more people like you looking out for their fellow man, we would have reclaimed Palestine." Such grandiose words of appreciation befit all Palestinians, and there's a duty I usually feel to give it in kind, but this time I can't. Hasan starts going over what's left on his to-do list. I barely feel my legs move as we inspect each aisle. Eventually we kiss cheeks, and he's out the door.

Being at the store chips away whatever's hanging on my shoulder. I orchestrate a playlist of rock and roll over the radio and whistle along to tunes, head banging when there's no one around chanting fuck the system. Even stocking the shelves puts a new spring in my step, and anyone who comes in gets a free piece of candy on their way out. A few shipments of different produce come in throughout the day, and it's nice to be remembered by the workers. We talk about light matter, like how hot it is for September, and a young couple down the street who got caught making out in their parents' car the other day. Apparently, you could hear the father yelling all the way in Ramallah. By the time night falls, I can't count how many cups of coffee I've shared with my community, but won't soon forget the ache in my jaw from laughing.

When I remember having to pick Leila up from the Compound it's nearly nine. It's goodnight to the last of my customers and time to close up shop. I run up the stairs to my apartment and scurry to my room where I pass Aylul's, sliding on my socks to a stop at the cracked door. Everything's exactly as it was on the day they decided to leave. In the first few months, I used to keep it closed, hoping that one day I'd find it open. They'd be reading a book or eating junk food while watching a movie, and turn to me saying something casual like, "Hey." But opening and closing that door became something of a habit, one I'd return to a dozen times a day. So now it stays open, as all doors should. My room, on the other hand, looks like a hoarder's nest if they didn't have many things to own other than takeout boxes. So I just reach on the floor for some shirts to smell a few, decide the black button-down hides the wrinkles best, and change on my way back out. As I enter the store again, the front door opens.

"Sorry, we're—" I look up to see Teta's wrinkled face illuminated by neon light.

"You said you had some olives with my name on them?"

It takes me a second to remember what she's talking about, but I quickly remember where I left those jars of Nablus green olives and jog over to the storage closet.

"You know," Teta hollers over from the register, "I saw the white car out front and thought I'd finally get to meet *her*."

"I borrowed the car, and you know her name," I chide, making my way back with a milk crate of olives. "Isn't she like your second cousin's grandkid?"

"Third," she corrects.

I raise an eyebrow at her. "Leila's working, but I promise I'll put something together soon. I've actually gotta go pick her up now, so if you'll excuse me—"

Teta grabs my sleeve. "Well, what do I owe you for the olives?"

"Register's off; too much trouble booting it back up," I do my best to look helpless in the situation. She doesn't laugh or loosen her grip.

"You know how thankful I am for everything you've done for Hassan," she starts slowly. "But I know what she is; so many of us do. I know where you've been spending all this time. It took me a while to figure it out, but enough whispers confirmed my suspicions. I didn't tell anyone," she says in reaction to my shock. "I think –" her voice cracks. She puts a hand up to her mouth as though she's going to be sick. "I think part of me understands why you felt the need to join them. But you've spent far too much time in echoes of defeat, Laeth, and it's time for you to think outside of that chamber. Please." Her hands shake in mine. "Please come back."

My first impulse is to apologize for everything I've done, and my second is to ignore the first. I can only nod with a sincere, vague promise that I'll try as she kisses my hand in hers. And somehow, that's enough to make her smile through tears. Together arm-in-arm we walk out the front door. By the time I lock the store for the night and turn to ask if she needs help carrying the case, Teta's already halfway across the street.

"Thank you, for –" I call out, but think of anyone eavesdropping.

Teta looks back under the crescent moon, black 'abaya billowing in the wind as though gowned in the night itself. "What are we here for if not for each other?"

٩

The road to Al Khalil – or Hebron as it's known by those who are wrong – is completely out of the way from our rally in Huwara. As much as I hate sitting next to Meir for any extended length of time, I do enjoy feeling the wind in my hair as we speed through curves in his cherry red convertible. I lean back to stretch my arms as a commercial plane disappears into the clouds overhead. This is the closest I'll ever feel to flying. I catch a glance over at the commander and worry about the absence of his typical chill. In its stead, his eyes fix forward unblinking, shrapnel scars twitching when he chews the inside of his cheek. After our first encounter at my father's shop, he reappeared a week later with news of Aylul. The caveat to sharing this information was driving me to Al Khalil. I thought it strange at first, but too easy of a trade to ignore; especially back then when I was having panic attacks thinking about where my cousin had gone. It was here two years ago in this cursed city that our pact was made, and I became one of the Forgotten One's guardian angels.

Thought I stumbled upon a zero-sum game. Meir offered protection for Aylul against his government in trade for me to help bolster TFO's ranks. In this thing, he's been true to his word. Aylul's eluded capture or assassination on a number of occasions thanks to Meir's moles within Al Mubarizun. Contact with them has been scant at best in recent months since the summer exodus, however. Apparently, Aylul now rules with an iron fist. As well, they should.

Our path breaks over the ridge and down below the tall wheat valley, sprawling into a metropolis teeming with life. It's a marvel of modern civilization built on gunmetal pillars and obsidian glass. I wouldn't be surprised to find out there are as many skyscrapers here as there are buildings in Ayn Yassin. When annexation over the long-contended land had been declared, most of us in the occupied territories saw it as the beginning of the one true end. Just as it was with the Byzantines and the Rashidun after them, Al Khalil is the second most prized jewel of Palestine after Al Quds. Birthplace of Abrahim, the resting site of his son Isaac, and now home to one of Israel's worst secrets.

With resistance forces significantly culled and the city taken, there were whispers of a labor camp deep within the mines of those very same brigades, but that's all they ever were for me beyond the paper trail proof online: whispers. But now I've seen them. Now I know what lurks beneath this glimmering city are not whispers, but rasps. It worries me that Meir decided to bring me back here.

"Don't you think our time's better spent securing Huwara?" I ask to shake the feeling.

"Trust your comrades to get the job done," Meir says over the wind. "You do trust them, don't you?"

I think of Leila and Samira, Amir, Moshe, and the dozen others under my vague watch each, forging a hope to bring an end to their pattern by forgetting the past to create a coexistent future. I leave Meir's question unanswered.

We outline a circle through the outskirts of Al Khalil toward our destination. Even here, marble houses shine under the sun. Children play in swimming pools, their laughter following us as we speed down roads without potholes. Cypress trees on either side sway in the autumn breeze, carrying with them the scent of falafel from the vendors spotting the sidewalks. Other than Tel Aviv, Hebron is one of the only places in Palestine without M16-wielding occupiers patrolling every block. It's a message to all who would question: this city is ours. Meir once told me there's still a base of operations a few clicks away. Can't be too certain, it seems. Their doubt makes me smile in spite of it all. It's quickly wiped from my face when a tunnel into the mountain's base comes into view ahead. A small group of soldiers clusters around the entry, smoking cigarettes and taking jabs at one another. It takes them a moment to realize we're waiting at the gates, but the moment they do, the fun and games come screeching to a halt.

"My apologies, Sir!" A lieutenant fresh out of the womb scrambles to salute Meir from beside his door. He knows who he's kept waiting without having to ask. "We weren't expecting such honored visitors, there were none on the docket."

Meir bites his lip at the excuse, cracking his neck before leaning out the window. "Must I ask for permission from witless bums whose mummies and bubbies in Parliament ensured their children could fuck off? Have I fallen so far?"

Beneath his helmet, the lieutenant turns beet red. "You're our country's gift from God. I did my dissertation on your operations in Gaza—"

"– Did I ask for a lesson in my own history?" Meir snaps. His sour mood reminds me of when he nearly kicked Samira out of TFO for mentioning his accomplishments during a victory speech.

"Raise the gates!" The lieutenant barks at his subordinates.

The iron bars groan as they activate, lifting through an opening in the mountain. With one last look at the sun overhead, Meir presses his foot on the gas pedal for darkness to swallow us whole. He turns on the headlights to illuminate the twisting road turned gravel as we bump along in silence. Down and down we go through the narrow passage as the space between seconds stretches. The air thickens with dust when we finally hit the flats. It's then that I hear the clank of pickaxes in the dark distance. My throat stays dry as much as I swallow, heart thumping along with the irregular tones. We're eventually guided by electric lanterns attached to the rock face. I'd be grateful for the light if it wasn't giving form to those creating the tick against stone. The cave widens and on each side, hunched shadows toil. They disregard the roar of our engine, mechanically lifting and striking their mountain prison that stretches a kilometer in any given direction. They slave away wordlessly as thin vessels long succumbed to their fate. After all, these are the ones who know the truth better than most of us on the outside: no help is coming.

"Now would be a good time to tell me why you've brought me here," I say to push the bile down.

Meir's frown deepens from the break in silence. "Patience has never been your strong suit. It's no wonder ambivalence rots at your core." He doesn't say more until we stop in front of the cages. They stretch into a separate tunnel, disappearing into open-mouthed oblivion. Clouds of coal dust linger causing us both to cough. Meir ties a kerchief across his face, throwing one at me to do the same. "Even after all that's happened, we're still reliant on fossil fuels to keep us going," he laments to himself.

I let the man dwell on the other things while I repeat acceptances in my head that I'm here again. The tattoo itches something fierce. A pair of footsteps echo towards us until two guards form to greet us with a lazy wave.

"We were only just informed of your arrival." One of the armored mercenaries speaks on behalf of the rest. I note the lack of decorum, as I'm sure Meir does too. After all, these aren't properly trained soldiers of the Zionist entity but mercenaries of a private corporation. Swirls of black splotches dance beneath the man's skin like a Rorschach test, hiding whatever emotion he may have left. They're both dressed in tattered uniforms, coated thick with coal dust. "What brings you here?"

I've spent enough time with Meir Cohen by now to know when he detests a man. There's a gleam in his eye that scans the area around them to assess how many ways he could kill him. If he had one more drink in the trailer before we left, I'd have to witness this mercenary's head crushed against rocks, consequences be damned. Instead, Meir straightens himself to tower over the brute and leans forward. "Leave."

Neither moves except for the subordinate glancing at the other for orders. It's then that I notice the weapon holstered at their hips: razor whips fashioned with a taser at the length of the base.

"Hero or not, make any trouble, and you'll hear from your superiors," the brute threatens. He nudges the other with an elbow and cocks his head back, granting him leave. He turns to do the same, but then flashes a light attached to his wrist on me. "Mind keeping your dog on a leash? I'll not have him upsetting the cockroaches." With no patience for an answer, he turns into the darkness, footsteps echoing away into an endless abyss.

"Fuck this," I seethe.

Meir looks as though he wants to apologize, but I chalk it up to shadows playing tricks when all he says is, "Follow me."

We make our way through the columns and rows of iron cages, each just large enough for a person to stand. Groups of one hundred come to the mines on twenty-four hour shifts poached from different UNICEF camps. The cages stand ready for those who rest, if such a thing can be achieved on stone and coal dust. There are roughly two thousand Al Khalil captives damned to slavery on the other side of the mountain. Even covered by the kerchief, rank sweat stings my nostrils. In the faint glow of distant lanterns, some stragglers scurry to the back of their prisons. I dare not shine my flashlight and stare at my feet. I don't realize Meir has stopped at the center of the room until I bump into him.

"Why do you think I offered you employment instead of a cage when we first met?" The acoustics of the cave give greater authority to Meir's voice. "I knew you're Aylul Khater's cousin-accomplice, I could have killed you without consequence. So, why did I give you this purpose?"

I fear those eavesdropping in other cages. "I've wondered that myself," I admit.

Meir steps toward one of the cages, using the nail of his thumb to scratch at an iron bar. "Inevitability," he says so low I barely register the word. Then, turning to me, he spreads his arms wide at his sides. "These cycles we've accepted as reality, the very same that would devolve my dear ancestors – many Holocaust survivors turned Zionists – scheming until their children's children would smith these cages around us. It is on that same looped path that Aylul walks that will lead them to share the same fate as their father. That – despite anyone's efforts – is an inevitability; and a rather predictable one at that, if you ask me." He reaches out, but I recoil at his touch.

"If you're so sure, why protect them?" Sweat drips down my neck but does nothing to relieve me of the heat.

"Because it keeps you close to me," he says simply. "My task, you know, was tracking your cousin since the apple never falls far from the tree. It wasn't long after observing them that I found you, and my interests changed the longer I watched."

"Meant to bring you in for interrogation, but that risked leading you off a ledge like so many of your kind. God told me: here is one who sees the need for our coexistence, but more importantly, a guardian to protect our message as it's preached. That I could dare dream to change the inevitability of your demise, that..." He clears his throat. "You're what I've looked for since leaving unimaginable Gaza. Prolonging Aylul's fate is a small price to pay for a future without blatant ironies."

I'm not sure what to say, so I don't say a word. Part of me wants to take his hand and tell him we could change the paradigm. But *cui bono, Caesar*? For whose actual benefit? The answer's always been obvious. Before I can respond, one of the guards calls Meir over to sign some papers. He turns to leave. I take one look around me and move with him. "No," he says at a pause. "I'll be back shortly."

It's not until Meir's footsteps fade that I hear the existence of damned souls. Scuffling feet here, scratching lice there. I don't move for fear of them knowing I remain. I'm still as a statue and as cold as one too until a finger begs to be cracked. My bones snap and echo through the chambers like striking flint.

A voice rasps for air but fails to speak.

My heart pounds, nearly spilling from my throat. Somehow regain control of my legs and choose to wander in darkness toward the fading voice. It comes from a cage at the far edge of the cavern. What little light shines through from the adjacent room is unable to illuminate the back wall where there's a fetal form. The man lay beside his daily allotment of a bowl's worth of water. I lean my forehead between two bars and leverage myself to see more of him. He crawls forward, giving face to an elder whose features melt under wrinkles. He's bald from recent shavings, red cuts like chicken feet spot his head. Rags dyed with soot from coal hang from meatless bones. The specter mumbles feebly, so I pivot to the side of the cage, straining an arm past the bars as far as I can to retrieve his bowl. He grabs my hand, shaking it until all the water spills to the ground. He pulls with all the strength of a child, raising half his body instead.

"Forgotten," the word escapes his throat like razors. He releases his grip, sagging back into shadow.

Before I can ask whether he means me or him, footsteps approach from the guard room, so I straighten myself away from the cell.

"What are you doing, rat?" The brutish guard asks beside Meir. "And before you lie, don't forget we have cameras."

"Just trying to help," is all I can think to say.

The mercenary looks at me as though I've gone crazy. I think he's about to reprimand my interaction with the prisoner until he forces out a laugh like miniature implosions. He turns to Meir, shaking his head as if to say *Can you believe this guy?* Meir doesn't give him the satisfaction. "Alright then, if you've done whatever it is you came here for – I suggest you leave."

I turn away from the men talking to glimpse back at the cell for some proof that the old man's still there. I know he is; there's no reason he shouldn't be. Yet I can't be certain.

"Come," Meir commands, "the day ahead still requires more from us."

Without waiting, he makes his way back to the entrance.

The cherry-red convertible looks sorely out of place in the open-mouthed cavern as we approach it and climb in the front seats. We don't say so much as a word as we leave the way we came. My mind still lingers inside that cage, though I know the old man would rather die than share it with me. The tunnel ends, and the sky cracks open with cloudless light as we follow the winding, paved road up the mountain back toward Al Khalil. Its ebony spires glitter like the sea I've seen so often in movies.

"After this is over," I say, "I want to see Haifa." I'm already starting to forget the details of the prisoner's sunken face. "I'm going to Haifa," I revise.

"For what purpose?" Meir turns the radio reporting another thousand climate migrants killed at the U.S.-Mexico border down low.

"Does it matter?"

"For the paperwork approval, I suppose not, but it matters in almost every other way, Laeth, yes. I brought us here not to threaten you, but to remind you of what we're hoping to end. It's been some time, so it took me a while to see, but you're teetering. So, whatever it is you're looking for in Haifa, I'll just say this: find equilibrium, young man." He throws on aviators when the sun glares on his eyes, fingers combing hair back in the rearview mirror. "You'll fall through the cracks if you don't find some place to stand soon. Here or there, in Israel, you can't be nowhere."

I chew on his words for a moment, annoyed by the paltry words of wisdom. "Just sign the damn papers."

It's a long time before I hear the *adhan* ripple through the airwaves. Despite being so close to Nablus at this point in the trip, all the crooked factories block much of what's natural with the roars of their smokestacks bellowing fire. A large bulk of displaced people migrating from Jerusalem, Al Khalil, and Tulkarm fled to Nablus and its surrounding villages en masse. Ramallah only suffered a fraction of what this city's been burdened with. I hate to think in such a way, but it's difficult not to when I witness what's become of the only other last bastions of Palestine.

Like gunmetal-fringed scales, industrial factories coil around Nablus like cancer in a cell. The ground beneath us, where olive trees once swayed, blanches with rubble and rusted iron. In response to the dying land, some of these plants facilitate vertical farms funded by the same foreign countries that put us in this predicament. In fact, most of the factories have flags like neon billboards flickering against their sides: the States, Britain, France, China, and Russia – the gang's all here. Repurposed UNHCR tents that could populate an entire city themselves cluster in rows like a median, guiding us to the city center. They sell anything from fresh produce to thrift stores advertising their wares on dismembered mannequins. Few are used for actual lodging since many of the factories use their basements as shelters.

It's tough for Meir to navigate the streets without hitting someone trying to sell children's toys or playing cards with a Quran *surah* printed on the back. An outsider might suspect such madness to turn into chaos, but an elite hierarchy maintains the ghost of law and order. The manipulative hands of PA executives operating from Nablus proper function inside a crystalline egg shaped fortress accented in gold. It is our first destination on the list.

As a courtesy born from past mistakes, we've gotten into the habit of meeting with local authorities before a big rally. Nine times out of ten, our hosts refuse to lend any assistance with policing. Behind cordial masks, I'm sure they're more than happy imagining the crowds swallow us whole. Still, not all are indolent, and I can count on one hand the number of times sympathizers have outnumbered our aggressors. So before we pull the trigger, I'm meeting with the PA's Chief Permit Officer in the area. I rub my temples hoping it doesn't take long. Meir stops at a red light, giving me the chance to grab a cup of cardamom coffee from a passing belly-dancing barista and toss a shekel on her tray. With any luck, Leila and the others will have most of the work finished by the time I get on site. I've been tired since I woke up this morning.

Thirty minutes later, my head's pushing against my skull with a heartbeat of its own. Thirty minutes of arguing with that cheap son of a bitch to get valet parking. Meir outright refused to allow either of us to pay the fee when there was alleged free parking in an area with more people per capita than Manila. He takes this stance against injustice with unwavering conviction as though we haven't just gotten back from labor camps created by those he gives allegiance to. After weaving several loops through the surrounding city blocks, I threatened to jump out of the car if he didn't get over it. Just then, by the graces of hell, did a man leave work to get in his shiny sedan and bequeath his parking space to us. I sigh audibly as he reaps his reward. Not wanting to inflame matters more than they already are, Meir stays in the car while I elbow past people to get inside the tower. Obsidian floors like coal lead me to a wide circular receptionist's desk with half a dozen women fanned out in black hijabs and 'abayas hard at work.

"Ah, Mr. Awad – it's been a while." Jenan, assistant to the Chief Permit Officer, says flatly when it's my turn in line to approach. She holds a hand to her heart when I reach out to shake it. Always the traditionalists.

"Bayt Thul, yeah." I try not to shudder. "Please inform Mr. Odeh that I'm here for our meeting."

"Mr. Odeh has since retired from his position, you'll be meeting with Mrs. Shaheen today." Jenan taps her earlobe but hesitates, holding it down to drop the call. "If I may be candid, sir..."

"By all means."

"Why waste everyone's time with this farce?" She speaks low so as not to make a scene, but her voice is unflinching. "Did Judas confer with Jesus about betrayal before committing his sin?"

I'm more surprised by a reference like that coming from a hijabi than I am offended by the parable. "Just make the call."

Jenan complies without protest, a satisfied look pursing her face. I lean back against the desk facing away from my tormentor, letting what has been and will be today cloud my mind when the puzzle pieces fit together in my subconscious and flash like a warning. "Wait, did you say Shaheen?" Too late. High heels clack like gunfire heading in my direction. I glance at the exit doors with longing but suck it up and turn to face the CPO.

"Laeth?" Sundus stands tall, transformed from the girl with the dangling pinned-up denim jacket to cut an intimidating figure in an iridescent black suit, curls flowing like a mane. Pushing the buttons of her shirt to the brink, Sundus lays a hand over her pregnant stomach.

"Well, shit."

can't get comfortable in the armchair no matter which position I fidget into. Sundus guided me to her office without a word shared between us, but now that we're here, I just want to get out of this building. She taps her ruby-painted nails against the desk between us in a beat of her own. I feel like I'm inside the woods, with how many trees had to die to making this room shine. It could be my head hanging up on the walls at any moment, but I can't get over how much fucking wood is in this room; I've never seen anything like it. Getting access to real lumber requires no small amount of money. Abusing friends in high places just for the chance. Vibrant acrylic canvases framed in more thickly treated wood decorate the walls. I'm sure this is Sundus' work, but I don't linger on one long enough to interpret them. Behind her overhead is a sketched portrait of her husband Husam, slick-back hair falling to a strong-jawed butt chin tilted slightly up in faux demure. I went to school with him, but never really knew the man. Can't say much except the "I'm always watching" move won't work on me. *Tap, tap, taptap, tap* go her fingertips.

"Suppose congratulations are in order," I finally say.

The rapping on the desk stops. She gives me a look as if she's gauging whether I mean it or not. "He'll be here next month; never been more ready in my life for something to finally happen." She clears her throat and fusses with pens on her desk when I don't pick up the lead. "We're naming him Yousef after –"

"– Your grandfather. Right." I feel the need to show her that I remember. "May he live a long and healthy life." I pick at a nail on my chair. "I'm surprised to see you here. I mean, I know your old man's VP and all, but what happened to the studio?" I can only see it because I was looking for it, but sadness pulls her low before she corrects herself into a formal square-shouldered composure.

"I still try to get some time in," she says, "but pastels and watercolors aren't what this place needs right now."

"More color is exactly what we need," I retort. "It'd be nice to remember there's more than brown and red."

Sundus doesn't take the bait and clears her throat again. "Let's get down to business, yeah? You're here because..." she shuffles through papers as if she didn't already know why we're both here. "You want a permit for your little rally in Huwara." Her lips twitch as if I've told a joke. "Laeth, how many times are you going to do this? Whether it's in Ramallah or Nablus, you're not getting our support."

"It's always polite to ask first." After a dozen rejections over the past two years, I'm not delusional enough to think this time would be any different.

Sundus regards me coyly. "Or so your goons can have a reason to smear our name all over social media as a scapegoat for when things inevitably go wrong."

"Yeah." No point in lying to her, she'll always be able to see right through me. "There is that."

She actually laughs in those short snorts that make my heart pang for bygone days. "Just leave my name out of it, alright? I'm not sure how it's working, but your people's message is spreading like cancer. Did you know the last provost who crossed you got a brick thrown through his windshield?"

She has a point. Despite our talk of peace, love, and coexistence, there are sympathizers out there who demand it at knifepoint. Get enough notoriety and eventually, your fringes will become large enough to cause mayhem in your name every damn time. The last thing I want is Sundus wrapped up in that mess. "No names. You have my word," I promise with a hand over my heart as I stare past her to that goddamn portrait of Husam; thing's so huge it's the only thing the eye can wander to. "I should get going-"

"– Ya know," Sundus cuts in, "never thought I'd see the day you commit to something. No joke. It's, well, it's nice. I mean, it'd be nice if, ya know, it didn't mean the whole allying-with-the enemy-and-betraying-our-people-thing, but..." she draws out the last word.

I raise an eyebrow at the hypocrisy. "We considered adopting the P.A. model, but thought, why not skip the extra step of hiding our schemes?"

To Sundus' credit, I can't read her face as she slowly rises from her chair. "On behalf of the Palestinian Authority, I decline your request for a public permit to conduct a peace rally in Huwara."

"Excellent." I clap my hands together and stand to walk out, but look back at the woman clad from head to toe in black. "You –"

"Goodbye, Laeth. Be safe out there, yeah?" She reaches out a hand I mistake for a shake, but uses it to shut the door instead.

Meir doesn't ask any questions when I get back in the car, and it makes me think he knew Sundus had been waiting for me in the tower. Doesn't matter; if I don't want fresh ones, I better keep old wounds in the past and focus on what's ahead. We travel from the heart of Nablus through windy streets back to the suffocating pollution of the industrial district. There are so many people, you could populate half of Palestine with how many lost souls linger here. Refugees, beggars, soldiers of fortune, and thieves all coexist in this capitalist wasteland. You know who's originally from Nablus if they're wearing a suit or dress or anything that doesn't have soot on it, really. The way I can really tell is how they walk with purpose in a sea of wandering zombies like a bullet passing through a swarm of mosquitos. Huwara's not far south, but it'll take at least half an hour to wade through these murky waters. Meir cusses out some man forcing a windshield cleaning in the middle of traffic, but fills his hand with shekel when he finishes the job. It's the least the bastard could do after Gaza.

Like the obsidian claws of a demon buried under Earth, the international factories pretending to be relief organizations tower over us from every direction. Their names are advertised in neon lights, belching chemical clouds into our atmosphere. At a red light, another barista with a tray full of coffee belly dances her way between cars. The coins hanging from her yellow choli outfit clink together as she moves closer to me. Impressed that not a single drop is spilt I add an extra shekel onto the tray and grab a cup.

"You know, it's rude not to ask if I'd like some," Meir sounds annoyed. "Didn't your mother teach you any manners?"

I didn't forget to ask, and I don't like him even mentioning my mom. I'm about to say as much when I notice a barrel-shaped man sweeping the sidewalk outside the USAID mansion. He's hunched over the broom as if his back won't get any more obtuse than a ninety-degree angle. An analogy wouldn't do justice to the nothing he is to the hordes of Nablus ignoring him on their way to better places. He interacts with no one, eyes glued to the ground. It's only when he wipes his forehead with the sleeve of his jumper that I see the man for who he is.

"Mo'taz," I whisper in disbelief. There hasn't been a day that's passed these years that I haven't wondered what became of him. I never saw him again after the apartment in Ramallah. When Ibn Walid died and Hamas with him, I just assumed he'd cast his lot in with a similar faction like The Lion's Den. Meir stops the car for a crowd crossing the road, so I reach for the door handle. But what would I even say? "Hey man, long time since my cousin ruined your life. How's it been?" And that's if he doesn't come swinging at me first, though he looks frail enough to blow over from being yelled at. Gods, I would've pegged him for fifty back in the day but now he looks old enough to be my grandfather. Before I can reach a decision, the crowd passes, Meir steps on the gas, and Mo'taz fades out of sight.

I think about the specter all the way to Huwara. We dip down low into the valley where the tree-line breaks, revealing our destination. Clean pearlescent buildings shine like marble under the mid-afternoon sun while the *Adhan* echoes in warm welcome between heavenward spires. A sunbird's melody replaces the wheezing belch of Nablus and the smog clears, if only just a little. We drive toward the call to prayer as sparse homes with large gardens become one-story strips of salons, pawn shops, and convenience stores. I thumb at the muzzle of Aylul's pistol tucked behind my waistband, heart racing with anticipation. Too much coffee. Less awake and more aware of how much I'm soaking the back of my shirt.

People can say what they will about leaving a cow out to hang in front of a butcher's shop, but there's nowhere more charming to me than a traditional bazaar. Multicolored tents and wooden stands line the road and spill back half a city block. Hearty women and men raise their voices to sell everything from dates to olives and knockoff Rolexes. Stoop chess. If I were still a college student, I'd leave buying textbooks from the university store for the chumps with spare change and come here. People sit on lawn chairs clustered together in pockets to share a hookah or black tea or the recent town gossip. At a stop sign, a kid steals an entire rotisserie chicken from a vendor looking the other way and ducks out between buildings before anyone's the wiser. The heist makes me laugh but Meir tells me to get a grip, we're almost there.

Samira and the others have set the stage in the center square where all roads lead. The meter-long plywood platform they spent all morning constructing stands on the grassy middle of a large roundabout. It's enough space to contain our numbers while also being destructive to order if we get the numbers we're hoping for to spill out into the streets. Meir pulls up to the shoulder, but doesn't park the car.

"Go," he says, reaching into the glove compartment to retrieve Aylul's pistol. He weighs it in his hand for a moment, getting a sense of the balance and feel. He hands me the gun and closes my fingers around the weapon. "Protect our flock. Fool me once, hm?"

Meir's reference to Bayt Thul rubs me the wrong way; can't shake the feeling he's manipulating emotions. But for what purpose? And since when is it our people? I tuck the gun in my waistband, leaving without response.

Leila's directing a group of college students to sign-making tents, stressing to them that this is a nonviolent protest. Her hair's wrapped up in a kufiyah, face painted in the red, white, black, and green of our national colors. She leans against a six foot pole of a white flag, waving her arms this way and that as she commands the growing masses. She smiles with a brilliant confidence I yearn for. Taking a beat to hang back and admire this woman only seems natural. It's in these moments that I dare to love her. She's done so much to bring me back from grief. Maybe I won't say no the next time she asks for us to move in together at the Compound. Maybe. Donned in a white gown with baby's breath between her curls, Samira takes the stage to announce through a megaphone that we'll be starting shortly. It reminds me I'm here to actually do something.

"Hey," I greet Leila. "How's everything so far?"

She kisses my cheeks then pulls away, dusting off her linens before throwing up her hands as if I've done this to her. "Where've you been this whole time?"

I think of the man still stuck in a cage underground. "Just some last-minute errands." Looking around, I can't find my team anywhere. "Where's Moshe and Amir?"

She gives me an exasperated look. "Your team's fanned out scouting for undercovers, remember?"

"Right, right…" It's not that I've forgotten the plans – I must've studied them a hundred times over – but I definitely let time slip; which is a hard excuse to sell considering I've got a digital clock in my eyes. "I'm gonna go debrief 'em," I say before giving her a proper kiss on the lips. "Be safe, yeah? You know where I'll be when shit hits the fan."

"Don't you mean *if*?" She pats my cheek fondly.

I pretend to consider it. "No."

Not an hour into the rally, there are more people than can fit on the grassy area, disrupting traffic by spilling onto the streets. I'm standing just a few steps away from the stage where Samira's giving another rousing speech through a megaphone. She passes it on to vetted victims of all this strife to say their peace in the name of our cause. Every few minutes the crowd cheers and howls their support, despite most of them not being able to hear a word. Not everyone's a supporter. Much like Moshe with his face hidden in a kufiyah, there are those here implanted by the PA, Fatah, and Mossad who would influence this rally to destruction. All it takes is the right push at the right time and this tinder box blows. My eyes scan the sea of faces for anything out of place. It's the neutral parties I watch for.

"– and to honor the memory of my mother and sisters, today I stand with my father to plead with those who would continue to fight what's already lost: enough." Some guy they must've pulled from one of our university stints is speaking on stage with his elderly father solemnly standing beside him. Unlike his son, he looks pained. From recalling the memories or witnessing the present, I can't be sure. "Enough bloodshed in the name of borders that hold no bearing in a world drowning in flood and famine! Enough focusing on what we've lost, because if we do not accept reality, we will see whatever remains fade to nostalgia; enough!"

Using his pain to fit our agenda makes me want to join those on the outskirts shaking their fists. I watch their numbers trickle to swell into double our size. Many give up trying to move through traffic, so they exit their vehicles to give someone a piece of their mind. We're still facing an entire city threatening to collapse around us. As my eyes dart back and forth, I catch a glimpse of Amir and Moshe sifting between people like sand. They're even apart, but close enough to help the other if need be, just like we practiced: good boys.

I notice a man near the front clad in all white suit shaking a fist wrapped in prayer beads slow to a stop. His anger drains from his pudgy face. He looks over his shoulder at the anti-protesters once, then twice, then back at the stage. I follow his line of sight to Samira, who's trying to educate on the difference between surrender and defeat. She glows like a person standing exactly where they should be. I'm jealous. I look back at the man, but he's no longer standing where he was. Standing on my toes, I search for him but can't find the bastard anywhere in this protoplasm. I tap a bead on my wrist.

"Anyone got eyes on a sheikh in white? Gray beard. Early to mid-sixties." I wait, losing confidence in my vision as adrenaline makes things start to blur. People become colors, and colors become emotions. It's getting hotter and harder to breathe evenly.

"Can't find 'em, Boss," Moshe reports back in my earpiece.

"Me either," Amir's static voice crackles and pops, "but I think – oughta see –" and his comms go out.

"What about the Mubarizun?"

"Nothing to report," Moshe's voice barely registers.

"And you, Amir?" I wait. Nothing. "Moshe, tell Amir to respond." Static. I search for them over the sea of faces, but can't even keep count for boxed breathing. "Moshe?" Fuck this. Time to shoulder push my way through the crowd, glares be damned. Instead, I get elbows to the back as I wade through humid hot sweat and chanting. Men and women blur in waves of full spectrum humanity as I look for Amir over their heads. Going straight through the middle was a terrible decision; should've walked the parameter first.

By then the police have cleared the roundabout enough for a single lane to pass through unopposed. Unarmed and understaffed, they dare not interfere with the rally itself, remaining as a human fence between us and the anti-protesters now corralled to the opposite side of the street. They're steadily growing in number, maybe half our size, but their fervor rivals their adversaries. A few antagonists from our side of the rally detach and confront the naysayers, yelling with clenched fists from the start. My nostrils flare in anticipation of tear gas, but then I remember there are technically no IOF here. I finally catch sight of Amir three rows deep, arguing with a man twice his size, waving his arms like he's trying to fly. Two men draped in gray *dishdashas* tower over my assistant from each side.

"– You don't know what you're saying because you've been brainwashed by the colonizer!" The man is talking so fast he's spraying Amir with spit. "My son, just because you have only ever known defeat does not mean you should concede to normalization!"

I grab my comrade by the elbow and yank him back. "What do you think you're doing?"

He looks around him with a wild, lost look. "Was defusing a situation with one of our own when—" tears of pain well up between his kufiyah. He swallows and tries to start again. "I guess we forgot to charge our earpieces. I'm sorry, I know we're not supposed to debate, but one thing led to another, and—"

"Oh, thank God." Moshe runs up to his partner's side. He inspects Amir with pats on his arms and legs. "Are you hurt? Did they get you?"

"I'm fine." Amir cups his cheek but then remembers where he is, taking a step back. He gestures to where the three men stand not far off. "I was just saying goodbye to these lovely gentlemen. If you'll excuse us—"

One of the elderly men whispers something in the ear of the bear, and it seems to rile him up all over again. He marches a few steps forward and attempts to tower over me, but I'm not having it and square up to his chest. "You the one they take orders from?"

"Something like that," I say. To my surprise, he clasps both my shoulders with a look of sheer desperation, apart from the rage before.

"Son," he begs, "you lead our young ones astray. Maybe you believe you're doing what's right to keep them safe, but in the process, you're cleansing them of our heritage."

I push his hands away from me and forget to take my own advice. "What good's identity if you're dead?"

The man grasps at me once more, wrapping my collar in his fists. "Whatever the *Yahoud* are paying you, it can't be enough! I mean – what? – they know they can't beat us with attrition, so they choose to have us eat each other instead? Shouldn't that tell you there's still hope?"

Despite his demeanor, this one's a fine orator. I'm not sure what to say. I mean...shouldn't it? Before I respond, Moshe gets between us attempting to rip the man's hands off me. The three of us stumble clumsily locked together until Moshe claws the bear's grip free, but now the two of them are going at it like wrestlers, trying to get the other to the ground first. They fall. Allies come rushing to get them on their feet. I lift Moshe by his armpits, but realize too late; his kufiyah lays on the ground and his Arabic's shit.

"Yahoud!" One from the crowd points at Moshe. He shouts it over and again, garnering the attention of every person within earshot. I only have time to grab Moshe's wrist when nearly fifty bodies all surge forward like a torrent. Together, we leave Amir and run as fast as we can away from the rally and into a cluster of tents. My peripherals blind to blood pulsating tunnel vision. Keep pushing forward through the tarped canopy bazaar. Duck underneath her arms, push him out of the way, stop, pivot, pull Moshe's sleeve to keep pace; run, run, run. I can still hear them behind us shouting *Yahoud! Yahoud!* and before we know it, what's in front begins to collapse in on us with a rush of victims seeking vengeance. Samira is shouting something in my earpiece, but can't make it out. She sounds panicked. What the fuck is happening over there? Where is Meir Cohen? Alleyway to our left. I whip us toward it but slip on a spilled canvas bag of saffron.

"Go!" I push Moshe off me and we're back on our feet quick. They're on our heels. Brick skyrises on either side widen enough for a few people. It's more than enough for mob justice. Another hundred meters and we'll make it to the light on the other side. Moshe's just about to make it through when he stops. I slam my nose into the back of his skull, webbing pain disorienting the senses. I gather myself in time to see a titan silhouette in front of us. It's the man we were arguing with before, but this time without his entourage. He looks cruder than before, fists up. He has no words for his oppressor. He takes a step forward, so I move Moshe that we're standing back to back, perpendicular to the two waves about to crash against us. I rip free Aylul's pistol and thumb off the safety, aiming it first at the bear, then at the others. For a moment, I think it works to stop them. They do hesitate. But all it takes is a breath to stare down one side for someone to punch me in the back of the head from the other, knocking me to my knees.

With the last obstacle to Moshe broken, they all move in to swallow the boy whole. Few people step on me to get to him; most step over. My gun doesn't fall far, but my hand gets stomped on trying to retrieve it. I cry out, knowing no one's listening. Finally feeling the handle against my aching palm and grip it tight. Someone trips over me with a steel-toed boot, and we both crumple over. Panic turns the world upside down. It hurts to breathe. I think they cracked a rib. Moshe screams over the clamor of illusions of victory over the enemy. He's begging them to stop. No one's listening.

I raise my gun in the air and shoot. The snap-pop explosion ripples through my wrist, creating an invisible force that drives almost all around us back as far as they dare move. Almost. Some are too close to justice to care, the bear man amongst them. He straddles Moshe, wailing blow after blow against the boy's guard. Between flailing limbs, I can see his face puffed and blood mixed with tears, desperate and scared. I make a break to shoulder-charge him off my comrade, but someone clotheslines me and I fall to my back. Can't breathe. Darkness blinks reality in and out of consciousness. Fuck. Am I going to die? Moshe's screams stop. The silence sends a shiver down my spine and wakes me up. Coughing hurts flat against my back. Look to the side. Moshe's facing me, eyes puffed black and purple. Those near him cheer the man on to finish the job for the sake of those they've lost. He raises his arms overhead, grasping them together to bring them down like a hammer. Moshe's going to die. Nothing will change. I raise my gun, aim for the man's head, and squeeze the trigger.

Like a flock of sunbirds, the crowd scatters from the three of us. Behind where the man once stood is an inkblot of blood-stained limestone. His lifeless body slumps down on what remains of his head, facing down in an awkward position, still straddling Moshe. His mouth is slightly open with barely enough time to register the surprise, eyes slanting downward toward a constellation of congealed blood and brain matter. My heart beats hard enough to rise into my throat. I cough until I vomit on my lap. I can't look at him again; get the feeling I'll forget who I am. More acidic dry heaving forces itself up and out again onto the sandy concrete as I push him off my comrade. It hurts to breathe, but I manage to slide over to Moshe and press two fingers above his VitaStim to check for a heartbeat. It's faint, but he's still in there somewhere. At least I made it on time. I stumble back and try to breathe evenly but only slip into short bursts of hyper-ventilating. Distant sirens approach; we've gotta get out of here. I move to tap my earpiece, but realize it must've fallen out in all the chaos. Fuck. Even if I manage to carry Moshe over my shoulders, we're not going to get far. Where the hell is –

"Get up." A shadow blocks the sun. Meir's clad in familiar clothes. I know I've seen that black *dishdasha* somewhere, but can't think clearly enough to process where. He glances over at the man I murdered, nodding something to himself before reaching out a hand to lift me up. "You did what you must to survive. Hey—" He grabs my chin to face him. There's a dull satisfaction that he can't seem to conceal behind those pale blues. "You didn't have a choice."

I mumble something, but neither know nor care what. I don't feel here. It isn't the same kind of soul projection I've felt before with drugs, but the complete absence of one that barely remained to begin with. I'm shivering and before I know it, leaning into Meir's touch for warmth. "Moshe?"

"Vitals are weak but there's an ambulance on the way. He should make it, thanks to you." He falters as if not knowing what to say. There's a first. "Laeth – there's something I should tell you."

I try to avert my gaze from the man with a hole in his head, but the blood is starting to pool at our feet. "Leila? Amir? Samira?" Can't shake the smell of iron and concrete. Burnt flesh too, but I tell myself I'm imagining things.

"A little scratched up, but they'll be fine; regrouped and headed for the Compound upon my orders, but Laeth – listen – Aylul wasn't here, they..." He fidgets.

"Out with it," I say with malice and step away from his grasp. I hate this new side of him.

"They weren't here to disrupt the rally because Al Mubarizun was in Ayn Yassin bombing the checkpoint." He attempts to weigh my reaction, but I grant him none because there's nothing left to give. "Two shaheed. No idea the fallout."

I look around for something but don't know what at first. "When?" I say looking back and forth between Moshe and the murdered man as if they can give me what I need. Bits of skull litter the ground as if a burglar on the run dropped their rubies. I consider picking it through to see if it's there.

Meir raises the keys to his car in front of my face. "I got word while I was looking for you two."

"Hmm," is all I muster. I snatch the keys from his outstretched hand and start walking back towards the roundabout. I rub my hands clean but there's nothing to wipe off.

"Laeth," Meir calls out.

I glance back over my shoulder. "You didn't have a choice."

I'm ready to argue, but it'd mean turning around to face what I've done. So I continue heading away where my cousin waits. "Shut up."

don't know where I am on a one-way road. Blinking out of navigation guiding me home, I pull off to the shoulder. For the third time, I put little effort into leaning out the window to puke so that it splatters against the side of the convertible. The grip of the pistol in my waistband shifts every time I move to let me know I'm still alive. Want nothing more than to toss the damn thing in the dunes, but now that I've used it once, something tells me there's a chance I'll need it again. Death begets death or some shit like that. I spit what's left in my mouth and crash back into the leather seat. Even the clear sky can't shake the cloud I feel overhead; can't shake the image of scattered bits of something that was once someone. It burrows and brands itself into the folds of who I am until it dulls a migraine behind my eyes. Blinking through the pain, I flip through news channels for any glimpse into what's happening in Ayn Yassin, but no one's reporting on it. I consider returning one of Leila's several missed calls to check on Moshe and let her know I'm alright, but ignore the urge. By now, they should have all returned back to the Compound and safe behind its walls. Right now I've gotta worry about myself. Gotta focus. They're waiting – I just know it – and there's still security to get through.

Like open scissors through a dusk tapestry loom I cut through the kilometers in half the time it took earlier today. When I turn off Route 60, it's apparent that getting anywhere near the shop is going to be harder than I thought. Even an hour after the bombing, soft white plumes chimney up from where the northern and eastern checkpoints once stood. Splotched throughout the city, puffy clouds of soot from burning tires billow in the wind. I sincerely hope Lieutenant Haya's alright in the south.

I slow to a stop a couple of kilometers away and scrounge through the interior for anything useful. There's an erotic pocket book, a pair of binoculars, a flare gun without a flare, hair gel, and some folded fabric in the glove compartment.

I grab the cloth and binoculars, thinking for a moment about Meir's deceit before kicking the door open with a muddy boot. One thing at a time.

Getting to my feet is a painful lesson in breathing with bruised ribs. The binoculars can help me see the town, but I can't see much beyond the top half of buildings. There are people in the high rises waving to those below, warning them of the enemy's location. The same can be said for the Zionist settlers stationed in the crystal towers of Ma'al Luz. They wave their flags and encourage the occupiers below. That's when the faint *pop, pop, pop* of tear gas turns into the *brat-tat-tat* of live ammunition. Stuffing what I can in my pockets, I limp then stride toward home. Amazing what you can ignore when shit only seems to get worse.

Ripping the folded polyester from its plastic reveals it to be a poncho. I've seen this once before, back in a different time when Mo'taz still had some light of life. This thing refracts its surroundings to give the wearer near invisibility. Or at least it's supposed to; his was beaten to shit with the projection stuck on some cracked earth near Gaza. No surprise Meir's works like a charm. I pull the hood over my eyes, activating the sensors with three hard blinks. Still at a distance, I walk off the road on hard, thorny thickets and position myself between the northern and western checkpoints. The wooden outhouse I'm looking for stands in the middle of a field between me and a dozen parked Humvees, all pointed toward Ayn Yassin. If I'm right about Aylul, then the way's already open. Breathe. Walk with intention, knees high. Can't suppress the occasional cough, but there's no one close enough to hear me spasm.

I notice the steel dogs when I'm halfway there and crouch lower into the wheatgrass as if it'd do any good against their infrared sensors. This jacket's a cheap magic trick in the face of their camera-eyed chainsaw maws. They're quad-rupeds on duck-like rubber soles that can catapult ten meters in the air with a velocity that'll turn bone to dust if that's its programmed intention. I've only seen them in action once before in college, and it took Aylul weeks to get me talking again. As I inch my way forward, one of the beasts shakes moving the four Tesla coil spikes jetting out from its back as if it's got an itch. I've seen them roll like an armadillo with enough electricity surging through them to singe the flesh off people's legs. If they spot me, it'll be over before I can try to use Meir's documents as a shield. This poncho makes me feel like I'm trapped in a terrarium with how much I'm sweating.

I reach a hand out for the door when I'm ten paces away, eyes locked on the pack of dogs less than a click in front of me. Their human counterparts bark orders at each other under scarab-scale armor, flailing arms this way and that to contain the spread of revolution. Half their number breaks off toward the eastern bloc by the time my hand wraps around the copper door handle, but I pause before opening it until the group disappears behind limestone high-rises. It's only once I'm inside that I realize I've been holding my breath and exhale, relieved that the stench of piss and shit isn't here to greet me. The human-sized hole before my feet proves my prediction true. Finding a flashlight on the hood of my poncho, I fiddle with the settings a moment before turning it on low brightness. Sitting on the ground, I hoist my legs into limitless darkness, feeling around to latch onto the side ladder, inching down the porcelain cover then it goes over my head as I make my way into the deep.

There's an electric lantern I don't recognize latched on a metal hook waiting for me at the bottom. The soft echo whoosh of air keeps me company down here; can't hear anything happening above ground. It gives me anxiety and pushes my legs faster but the pain in my abdomen only allows brisk walking. The lantern illuminates a yard ahead. All around me is shapeless night. Anyone, any-thing, could break through the veil at any moment. If it's dogs, I'll be able to see their lenses before my shredded end. There's a part of me that half expects Mo'taz to rise from the abyss to offer Virgil guidance; hold a hand out and say, "Hey, I know it's hard, but I'll show you the way."

Something on the surface makes a large enough explosion to shake dirt loose from the domed ceiling. Panic grips my nerves. Whatever's happening up there, I just hope Teta and Hassan are safe. I tell myself I can't die in a place like this, but the thought of Mo'taz dispels the arrogance. After five decades fighting the good fight from Gaza to Golan, I doubt the bastard imagined his death would happen slowly in a shelter.

It takes twenty minutes for the small shaft to merge with the larger tracked tunnel Uri once guided us through. Unlike before, the overhead lights are off. Probably out of juice from lack of use over the years. I lift the lantern to the rock walls, rubbing a palm against flecks of dirt until I feel the arrow etchings left by diggers to point each other in the right direction. Taking a right, I press on with failed attempts to suppress coughs that threaten to puncture my lungs. More dirt sprinkles from whatever chaos ensues from above. It mixes with sweat to cover my face in a thin, crusty layer of mud. Despite the small digital clock behind my eyelids telling me how long it's been, untethered from reality down here. Shapes like ghosts of the past form and fade with each step. The gray matter silhouette of the bear-shaped man in Nablus floats just out of reach, mouthing something I can't hear. How do I not know his name?

When I reach the rusted ladder leading up to the walk-in freezer, I pause a moment to listen for any noise coming from the shop but there's nothing to be heard. Fear of the unknown forms nausea in my gut. No matter how many times I've been tackled, teargassed, or shot at – this shit always scares me. Wasn't meant for this life. Can't make a difference here. So why did I stay? Pushing through rhetorical questions, I climb toward the answer.

Hoisting myself out of the hole and into the pitch-black freezer, I push open the door to blinding white light, and the world goes upside down. Searing white pain radiates from my abdomen. I try to cry out, but there's a leather-gloved hand covering my mouth. A knee presses against the small of my back, and impossible strength leans against my legs. Another hand pats me down and finds the gun behind my waistband, tossing it away on the floor before restraining my arms back.

"Shhh," a voice-like static whispers in my ear.

Without further assurances, I try to thrash free of his grip but the behemoth has me in his claws. Try to bite through his fingers, but the gloves are too thick for my teeth to pierce. A pair of heavy boots thud closer. A second person bends down over me, lifting the back of my shirt to graze between my shoulder blades with something sharp. I know it's a needle when they push through the skin, but it doesn't hurt until I feel it open into a claw once inside. Hot flashes pulse from the source and panic seizes my senses in an attempt to wrestle free from my oppressors, but that just makes the pain worse and the hole larger. A gloveless hand rests near the puncture, softly caressing. The skin connection is soothing. Relaxing away from the reaction, I give into my circumstances and lay still with my cheek pressed against the cold concrete. The comforting hand lifts and the throbbing pain in my back resumes until I yelp at a sensation like picking meat out from between my teeth. Warm blood trickles down from the incision, seeping onto my boxer briefs. Then comes the burnt shock of cauterizing the hole. My screams muffled under the glove, but it is over as quickly as it came. Someone takes a rag to wipe my back before slapping a bandage patch on rather aggressively. Two hands like mitts grab the back of my arms and effortlessly lift me to my feet.

"What do you want?" They're facing me toward some kind of spotlight so it's hard to gain my bearings. "I've done nothing wrong."

"Oh, you haven't?" a voice like silk snaps.

"Enough, Uri," a familiar voice commands from the other side of the room. "Sakine, you're sure it's taken care of?"

"Aylul?" I call out, trying to turn their way but Uri has me locked in place. "Uri, what's –?"

"Of course it's done. At least, I think. Probably."

I'm not that surprised to hear Kurmanji from the left. "Guess we'll know in a minute or two if the doors come crashing down." There's a pause. "Alright, alright – not funny. It's done. Cross my heart, hope to die, stick a ten-inch dildo in my eye."

The person behind me sighs. "Get the light on your way out. Remember to set your clocks for ten. Don't care what's happening out there, stay off the comms."

With the informal dismissal, Uri releases me with a push. My wrists feel like they're going to snap off, but the pain is dulled by the hurt knowing these bastards ruined my tattoo. I'm so tired that my vision's hazy like I'm observing a dream. A trollish brunette typing on a tablet that's either thirteen or thirty crosses the room in front of me to exit upstairs. Before she leaves – Sakine, I presume – sheathes the computer, turns to face me grinning, and curtsies with her denim jacket as though it was a gown. Not waiting for a response, she giggles and disappears through the door. My eyes follow Uri to a shadowed corner of the basement. He reaches a hand out. From the darkness, an elegant one grasps his, and through the veil comes Aylul. Morphine relief washes over me. They're wearing gear like mine except their jacket scales flow as long as a trench coat wrapping around them like a shadow taken from the corner where they were hidden. Uri runs a hand through their thick curled hair, and before I can even say hello, the two are kissing in his arms. He whispers something delicate that makes their eyes glow with autumn adoration. Shooting one more look of disgust my way, Uri nods to Aylul and leaves to join Sakine.

"I must be dreaming," I say to his back when the door latch clicks.

Aylul turns to me with a coy twitch on her lips. "Why, because he wears a yamaka and I'm – well – me? It's been two years, Laeth; with everything that's changed there's no way you can be this boring already."

"I was going to say because he's old as fuck." Pulling a crushed pack from my back pocket, I slide out a cigarette and walk over to offer them one. They take the olive branch but choose to light it themselves. Pushing a plastic chair toward them, I grunt through pain to take a seat across from Aylul.

"What's fifteen years in a place locked in time?" They sit crossing their legs and weigh me under a thick puff of smoke while I itch at my back. "Sorry about that." They raise a microchip between two fingers for me to see before tossing it on my lap.

"What is it?" Holding the nickel-sized square in my palm, pinkish tendril wires grasp at my skin with futility to burrow back inside its host then wilt, frayed, and dead.

"You mean you don't know?" They're not even trying to conceal their mocking tone. "All Zionist collaborators carry these on their person. They link up to the communicator in your bracelet and lenses; whoever's got the switch can see and hear everything you do. I'm sure you understand why we had to disable it before meeting."

No point in masking my surprise. "Makes sense."

"Oh, don't get all dramatic and break it. We can't completely destroy the thing without alarming your commanding officer."

I flinch when they refer to Meir as my commanding officer but let it slide, pocketing the chip to deal with at another time. Aylul uses a foot to bring my gun over to them, picking it up with amusement in their eyes. "Wasn't expecting to ever see you again," they say to the weapon, cradling it fondly in their hands. They slide the magazine out and fiddle with it for a moment before arching an eyebrow at me. The unspoken question hangs in the air.

"Wasn't gonna let another Bayt Thul happen," I confess, waiting for the other shoe to drop. It doesn't. Aylul merely pouts their lips and nods with some general understanding. We sit in the storage room in silence, ignoring the seconds counting down from ten minutes for as long as we can. Last we were here together, we were waiting to meet Uri for the first time. Another life ago, but somehow it doesn't feel like we're different people. Never wanted this for either of us. Leaning back on the plastic legs of my chair, I wonder how to break the hush.

"So you're fucking my ex-girlfriend," Aylul chimes in.

Blood flushes my face and I lose my balance, nearly falling back on my ass. Aylul chuckles into a laugh, waving a dismissive hand. "It was always so easy to get you worked up," they say when they calm down. "Just wish it'd be about the right things."

The added comment brings me to my feet, but once I'm standing, I don't know where to go. Pretending it's to light another cigarette, I sit back down and shoot them a warning look. They respond with one of their eye-rolls and stamp out their smoke. "Is that why you're here?" I ask. "To ask me to join you?"

They stare at me hard without malice. "No. We're warriors, Laeth – not children parading around with plastic talking sticks."

It would've hurt less if they said it in anger. "So then, why?"

Aylul reaches the pistol out to me, and I take it back, tucking it in my waistband. "The people must know we haven't forgotten them," they say, "Al Mubarizun will take Ayn Yassin back and herald in the fifth Intifada."

I scoff at what sounds like lunacy. "What, today? You're about two years too late."

"No, not today. I wanted to back then..." they drift sadly, "badly. But Wissam wouldn't allow it. Not enough intel. People. Weapons; no resources at our disposal. He was right, of course, though I'd never admit it to him."

"So you're Wissam's dog now?"

Aylul shrugs, unbothered. "The devil you know. Better a rabid hound for my people than an obedient mutt for my oppressor."

I barely have time to register that when I hear tear gas popping not far from the store. Distant muffled screams from either side call out unintelligibly, and we both wait on edge for something to happen. I half expect Uri and Sakine to come running down the stairs, but they never do. The sounds of anguish and grinding metal eventually recede deeper into Ayn Yassin. There's no change in Aylul's demeanor as they pull a smoke from their jacket pocket and light another one up. "Are Teta and Hassan going to be alright?"

"That's subjective, isn't it?" they say in a way that pisses me off. "How can any of us be okay under occupation? If you're asking if they're safe – then yeah, probably – our numbers are taking the fighting to Ma'al Luz. They're unarmed without uniforms. I told you: today's not about battle, but sending a message. It is always the message."

"If not today, then why are you here? For two checkpoints? They'll be refortified with even more soldiers by sundown."

"That's the hope," they say.

"No, you don't get it..." I hesitate, unsure whether to tell them about the mole Meir planted in the organization. Don't want to spend what little time we have left angry at each other. Still, I'd rather that than Aylul dead. So I tell them. About the mole. About the surveillance around Cid ever since we found out they commissioned him to manufacture explosive belts in his garage. Everything. By the time I'm done, I have to catch my breath. "They'll know you're coming before you leave Jenin."

Aylul doesn't seem angry. "Good to know about Cid." They're confused by my surprise. "We've known about the plant for some time now. Took a while to figure it out, but Uri has his ways of flushing out rats."

They make a good point. I'm less surprised at them for knowing and more at myself for underestimating them. "Is he dead?"

"No." I notice an insecurity nip at them in the way they fidget with the sleeves of their jacket. "One of us now, actually. Why do you think Meir hasn't been able to pinpoint our movements? Not that it matters. Uri says where there's one, there's many. Just like –"

"– Rats. Yeah, got it."

A blinking red dot forms in Aylul's iris, prompting them to raise a finger to shut me up. "I haven't said half of what I wanted. Listen, cousin, and listen well: I'm here to tell you that we're recapturing Ayn Yassin in a month; the sixth of September. Do you remember Jabriel? The boy from way back when? He will sound the alarm in Ma'al Luz, and unlike today, I can't make promises." They step closer to me, combing their fingers through my disheveled hair and flicking out a piece of dirt. "Not much surprises me anymore, but I can't tell you how happy I was to see the tunnels operational. Please keep it that way; it's one of many we will require. Take Teta and Leila; whoever else you can scrounge up and make a run for it once the fighting starts." Their stance resembles their father's commanding presence: shoulders back, arms folded. "I'll send someone to bring you all back to a home as you remember it once we've liberated this bitch."

They're barely able to convince themselves. Standing to my feet, I crane my neck to meet their eyes. "Our home was lost the day we stumbled on that construction site. There's no reclaiming it. Even if you succeed at first, they'll only double – triple – quintuple their forces to fucking infinity until it's theirs again. They'll send their legions; legions, Aylul. Even if you manage to cut through them, you'd still have the States; the European body. Leviathan tanks and armored behemoths, biological and nuclear; read the other day they're closing in on nanotech, which means they already have it. I won't pretend to know your strategy, but whatever it is won't shield us from twenty-meter tungsten spears shooting from space." I clasp their hand in mine, and Aylul squeezes tight. "There's no fucking hope."

They don't pull away. Somewhere beyond us frozen in space, the clock's still ticking. "Maybe," they admit with just one word.

After some time my mind drifts to the boy in white we saved all those years turned lifetimes ago. "How did you convert Jabriel?"

"I told him..."Aylul straightens their shoulders, clears their throat, and grants me a translucent smile. "I told him: 'So long as a Palestinian breathes, there's more to life than—" their voice falters. Another red dot alarm blinks inside their cornea. Before more is said, two pairs of feet stomp down the staircase to our left. Uri and Sakine come out the door with stern expressions. I get the feeling Sakine's just doing it for appearance's sake from the way she skips along after her comrade.

"Don't give me that look," Uri says to Aylul, "you said ten minutes, and it's about time we leave." He pauses. "They got Ja'far." Pulling Aylul out of earshot, they leave me with Sakine who slurps at a lollipop-like ice cream.

"Handsome, isn't he?" she asks. "Don't get me wrong – the sideburn thing is meh – but sheesh."

She's not wrong. He looks like some mythic warrior clad in modern gear, but her comment doesn't warrant a response. When the couple finishes whispering, Uri nods to Sakine, and together they head towards the walk-in freezer. She climbs down first whistling to the tune of "Wein 'a Ramallah" until she can't be heard. Uri clicks the visor on his helmet into place and faces me.

"Ekh," he says, shaking his head. "Nevermind." With that, he swings over the ledge and disappears into the tunnels.

"Yeah, fuck you too."

Aylul walks back into the light. My heart pangs to witness their puffy eyes. "I'm sorry about your friend."

"We should all be so lucky to die for a cause greater than ourselves."

I reach out to grab their hand and miss, though Aylul tarries at the latch as if I hadn't. "Doesn't have to be you. Really. Think about it. We can figure out some other way. Together. We could start our own nonprofit..." They snort knowing I'm grasping at straws. Never really thought of it until now – probably didn't want to – but there was never another path for Aylul. The more I try to think of any real alternatives, the closer I get to what I've known all along: they're not wrong in their method, it just doesn't fucking matter. Doesn't matter because the world forgot about us; forgot how to fight; forgot themselves for comfort and consumption. "When you're given a broken pile of corrupted shit, suing for peace is the only way we get out of this alive."

They stare down at the hole in front of them with their back to me. "Four hundred and forty-two illegal settlements erected in razed Palestinian cities. Forced migrations, concentration camps disguised as UNICEF tents. We beg rain catchers for life when we're an hour away from the Mediterranean and Galilee." They lift the hood of their trench coat over their head becoming a mere outline against the shadow. "I love you, Laeth, I do – but you've been asking the same question since the day I've known you: why do it?" They turn on their heels, shrugging in a way that reminds me of the kid who showed up on our doorstep all those years ago. Reaching into some inner pocket, they retrieve my pistol and hand it out for me to take. "I asked myself for longer than you think: how can't he see it? Only now I realize it's not that you don't, but won't." The glisten of tears is the only proof that they see me. "Whether five or five hundred years passed, they endured as a people who came from distant lands, wielding tragedy to lay claim to revisionary mythology. Manipulating the hard truths of the world through their suffering, they come to conquer as monsters – armed by their masters – ready to burn and devour everything in their path to see their people behind the ethnostate gates of *Shamayim*."

They kick some rubble down into the hole, and we listen to the pebbles clack down against the ladder. "From the river to the sea," oddly enough, they chuckle like they've told some inside joke. "It's simple, really. If you assume there's nothing we can do, they've already won. Underneath all the made-up complexities our philosophies create, saving our people from invading monsters has always been the right thing to do. You know it in your heart. I know you do because you're so bad at hiding your shame from trying so desperately to find some alternative method. Neither my faith in God nor Self holds a flame to my belief that if we endure this nightmare – whether it's in five or five hundred years – an indigenous liberation will reach victory over these parasites on Nahasdzáán."

Aylul peers down the hole with curiosity parting their lips upward. "But, hey: next time might be our last. When it happens, can we please talk about anything other than this?" Without looking back, they lunge down into the tunnels. Forever moving forward.

Most of the fighting recedes into mass arrests by the time I reach the store's rooftop. Like boiling warts throughout the town, crowd-control ultra-sonic domes radiate cerulean light under the setting sun. Ayn Yassin's screams hush under the muffling savagery. Small plumes of smoke – black, gray, and white – rise between glass and limestone from every direction but much of the town's still intact. Drone and vehicle traffic move without detriment on the main streets as if it were any other day. A notification blinks in the corner of my lenses telling me Leila's calling for the tenth time. It goes to voicemail before I can think of what to even say. Instead of returning it, I saunter over to a lawn chair and plop down with a grunt. It's getting harder to breathe. Should probably make my way to the hospital but by now it's either too full or too under stocked for any real healing; might as well catch the show from here. Not thinking through the exhaustion of the day, I light a cigarette and take a deep drag. It's like inhaling cinders from a fire, making me hack a lung until I spit phlegm blushed with blood.

On the block across the street, Teta and Hassan stand around a felled per-simmon tree torn from its roots. Hard to make out the details from here, but looks like Teta's crying from the way Hassan has his arms around her. It's enough to get me off my ass and down the stairs faster than I thought I could move. When I open the front door, faint remnants of pepper spray and sewage sprayed from Humvees do my condition no favors. I push through eye-watering revulsion, running a palm along the hood of my truck for balance as I crunch across the gravel lot. Not fifty meters away from my untouched shop, broken windows and dumped garbage bins litter Eran's bakery. He's hunched over a broom, sweeping the debris with spray-painted swastikas on the backdrop wall. The old man notices me from under his bifocal glasses, giving me a meek wave as though he's not sure if we're cool or not. I struggle to even nod some vague acknowledgment in his direction. Part of me wants to help with the cleanup, but there's a mob of his settler-countrymen surveilling the streets incoming so I leave.

My neighbors notice me waddling over when I cross the grapevine pergola threshold. Hassan says something to me, but I don't quite make it out; a question, maybe. The field's littered with bent canisters fresh from the States and broken Molotov cocktails. Tire marks from three different vehicles shred the earth, swerving in semicircles from where I entered to the opposite end of the orchard. Tracing them with my eyes makes me nauseous-dizzy, my stomach turning like a washing machine. I do my best to limp through it by staring at my feet.

I've never been good with pain. When Aylul shoved me down the stairs all those years ago, I could've been released from the hospital days before I actually left. It wasn't until they showed up to call me out that I was discharged later. Still. No matter how many times it comes, I'm desperate to deny the end. How can it all be over when I've only known recycled epilogues? Sensing my own mortality brings me to my knees. Blood rushes to my head, melting me down 'til I'm flat on my back looking at the sky. Doves fly in linear formation toward some hidden horizon out of my periphery.

Hassan's chubby cheeks obscure the perfect view. He looks so much older with all the worry written on his face. I tell him it's fine but with the way I croak through cottonmouth, I know there's no convincing either of us. Should've taken Meir up on a VitaStim, but dealing with the hassle is the least I can do. I'll be right as rain after I get Hassan to roll me over; there's a twig digging into the wound Sakine left as a gift.

"We need to get you to the hospital," Hassan says incredulously, "you look terrible."

His sincerity makes me laugh. "Pretty sure avoiding the barber for months doesn't help."

Screeching tires from slammed brakes wakes me up a little bit more. Hassan looks up. I'm trying to read his face so I can prepare for some eventuality, but his confusion and disgust means it could be anyone. Wish they'd all just leave me alone for a while longer. A familiar voice calls out my name, but I'm more interested in watching the sunbirds overhead sharpen and blur. Hassan's face is replaced by Leila's and the painting's made only more beautiful by the concern wrinkling the corners of her nose. I've got an urge to reach out and kiss her, but

I'm pretty sure there's blood on my lips. Wonder if she'd mind. Before I try lifting my head, I remember Teta's not far away. She's gasping with worry, but I wouldn't put it past her to beat me with a shoe for doing something so *'ayb* in public. Leila's dark locks tickle my nose, and I sneeze on her face.

"Lovely," she says, wiping her cheek with a sleeve. Then to Hassan, "We need to get him to a hospital."

"There is no 'we' in any of this," Hassan snaps. "I'm sure you've forgotten, but the hospital's overrun by now. Run back to your masters, *khayina*; I'll take care of this."

"Huh…" Leila gets on her feet, tapping a finger to her chin. "That's not a bad idea, actually."

Credit where credit's due, Leila's never been one to take the bait of someone else's petulance. It's why they drive that white sedan Meir gave them even though it means replacing the windshield once a month. If you ask me, it's not worth the hassle, but it does have the benefit of highlighting hypocrisy. Why's Hassan so worked up over her when he sees me climb into the passenger seat every morning? "Help me get him in the car," Leila commands Teta's grandson, bowing her head to her elder before walking off to bring the car up. It takes a few different approaches to get me in the sedan without making me squeal in high-pitched death throes. Luckily, some neighborhood kids notice the commotion and assist Hassan as a gurney of arms to carefully lay me in the backseat.

"Drama queen," Teta calls from the sidelines when I yelp.

Crusted bits of mud hide my heated cheeks while everyone laughs outside. I listen to Leila thank the group for their help. Exhaustion nearly pulls me down into sleep like added gravity until the driver's door opens and slams shut. At first I'm sure that once we're out of sight, she'll dig into me for ignoring her calls, but minutes pass with nothing said between us. I consider drifting into slumber but decide to clear my throat to grab their attention. It spirals into a coughing fit that leaves me feeling brittle.

"Give it a couple of weeks, you'll be fine," Leila waits to say after I've settled down. "I remember my dad breaking four of mine when he caught me with a boy back in secondary school." She chuckles with rancor. "Can you imagine if it'd been during college?"

I'm not sure what to say because there's only one answer we both know: she'd probably be dead. Always knew Leila came from a strict home, but didn't have a clue it was that bad. I guess I never asked. "How's Moshe? The rest of 'em?"

"Everyone's back at the Compound. Moshe hasn't woken up yet; his face..." she pauses.

"What is it?"

"The doctors say he's past the worst of it," Leila skirts around the question. She digs through the glove compartment then reaches a hand back to plant two crimson pills on my chest.

I don't care what they are and shovel them in my mouth with a bitter crunch. Knowing I'll see Moshe in the next couple of hours, I drop the subject and settle as best I can into the cloth cushion. The cauterized scar on my back makes it impossible, but my core begins to sloppily shut down from fatigue anyway. Closing my eyes, I'm reminded of the man I killed today. Just gotta wait for the pill to drop, then its smooth sailing. By now, families in Nablus are dealing with their whole world being destroyed again, only this time the crime was committed by their own. Surprised Leila hasn't mentioned it yet; not that I want to talk about it. Riding the penumbral cusp of sleep, she finally brings up what's really on her mind.

"Did you find Aylul?"

My heart pangs with jealousy in the midst of more painful and important things. Rather than address it, I choose to plunge further into the siren song of sleep's sweet nothing.

I don't recognize where I am when I wake up on a twin bed. A soft fluorescent buzz of white noise greets me before my vision sharpens on a beige ceiling. Without thinking, I throw my legs over the edge, ripping an IV out of my wrist. I yelp at the pain shooting across my abdomen and shuffle back onto the mattress. Grasping underneath my gown, I feel rubber gauze bands cool like ice in reaction to the stress. I find more gauze in a drawer beside my bed and slap it over my wrist to stop the bleeding. Shades of purple irises decorate the window where it's dark outside. Noticing a curtain divide in the room I pull the veil back.

Moshe lays across from me on a bed like my own, only he's hooked up to about six different machines attached to his body like shards from a coffin.

His usual sunlight hair mats against his forehead, brow furrowed with strain. Carefully bearing weight on my feet, I shuffle over to lean over him with great effort. Given his condition, I'm surprised he hasn't been MedEvac'd to Tel Aviv. Stripped of his uniform, he doesn't look as tired. It's unsettling how much he smells like chlorine. Averting my gaze, I notice a pair of crutches leaning on the wall and grab them to make standing more comfortable. I thought seeing Moshe alive would've made me feel better about killing that man, but I still don't know his name. Can't help but feel the same way I did when Aylul showed up on our doorstep with those see-through eyes: this isn't fucking fair. Couldn't hold the tears back then and I can't now. It's a grief from hidden, stowed-away places long forgotten, swelling until I'm so aware of the pain I'm mourning the state of my sorrow. I tell myself it's pathetic. The door behind me swings open. Leila swaggers through in a lovely red dress. I can smell the tequila limes long before she gets close.

"Surprised you're awake," she says, combing my hair back with her fingers. When it's to her liking, she notices the puffy eyes and kisses my forehead gently. "How do you feel?"

For as long as I can remember that question never fails to make me laugh. Now's no different, though I'm sure it's far from cute with what a mess I look. Then there're concussive bangs outside followed by bright lights shining through the window. Dropping my crutches, I squat down instinctively with my arms over my head. "What – ?!"

Leila rushes to my side, concern wrinkling her face. "It's okay, they're only fireworks." She bends over to help me back on my crutches trying to soothe me with soft shushes. A warm hand cups my cheek, and I lean into the comfort of her thumb running along my jawline.

Moshe's tube-wired sweat-blanched body blurs in my periphery over Leila's shoulder. I'm not sure which of them to focus on. More short bursts boom neon spectrum lights casting shadows in the room until the shaking stops and by then, Leila's holding me tight. Her lips kiss my temple until I remember the party Samira mentioned earlier today. "Everyone in the mess hall?"

She nods against the nook of my shoulder. "There and everywhere else. They practically carried me and Amir out of here about an hour ago, you know how it is."

I do, but watching Moshe while she speaks sparks a desire for some reminder of the brighter side of this ideology. "Where are my clothes?"

Leila crosses the room to a cabinet where my outfit sits neatly folded on the shelf, leather jacket on a hanger. She holds them hostage when she returns. "Wanna tell me what happened to your back?"

Only took my first week here to realize every corner of the Compound's been bugged, but it's difficult to speak without knowing if they've tapped Leila. A lack of privacy is far from being my issue. Learned young that's one shared problem every poor bastard on earth inherited. But staring into her eyes feels like looking at a one-way mirror with Meir on the other end. Withholding information and lying have always been separate things; I repeat that lie again and again as I tell Leila everything that occurred between running after Moshe in Nablus and finding me in Teta's field. That is, everything except Aylul's plans for the sixth of September. Even if no one was snooping, Leila would go straight to Meir with the information. Reaching into her folded arms for the inside pocket of my jacket, I retrieve the tentacle microchip with two fingers and raise it eye-level. "They've probably gotten you too."

She doesn't ask about it as if she expected as much. Leila tosses my clothes on the bed and stands close enough for us to share the same breath. She unzips her dress down right below the shoulder blades, holding the bodice with one arm and, with the other, grabs my hand to run my fingers along her spine. The up-down motion gets smaller and smaller, pressing hard against what feels like vertebrae until I sense solid square edges. "When I first joined up," Leila answers the unspoken question.

"Why?" is what comes to mind after the shock, but "did you know they planted one on me?" shortly follows.

A sense of betrayal at the accusation steels her side-eyed glare. She moves away from me and zips back up. "Alright, sorry," I say.

Whether it's because she's drunk or not, Leila shrugs the matter off and steps closer, looking from me back at Moshe. Vibrant chartreuse light from the fireworks cast fractal reflections over her charming figure. She grabs my hand, twirling me away from the boy in a coma. Stepping slowly from side to side, Leila encourages my hips with her hands to slow dance. I'm weirded out at first, but she gives me a look that tells me I'm being a bummer. It's silly – inappropriate, even – but a nice change of pace.

"How about we put a pin in the questions?" she offers, "and join everyone outside? Seeing you up and at 'em would do a lot for morale."

Seems crazy at first with so much left unsaid, but when tangled emotions begin to constrict, it's easy to drop the complicated matter entirely. What's left to deal with when it can all be erased? It almost comes naturally after Leila pops two pills on my tongue and tells me to chew. We sway left, side to side while we wait for the pain to subside and my body to unstiffen. For now, at least, let's drop it for now. That's what we tell ourselves, swaying right then left, side to side. For now and for later, we sink into soft exhales of humanity stumbling on each other's feet toward the present. Laced fingers and holding each other close enough for Meir's jasmine perfume to pierce through the tequila and cigarettes. The celebration outside parades us in heavy droplet showers of translucent purples and gold. Seems they're doing fine without me; everyone's doing just fine without me, except in this room because Leila and I need each other to dance right now.

I'm positive not enough time's passed when Amir comes waltzing into the infirmary, spilling porch light onto our crystalline moment. His skin glistens with sweat, eyes bloodshot-dilated from cocaine that probably isn't just cocaine. The shit-eating grin across his face when he catches us in our awkward moment shatters when he notices his partner lying out on the bed.

"Hey," he says to Moshe instead of us.

Expecting him to break down in tears with the way he kneels on the floor clutching Moshe's hand, I break off from Leila, ready to be there to support my subordinate, but the grieving never comes. Amir kisses the hands of his lover and neatly places them back at his sides. Standing over Moshe, he nods as if remembering something. Before I have time to react, he crosses the room with three long strides and wraps me in a hug, squeezing tight enough for a fond farewell. "Thank you for doing what you did to bring him safely home," he says with his face smushed into my gown. He's got the jitters like an alarm going off inside him, cottonmouth breath downright putrid.

I peer over at Leila and she gives me an encouraging smile, so I wrap an arm around him. "Is there anything we can do to help?"

Amir pulls away from me with the energy of a child. "Uhh, yeah! You can join the fucking party, man! Come On!" He grabs my hand and pulls hard, making me gasp from the pain.

"Why don't we leave Laeth to change and he can join us in a bit?" Leila grabs his hands and pries them off me gently. Between Amir's profuse apologies, she leans on her toes to gift me a kiss on the lips that makes my heart pitter-patter flush and flutter. Like an aerial silk dancer, she twirls around Amir to divert him across the room and through the door. "Take your time," she says before shutting it tight behind them.

With nothing to eat but breakfast all day, the opium's a dip in the pool. Still hurts to breathe, but the pain's tolerable enough to let me twist over to my clothes on Moshe's bed. Clear acid-green bubbles feed through the tubes attached to his mouth, wrists, and stomach distract me from what I was doing. Their direction ebbs forward and back, taking my imagination to a place where the machines are sucking him dry of all his soul. Somewhere underneath all that gauze is a tender person who got awful marks on his *Te'udat Bagrut*, the driving force which would eventually lead him here. I struggle to muster empathy, yet some receding part of me whispers hollow well wishes. What I need is a beer and someone to make me laugh to get this stick out of my ass. Unfurling my shirt, I pause to notice the wash couldn't completely remove soft stains of blood. The drugs help me not overthink things; I just have to crumple it into a ball then toss the damn thing on the other side of the room. Jeans and a leather jacket will do me just fine if I zip them up. Sliding my feet into the furry white hospital slippers makes me giggle.

According to modern seasons it's nearly winter, but a cool autumn breeze welcomes me when I step out into the night. To my surprise, it's Samira waiting for me in front of the infirmary. She's alone, back leaning against a guardrail with two unopened beers at her feet, as though she can read my mind. Grinning at the grisly sight of me, she walks over under the porch light and pops the bottle tops off with a lighter. The flame from mine reflects off the iridescent thobe she's wearing. Cascading geometric embroideries trap me in a trance until Samira bends forward to catch my attention. Under her lion's mane of curls, she winks at me with cat-eyed makeup before clicking our glasses together to take a swig. Any insecurity I once had gets buried under barley with just one sip.

"I'm glad you're okay," she says with her bottle half-finished. "I mean, not 'okay,' but you know what I mean – safe." She hugs me quickly like getting caught in the act would be a scandal, but she stays just long enough instead for us to sink into each other's broken heartbeats.

Amused by how the alcohol mixes with Leila's medication, I chug what's left of my beer and do what any Palestinian who loves their country does: toss it over the fence to see how far I can throw it. The fireworks have ended, but a cheer goes up in the direction of the mess hall as if something fantastic has happened. "Come on. I hear there's a party, and you know how much I love being fashionably late."

With a chuckle, Samira weaves an arm into mine. Together, we take our time walking through chest pain gasps and moans toward some promise of opulent delight. The clock reads one in the morning, and the few people left outside are the poor enlisted bastards pulling graveyard shift guard duty. Most of our Israeli counterparts in the organization will probably be in their barracks by now adhering to strict military guidelines; it is Tuesday, after all. When we pass by one of the dormitories, an open door wafts melodic oud and flute sorrow, luring me away from my destination. Samira and I stand quietly in the doorway watching a man and woman perform for a small audience sitting cross-legged around them. The middle-aged couple stands facing each other in their underwear playing a song of longing I find faintly familiar. One plucks away with his fingertips while the other lets the wind sing.

I nudge Samira with an elbow to leave, but recall that my mom used to hum this tune when we'd do chores together around the house. If I focus on the memory, I can almost hear her pitch-perfect alto and the smell of fresh linens. These two managed to compose an even more depressing version of Umm Kulthum's "I Now Have a Rifle." Holding my breath, I close my eyes. The song ends the moment I do. It's followed by soft clapping and snaps

When I hear the stomping cacophony of circular flowing *dabke* coming from the mess hall, I want to throw up. The corkscrew pop of champagne flowing raises cheers that echo out into the dunes.

"Recruited seven new people thanks to Huwara," Samira says with pride. "Hate waking up to construction in the morning, but it's easier to deal with when it's for new dorms. Can you believe it, Laeth? Took us all last year to hit those numbers and now look at us struttin' our stuff. Who knows, maybe before we're dead we'll make homes for all our people..." her voice trails off into distant fantasies still trapped behind apartheid walls.

Watching her stare up at the stars above, I know she's found where she's meant to be. Being close to me will only serve to take her away from it, and it'd be wrong to. When she tilts her head further back, I stick a finger down my throat and projectile vomit acid bile against the side of someone's tent. Samira rushes to me, but I put a hand up to stop her. "I think it's best if I lie down instead; the others will have to wait 'til morning."

Wanting nothing to do with Moshe, I let Samira guide me to the room Leila and I use whenever we're too tired to head back home. After declining offers for food or water, I convince Samira that all I need is sleep.

"Alright, alright," she says, "I'll let Leila know you're here."

Inching my way through the door, I thank her for her kindness but something comes to mind before it's shut. "You don't know where Meir is, do you?"

She looks suspicious at first, but I can almost see the liquor pushing the train of thought off its tracks in real-time. "Once we were all accounted for here, he told me to grab every bottle of champagne from the officer's closet and ran off. Who knows where; but he seemed…"

Knowing what she's going to say, I grit my teeth down 'til my jaw tingles numb. "What?"

"I dunno? Happy, for once."

When Leila stumbles into our bedroom, a bloodshot eye reads 03:38, and I swear the matte black splotches on the ceiling are looking back at me. She has the good grace not to turn on the lights as she undresses for bed and throws her body on the mattress beside me. I'm touched she thought to shower and brush her teeth minty fresh because I know how much community bathrooms freak her out. She's still chilly from outside, so I wrap an arm around her and bring her close to my insulated warmth to kiss the top of her head.

"Told those assholes not to let you drink," she says with her lips fanning my shoulder.

"I think I'm a big boy who can make decisions for himself."

Leila doesn't move from her spot, sinking further into the mattress. "Mmph; that's why I told 'em."

I wait for her to make any mention of what happened in Huwara, but there's only the soft, comfortable coos of her getting closer to sleep. Must be nice.

"What're you thinking about?" A pathetic attempt at bringing the subject to light, but maybe the nightmare won't come if I give it a voice.

"This room would feel more like home with more of our stuff in it," she mutters dreamily.

I give Leila no reason to stay awake and feel her body slump as she gives into sleep. With her snoring comes the hollow ceiling darkness that takes its final shape, and all I see is him.

With the media frenzy Huwara caused, it didn't take long to find out his name was Subhi Abdul Rahman Sa'adat but researching for two days more led me to discover that his only son Mahmoud flies the white flag. On the fourth, around midday, I'm in the store's back office sitting at my desk waiting for him to arrive. I found his name in our database under those who recently joined, and it wasn't hard to put two-and-two together from there. It's clear to me that his father was at the bazaar that day to guide his son back home. What surprises me most is that Mahmoud's still scheduled to move into the new dorms. Yesterday, I lodged a note in the zipper of his temporary tent asking if he'd consider *Sulha*. So here I sit biting the nails off my fingertips wondering if he'll show. Took all morning to decide whether to leave the pistol in the truck just in case this guy seeks vengeance, but I figure he had his chance at the Compound a few nights ago. I guess it's not fair considering I haven't been there since, but working in the shop's been healing me better than the medical supplies I stole from the infirmary before I left. The front door abruptly opens, and Hassan pokes his head in.

"Laeth? There's a man here to see you."

I smile through my blood pressure rising so as not to raise any suspicions; the last thing I want is Hassan putting two-and-two together. "Please show him in and put some coffee on the stove." He disappears from sight, addressing Mahmoud from the front of the shop. Time to rethink whether I need a gun or not. Scanning the dingy file cabinet room for anything to use as a weapon, I come up short when there's another knock on the door a few seconds later.

"*Ma'lim*," Mahmoud's voice gravels the small sign of respect like it's coming from deep below the earth. Wearing nothing but a plain white tee and jeans for the ritual, I feel silly sitting here in a suit. He's a thick-necked man just a few years my senior who looks more like a bar brawler with that flat nose than someone seeking peace. It's a miracle to me that I'm not dead already. He certainly would be if the roles were reversed.

"Thank you for coming today," I say then try to sound stronger. "Please, take a seat." When he doesn't, hot flashes prickle along my spine despite the whirring fan nearby.

"You mentioned *Sulha* in your letter," he cuts right to the chase, crossing his arms over his chest. "What did you have in mind as far as *'atwa* goes?"

Thanks to Teta's coffee cart gossip, I learned that the Sa'adats were a family of bakers who sold their produce outside of elementary schools on weekdays. Doesn't take a genius to know that they can't afford a decent funeral. Their patriarch's already in the ground, but their debt's going nowhere. I reach into the bottom drawer of my desk to retrieve a manila envelope stuffed with ten thousand shekels and place it between us. Two years ago, I couldn't imagine affording this but cooking the books so as not to raise any alarms with Hassan came surprisingly easy. Really do owe him a raise for all he's done for this place. "In light of what happened in Huwara, it would be my honor if you would accept this as a token of restitution." Reciting the words of formality I found on the Web feels like translating languages with free software.

Mahmoud takes a step forward, picking up the envelope to count the bills one by one. When he finishes, he slides the bulk into his back pocket. "Okay," he says, reaching out to shake my hand to seal the *Hodna*. He could crush mine with little effort, but he squeezes just enough to warrant the worry. Without further ado, he stalks off before more can be said.

I sigh but hardly feel relief when the door clicks behind him. Nearly two thousand years of tradition boil down to just a few minutes, and the concentrate tastes bitter. Back in the day, there'd be entire event halls rented out for such an occasion. Representatives from each family would sit across from one another while the immediately affected by the wronged and accused would confer with village elders and sheikhs they assigned as *Jaha*. It was a ritual about more than just payment and punishment, but peace and resolution between members of a community striving to move forward. Looking through the block window at Mahmoud's distorted figure climbing back in his car, all I sense with me now are the ghosts of my ancestors hanging their heads in shame.

Meir sends one of his messengers to the shop with a letter one fine day in September. A buzzed-cut twelve-year-old in a Spiderman cutoff daring to wear jorts waltzes right up to me at the cash register, slaps down an envelope, and holds out a hand out for a ten-spot. The way he grins all smug with his buckteeth makes me want to throw a jawbreaker at his head. I've seen this son of bitch kicking a futbol way too close to where I park my baby. Being at the store as much as I have these past few weeks got me noticing neighborhood behavior – the uptick in these ruffians. I've resorted to screaming with the threat of a broom until he runs off laughing.

"First admit you're a little shit." I retrieve my wallet and flap twenty shekels over his head just out of reach.

With better reflexes, he snatches the bill on his second try. "Okay," he puts simply, pushing the money back onto the counter. "Two packs of American Spirits, please."

"*Welak!*" I raise a hand like I'm going to hit him, but he doesn't flinch. Something about his sweat-slicked hair and chubby cheeks reminds me of Mo'taz. Throw some fool's gold chains over his neck, and I'd swear I'm looking at his son. Reach behind me for one of the small Pringles cans for old times' sake but pick a bottle of water to toss at his head. Hassan's going to have a meltdown when he finds it missing from inventory, but without gilled wrists, this kid will be dead before spring. "Now get out before someone sees you in my business."

He gives me the middle finger but doesn't forget to grab the bottle on his way out. There's nothing written on the front or back of the envelope, so I slice it open with a box cutter and wiggle out an index card.

> *Abdullah's Roman Bathhouse, 16:00*
> *Pack an overnight bag*
> *– M*

All this time, I've woken up thinking this is the one he'll call on me. Took weeks not to think I'd shoot him for setting me up in Huwara. Still not sure I'm there, but you don't have to give it up to let it go. Technically speaking, I never resigned from my post with the Forgotten Ones, but I figure I never really had one to begin with anyway.

TFO grows nearly as steadily as the Mubarizun, so it's not like I'm missed. No doubt Meir is ready to dangle Cid and Aylul above my head with some new initiative he wants my help with. From what little I've heard from Leila, Meir's been absent from the Compound for weeks; scheming in some hidden place, I'm sure. I blink out of old threads on my phone of everyone at the Compound telling me Moshe has finally woke up, checking the time instead. Already noon. This asshole better not expect punctuality with the way the checkpoints have been lately.

Throwing the keys over to Hassan, I toss on a hoodie and jacket from the rack and step outside into a thermal winter. Always hated the cold, but love the snow; each unique flake is a distant memory that blurs. Now the best I can hope for is slush two months out of the year.

Squishing around like a duck towards Teta's, I take a good look around crossing the street. Less IOF troops than usual patrol the area. In their absence Ayn Yassin seems to glow brighter. Sheikh Omar's *imam* crackles over a loud-speaker system at the mosque a few blocks away, his old man vibrato starting the *Adhan* with a deeply pained gusto. There's a group of children playing a game of judge and executioner down the road. Some curly-headed kid with forehead wrinkles swings a ruler around at his friends, ruining the game entirely and sowing chaos among them. Their shrill squeals of horror and glee echo out, bouncing off the concrete high-rise apartments as they try to escape his tyranny. Crossing onto Teta's property, I walk through rows of leafless trees until I reach her plywood door and knock twice. Then thrice, then twenty times more in quick succession until I'm drumming on it like I'm in concert. The door swings open.

"How many times do I have to tell ya that shit annoys me?" Teta glowers, hands in her pits as if she's about to die from hypothermia.

I kiss both her cheeks. Through the door, a waft of sumac chicken cooking in the oven greets me like temptation's mistress. Poking my head into the kitchen around the corner, I see the table's full of taboon dough waiting to be baked. There's a large cast iron wok on top of the stove sizzling with coriander, cardamom, and allspice onions on the fire with roasting pine nuts. Teta smiles like she knows she's hot shit when I turn back to gawk. "Oh my God, it's *musakhan* day?"

"Don't blaspheme," she's too busy gloating to say with any conviction. "What's the matter? Thought it was your favorite?"

"Something came up; wanted to tell you I'm gonna be late for dinner tonight. Might be too late to come at all..." Deepening my frown, I try to pull off my best doe-eyed look.

Teta pinches my cheek and gives it a hard slap. "For you, *habibi*? I'll set aside two in the cupboard where Hassan can't reach." She encourages a smile out of me with one of her own that pulls at her wrinkles. "Come home safe."

Pushing aside the pillow and blanket, I climb into my truck with enough effort to remind myself that my ribs haven't fully healed. Driving through Ayn Yassin gives me more anxiety than any protest I've ever been to. There's no telling anymore when rubble from unfinished buildings will come dropping from the sky. Any road you turn down can suddenly be blockaded with burning tires. The other day some dumbass throwing Molotov cocktails with a sling nearly splashed liquid fire on the hood. There's been an uptick in Mubarizun activity. I visited Cid and Diwa's about a week back to see what's what, but no one answered the door. I've called every day since, but I'm only met with a dial tone.

As I pass by a gleaming glass egg surrounded by flora not meant for this environment, Ma'al Luz bustles with bored people waiting outside for their ticket to be called. Seems a new bus packed with American and British immigrants called expats who bought into Birthright comes rolling in every week. Add in the constant stream of young Zionists waiving their mandatory two years of military service for five years' civic duty squatting in settlements, and Ma'al Luz has more or less become a small city with its own identity beating at the heart of Ayn Yassin like haute couture tumors. Dozens of U.N.-affiliated flags obnoxiously litter the hotel campus as if it were an embassy. After all this time, I'm still not sure what to think of Jabriel's mission tomorrow. What am I going to do? Point a gun at his head? Can't grasp my role in all of it; feels too big; too real, and utterly violent. A pair of boys swing on the playground as I make a right turn reaching into the glove compartment for my medication is the only way out. I palm the last two pills hoping to lessen the guilt by pretending to wonder if I should ration them. I'll give Leila a call for more once I'm done with whatever this is.

Lieutenant Haya finds my truck waiting in line ten cars back at the southern checkpoint. It's too bad I don't carry Meir's documentation with me anymore, but without having to mention that I'm headed to Ramallah to meet him, she clears me for passage. For the price of a box of assorted halvah and dealing with my people slinging every slur in the book at me as I make a hasty exit, I'd say it's a steal.

Ramallah's a strange place to visit nowadays, but maybe it's becoming what it was always meant to be. A vertical black sea of flags flap in the windows of nearly every residential tower I drive past. To contend with the surge of support toward their rivals, the Palestinian Authority and Fatah have made it mandatory for all commercial businesses to fly their pee-stain flags in a campaign to rally the people. All it accomplished is what any power grab from a government that realizes it's lost the support of its people does: further polarize our nation. Unlike Ayn Yassin's fever-pitch reaction, the people of Ramallah revolt like the city's one big EDM festival. From dusk till dawn, pockets of heavy bass raves can be found in nearly every borough, turning night to day with their drone-choreographed light shows. As I pull the car around and cross the cobblestone threshold of Old Town, where the younger generations work and older people live, small clusters of white flags begin to bloom around like a sea of stars. Blinking out of the GPS, I splurge on valet parking since I want to be in and out as quickly as possible.

It's no wonder I've never heard of this place. Abdullah's Roman Bath-house squats between two skyscrapers with a greenstone entrance like you're heading down into the Cave of Wonders. The spiraling staircase descends into a red velvet room with chairs lining the linen-draped walls. I walk up to the front desk, expecting an AI host to appear, but there's nothing in sight. Smells like someone's using olive oil soap steaming from the *hammam* someplace beyond the curtains. I notice a loincloth neatly folded to the side with a bar of soap on top with a note that says my name in chicken scratch Arabic. Crumbling it with a fist, I push through the drapes stepping into a stalactite cavern humid with the stench of salt and body odor, the natural dripping pillars glowing bright with seductive pink LEDs.

In the center of the cave is a small hot spring in the ground big enough for five or six people, but now there sits only one. Sitting with his arms spread over the edges, head back as though he can't hear my footsteps approaching, is

Meir Cohen. The top half of his body's chiseled from stone but marred by scar tissue lacerations. When I stop at the edge of the pool, he lifts his head to wink with the same eye as two years ago before killing one of his own. They're the same nautical blues that looked me up and down before whispering enraged words in Subhi Sa'adat's ear. Takes a moment to realize I'm shaking. Need to calm down. How I feel doesn't dictate the reality of the situation and right now, this man holds all the cards with enough Krav Maga to pummel me back into the Stone Age.

"It's good to see you, Laeth," Meir's chimera voice reverberates around the cave. He looks me up and down, pursing his lips. "Not joining me? Smart thinking, really. If the owners of this swamp were allowed to visit *Hamat Gader*, they'd kill themselves from shame for calling this a Roman bath."

It hurts to breathe for several reasons and the humidity's not one of them. "I'm not sure what you want me to say."

"How about 'thank you for erasing the Huwara footage before it got into the wrong hands? 'Thank you for keeping me out of jail for the rest of my life'? I think that'd be a nice start." Bathed in ambient light, he turns just enough to reveal the Desert Eagle on the ground behind him. He follows my line of sight and shrugs like it's my fault for being surprised. Picking it up, he raises the chrome cannon slowly until it's aimed at my head. He waits for me to say the words.

"Go fuck yourself," I spit.

Meir rolls his eyes, dropping the gun. "I'm beginning to realize just how badly you need what I have in store for you," he teases.

"Enough. Why not cut the shit and say what you want?"

His eyes slit in warning for overstepping boundaries. "You know," he says, getting out of the pool to dry himself off. "I've been back in Tel Aviv hoping to take TFO to the next phase – grant writing, stuffy dinners, lobbyists – things that would bore you to tears because they did for me." He walks over to a shelf carved out of the cave wall to retrieve his clothes from a duffle bag. Rare to see him in anything but military dress, but today it looks like he's sporting a polo and khaki pants like we're about to go yachting. "One day, I received a message telling me your request to visit Haifa got denied – sorry about that, by the way – but then a wonderful idea occurred to me." Meir slips on his loafers and crosses the distance between us to grab my shoulders. Even having just bathed, he smells like iron. "When's the last time we allowed ourselves to have a little fun?"

It's hard for my brain to transition from desperately wishing I hadn't left the gun in the glovebox to processing what he just said. "What?"

"So I filed the requisition forms myself," he continues, "and wouldn't you know, they approved you to stay with me for a couple of days –"

"– in Tel Aviv?"

He gives me a look like I just asked the stupidest question. "Well, yes, in Tel Aviv. Come, I believe the parking meter's running out, and we wouldn't want to start with a ticket." Meir pats me once more and heads for the staircase.

I knew this was all a setup to get me away from Ayn Yassin tomorrow, but didn't think the attempt would be so pathetic. It's enough to make me laugh, and I do. "I'm not going anywhere with you."

Meir pauses at the first step before turning to face me, clicking his tongue. "Look around you, Laeth. Why is there no one in this bathhouse?" He raises the cannon at my head again, but this time pulls the hammer back with a grating click and lock. "I could kill you right now and have the PA clean up your mess for me before the old lady finishes her next batch of *Musakhan*." He nods along as I process the double threat that validates all of my paranoid suspicions. "Good. Now that we're on the same page, come with me and get in the goddamn car. It's time we have some much-needed fun."

When we're back on the street, I convince Meir that we should take my truck. Bet that bastard hasn't worried about overnight valet fees a day in his life. Not many roam the sidewalks here this time of day; just a few scattered souls bundled up in jackets walking with their heads down to some final destination. When the valet brings my Warlock around, I toss him a coin and slide into the driver's seat. Meir hoists himself beside me while I find something we can both appreciate and settle on death metal.

"What am I punching in?" I ask. Keeping the windows up, I light a cigarette mindful to take deep drags. The look of disgust on his face satisfies some pettier sides of me.

"We could be in Paris and I'd still know which direction's home," he boasts, pushing the button for the window over and over until I turn the child lock off. "Take the 443; we'd do well to avoid *Yerushalayim* today."

"*Al Quds*," I correct. He's surprised I care to make the distinction without asking why, but the why's obvious; the city must be on fire from another twelve-hour Cain and Abel rebellion.

"*Yerushalayim, Al Quds*, Jerusalem; what does it fucking matter?" Meir pulls a flask from inside his vest jacket and motions with it for me to get moving.

Despite being with the man I hate most, there's an excitement about going somewhere I've never been that overcomes my reservations. All we need is for Meir to bat his lashes for us to blast through fourteen iron dome checkpoints like a dart through balloons. When we push through Ramallah's dilapidated concrete outskirts into rolling steppe hills, Meir sifts around his duffle bag for a white box wrapped neatly in a bow. He rips it open like a kid on Rosh Hashanah morning and pops two iridescent marbles onto his palm. Tenderly plucking one with his fingertips, he wiggles at me as an offering.

With Leila's meds still working their magic, I'm not sure I need the extra push, but it's tempting. "What are they?"

He answers by ingesting his like some Roman dignitary feeding from a grapevine and shivering as he swallows. "The best part of freedom is experimental lab-tested drugs that make you forget what it costs to get there." His victimization falls on deaf ears, and he sighs. "Come now, Laeth; we said we were going to have fun."

I don't remember agreeing to anything, but it's another hour to Tel Aviv, and it'll certainly help me tolerate this piece of shit. Thumbing it around in my hand, it looks like it'll break my teeth but when I mouth it whole and crunch, I know I'm screwed. Cotton candy spores cake my mouth and throat. I gag into a coughing fit, swerving us off our lane onto oncoming traffic. Meir grabs the wheel laughing as we just miss a semi-truck while I regain my composure to take back control. There's a call from Leila but I let it go straight to voicemail. Why answer the byproduct when the source is right here beside me.

Brown-beige steppes lined with Bedouin tents and anorexic sheep gradient fade to grassy plains of palm tree farms and olive fields. We bump along the four-lane freeway with the volume back up enough to hear a thump. Scattered shacks selling anything from shawarma and coffee to plastic toy guns begin to dot the rural country as we near the outskirts of a Zionist settlement. An encircled wall of ten-meter concrete slabs with pearlescent temple spire skylines almost makes it look like a medieval castle stronghold; all it needs is a good moat. Their fantasy can't hide the thousands of Palestinian bodies, no matter how deep they unceremoniously threw them in a ditch somewhere underneath its foundation. Lucky for Meir's jaw, the road leads us out of sight into a tunnel through a mountain. We plunge into shadow with nothing but the soft red hue from the dashboard and reflective sticker medians in the headlights to guide the way. In the void, my mind goes to the children swinging in Ma'al Luz to the curly-headed kid who ruined the judge and executioner for his friends. Locking Aylul out of the hatch under the store should be easy enough, but what about all the other tunnels throughout Ayn Yassin? What about Jabriel?

"Can I ask you a personal question without turning this into a Turkish soap opera?" Meir asks. He takes my silence as something I never agreed to again and continues. "Why did you leave?"

It's only been twenty minutes, but the anxiety of the come-up rushes through my veins like synaptic lightning. It's a good thing the road's empty. My anger flickers and wanes, flames burning any damnation I've saved for the Captain to smoldering ash, collected and swept away for some other time. The only possible answer that remains is the truth. "Was reminded what it means to be under the heel of Fortuna's wheel."

"Has anyone ever told you what an outrageous bummer you can be?" Meir groans from his seat. The reflection of three different windows opened in his lens close out and he glares over at me. "In your hurry to leave, it seems you didn't stop to think what would happen to Cid and Aylul in your absence."

The threat hits like a slap against a brick wall. I'd rather focus on the reflective light strips on the road merging into a straight line the more I lean on the gas pedal. "Can't believe you didn't wait to give me this stuff 'til after we get where we're going."

"Always blaming others for your misfortune," Meir scoffs, "no one told you to take it now."

The tunnel opens up with a flash of sunlight, blurring my vision with hexagonal orange phosphenes. I roll the window down for a cigarette but forget to strike the flint when tall smokestack peaks billowing fire break over a hill to our left. Electric fences and concrete slabs tear the earth a thousand meters long and four hundred meters wide around a compound with two towers. Eight squat stone buildings cluster together on the opposite end of the umber dirt courtyard. Not an hour away from Ayn Yassin and I'd have no idea what I was looking at if it wasn't for reading about these places in the news my whole life.

Once the U.S. pivoted to become on the ground colonizers of Gaza, Israel ran into a problem. After a century of abetting in their scheme for better oil deals, the Kingdom of Jordan couldn't accept any more than the millions of Palestinian refugees they already had. The Senate and Knesset unanimously voted in favor of taking a leaf out of the CCP's handbook with cleansing the Uyghur people in vocational education and training centers. They erected four in Gaza those first few years, but once the Great Climate Migrations flooded the global spotlight, it was easier to move in the shadows. A little boon to black market organ harvesting kept the right coffers satisfied, and without expansionism on the menu, no country in the world would dare sacrifice its own to save genocide. We ascend the pothole road, driving through cracked desert earth as we snake back and forth up a mound. Clouds break once we're at the top, sun shining dull on fields of panopticon structures stretching south as far as the horizon dares end. My cauterized wound itches something fierce so I swivel my back against the seat to scratch, taking the western road facing away.

From then on the landscape transitions to a more mild, wet Mediterranean climate with not a wall or soldier in sight. The freeway's smoother to ride on as we pass horse ranches and tropical mansions populating wheat fields. Bus stops with everyday folk heading into the city blur through the windshield as I continue to ignore speed reduction warning signs. The 443 thins to two lanes as we pass through a town I could've once pronounced properly a hundred years ago. I peer up at the azure sky noticing the absence of obstructions. Spaceships like distant day stars replace the usual commotion.

"Where are the drones?" I'm so enthralled that I nearly smash into the car in front of me.

Meir doesn't flinch when I slam on the breaks. "There's an underground network like a sewage system running from here to Golan," he responds. "Oh! Oh! Stop here, they have the best Americanos."

It's more evident than ever that I'm three forgotten showers past belonging here when I pull over to park outside a log cabin called Café Café. It's like I'm sitting in a hulking mass of scrap metal docked at a sea of smooth curved gunmetal and chrome self-driving vehicles. Meir gets out of the car and shuts the door without asking what I want. Looking around the strip, citizens on their lunch break bustle about an upscale shopping mall with bars and restaurant patios. They chatter and laugh under levitating Tiki torches, augmented reality animals looping through some kitsch jungle simulation through plastic canopy roofs. There are little flourishes of self-expression that catch my eye every now and then; different piercings and hairstyles, but I was expecting something...different. Thought it'd be more occupied with augmented freaks; bluetooth antenna horns jacked to their brains. It exists; it's there; but there's none of that, really. More pretentious and advanced, sure, but the biggest difference here is people throw their trash in bins.

Meir climbs back inside the truck whistling some slow tune with Americanos in his hands. We exit the town and zigzag our way up another mound of terraformed earth lined with palm trees swaying under the cold winter sun. A pair of vultures peck at a dead dog on the side of the road, flying off when we rush by like the wind. My coffee gets cold in the holder barely touched; now I know why some people think it's just bean water. Steam-roasted beans and nicotine make for a good candle though. There's a cozy budding sense of euphoria blooming in my sternum. Meir jerks upright in his seat and leans his head out of the window, pointing forward. The idiot's saying something but doesn't realize that at 100 kmph I can't hear a word he's saying.

"I was saying," he says once inside, "pull over when we get to the top. There's something you should see."

When we step out of the car, Meir leads me further up the grassy hill another few yards until he stops for me to stand beside him. Breathing into my hands to rub the cold away, I can't seem to inhale again from what I see before me. Down the ridge, along the coast glimmers a monolithic metropolis under a perfectly beautiful midwinter's day. The thick bristle of vertical glass spires is surrounded by white stone buildings with orange-tiled roofs tightly packed in squares and blocks spreading out until they dissipate into the sand. Craning my neck for a better angle, I search for the dark blue of the Mediterranean Sea, but it seems we're still too far away. Halfway to giving up, my eye catches a ripple between pillared mansions. I gasp loud enough for Meir to smile wickedly.

"Welcome to Tel Aviv."

١٤

Meir directs me inland through tangled web highways leading away from Mediterranean waves toward downtown's crystal rose towers. My vision breathes geometric mandalas into the pores on my hand gripping the steering wheel. It bleeds up the windshield from the hood of my truck to the traffic in front of me. Just have to focus on brake lights to get us there safely.

"How much longer?" I'm sure he can hear the panic in my voice.

His delayed response comes because he's too busy marveling at a bronze statue of Ben-Gurion sitting by the entrance of a park. "Not much," Meir mutters. Much to his dismay, a magnet-powered tube train whizzes overhead in the opposite direction toward the beaches. "We must get you changed at my apartment first. Sorry to break this to you, but looking like a vagrant doesn't work everywhere you go."

Ten minutes later on a street lined with glass hotels and picture-posing tourists, Meir tells me to pull into a garage door sliding up directly into one of the towers. As soon as we're in, a red light glows followed by a feminine voice asking us to vacate the vehicle in every language. A strong leftover musk of vanilla spice cleaning product makes me sneeze in the car lift elevator. Meir walks over to the back doors, where a small screen opens in the metallic wall for facial recognition scans.

In an instant the lift hums to life, shooting us upward sixty-seven floors, then slowing down to move horizontally until a chime announces our arrival. Heavy gated doors open to a hardwood-floor condominium with a wrap-around wall of windows overlooking the city. The elevator closes behind us to store my truck in the garage. We step into a living room with industrial lights hanging over flat gray couches that look uncomfortable to sit on. Across from us is a kitchen outfitted with stainless steel appliances and a small island without stools around it, but what seems all too familiar is the lack of décor on the walls. The only proof anyone calls this home is a gold-sheathed *saif* hanging on a mantle above the fireplace.

"Why would you buy a hotel suite?" I ask as Meir disappears down into the hallway.

"Housekeeping came with the closing costs," he calls back before shutting a door somewhere out of sight.

There's an exit between windows leading out to a balcony, but on my way I notice a standing clock nestled in a corner down the amber-lit hall. It stands apart from anything else in this place like someone stashed it here from somewhere else. Wooden metronome ticks resonate; hypnotic. More intricate details cover the maple-stained frame, exposed golden shafts meticulously turning wheels and pinions as seconds turn to minutes. Chains and nylon pulleys cascade down tied to a swinging pendulum knocking hollowly at the height of each turn. Encasing the white face of time sits a spired temple etched from oak like a helmet. The temptation to reach out and touch one of the spinning gears overcomes me, but it slices through my fingertip.

"Laeth!" Meir barks two doors from the left like he's been calling my name more than once. He's changed into a milky wool trench coat with stitches slithering along the seams as if they were alive. The gray spiked animal pelt woven along the back collar makes him seem not of this world. There's an amused twitch in his lips when he steals my attention. He lifts some folded clothes up and cocks his head to the door beside him. "You can change in the bathroom, but don't get lost in there. The show starts in an hour."

"Show?" I wonder aloud, but all the man answers with is a playful giggle I never imagined possible from the Butcher of Gaza.

I'm sitting on the toilet wearing Meir's clothes facing a full-length mirror after he insisted we couldn't leave until I combed my hair. Not one bit pleased with my first attempt, he stands over me now in the steam-damp room huffing as he pulls at my knots. The bristles scratching against my scalp soothe me into some warm place of nurtured tranquility. Much to his credit, Meir chose an outfit I couldn't oppose wearing. It was a type of black romper suit that flowed like a montsuki with delicate floral vines changing color along the uraeri, tying a red silk sash to accent the look. My confidence swells enough to make me think I might be handsome.

"All done," he says, patting my shoulders. Squatting to inspect the messy comb over with me in the mirror, he hums a tune delighted with himself. He glances over at my reflection to gauge a reaction, and I beam up at him with an excitement I haven't felt in ages; a heightened elation for what's to come.

Back outside on the sidewalk curb, I stretch my hands out toward the chill muted sun to bask in its energy while Meir hails a taxi. A slick white sedan pulls up, and we climb into the plush leather seats in the back. When we strap on our seatbelts, a screen divides the car into two flickers to project the simulation of a driver in the front seat. At first glance, the handsome Indian man in a dark sherwani asking us where we'd like to go seems real enough to reach out and grab his shoulder. My suspended disbelief ends when my finger presses against the glass. Widgets brighten with options to change the settings and menus I don't care enough to read. Meir slaps my hand away and commands the vehicle to take us to an address he seems to know off the top of his head.

We're in the car for much longer than I thought we'd be, but I have trouble seeing the rush when there are ready-made Moscow mules being served on Meir's tab. We leave the dividing screen blank to reflect our opulence while we toast without speeches to throw back a few copper mugs.

"Give me a hint," I implore him.

Meir's brow twitches at my third time asking him. "Good God, man; can you not enjoy the suspense of a surprise?"

"No," I put simply, "I can't." Feeling nauseous, I crack my window to breathe in the fresh air. There's an absence of honking midday traffic filled instead with bird songs and bicycle bell hellos to a waving bookstore owner. Children on lawns outside their school laugh around vibrantly colored building blocks floating off the ground or shout victoriously at the goalpost at the corner pitch. Two-story family homes neatly spread out in front yards with driveways and Ikea dream catchers. By all rights, it seems we've found ourselves in suburbia. "Please?"

Meir grins over at me, eyes glowing red through slits. "Ever heard of Gladium?"

"You will arrive at your destination in *thirty seconds*, thank you *Meir Cohen* for your patronage with us here at The Magic Carpet Express," the AI system says over the speakers. "You have *one minute* to vacate the vehicle, otherwise your credits will be charged every minute incurred after. Goodbye."

Anyone with an internet connection and a curious mind knows about Gladium, but the sport's been banned in most countries for well over a decade now. It was one of those unilateral agreement bibs the UN cobbled together for the world to sign so we can all continue pretending they're actually benefitting society. It's easy to access old videos though; some of my favorite memories growing up were watching the Battle of Yarmouk reenactment with my family on Eid al-Fitr. The thing is, when you can willfully change the appearance of an android made of ballistic gelatin to look like anyone dead or alive, society's bound to take things to weird places, and sexual fetishes are a bottomless pit. The Gladium entertainment industry nearly flatlined after the UN Resolution, but shows still surface on popular forums from time to time. A shell now from its short-lived tradition of reviving milestone moments in human history, the stages are typically set in abandoned warehouses from the Eastern Bloc. That's why it comes as a shock when we step out of the taxi to stand at the iron arrow gates of a colonial brick mansion.

There are two guards facing us on the other side, and Meir walks over to talk with them in low voices, though I'm too distracted by the garden world surrounding this castle to eavesdrop. Assorted bushels of cyclamen flowers and lilies paint pinks, purples, and blues along a curving concrete path leading from the gates to disappear back behind the terrace. Without the buzzing of overhead drones, I can faintly hear the soft humming of pollinating bees or a neighbor across the street dropping his toolbox and cursing his family name.

"Come," Meir says, tugging at my sleeve. "Don't wander far from me."

The two guards, one short are interchangeable in their white button-up, black suit attire. I wouldn't know they were security if not for the baton they carry where I expected a holstered gun. Unlocking a side door to enter the premises, they lead us down the winding path toward the backyard where the grass is cut into neat squares of different sizes with meticulously trimmed sphere bushes. Palm trees thicker than I've ever seen run parallel down a path leading away from the house toward a statue of Bacchus holding bushels of grapes in one hand and knocking back a glass of wine with the other. Water flows freely from the goblet into his mouth, siphoned down into the pool at his feet. We reach the cellar doors shaded by a pergola wrapped in wires with antennas like a rose bush. The guards give us a short bow shoulder-to-shoulder before heading back the way we came.

"Whose house is this?" I finally get to ask once they're out of earshot.

Meir turns to me, fidgeting to straighten my sash. "An old friend's," is all he thinks he can get away with saying, but after a look from me, he presses on: "His name's Si; one of our lobbyists from AIPAC. Where do you think I've been getting the money for our little ventures?" When he reaches for the doors, a small section in the wood separates to reveal a fingerprint scanner that Meir presses his thumb against. The way hisses open like pressurized steam, greenstone steps descending into the center of the earth. He moves forward but staggers back with a raised finger like he's just remembered something. "Stay close. It's a members-only venue, but I don't know everyone attending."

Ancient torches on the walls blaze with fire the moment we step onto the staircase, but I still can't see the bottom until we've been walking for quite some time. When we reach the end, Meir knocks at an oval crimson door in an arrhythmic beat. The door swings open as if someone had been waiting on the other end, and some blurred creature comes barreling out to jump Meir with arms and legs wrapped around him like a succubus.

"Uncle Meir, Uncle Meir!" The tender voice of a sweet little girl echoes throughout the dungeon.

Meir lifts the girl in striped pajamas from under her armpits and twirls her around like a carousel. He ruffles her blonde locks when he sets her down, kissing each cheek with the formal reverence one might expect toward an elder. "It's good to see you too, Golda. My, how you've grown in just a day! You'll be talking down to me like your father by month's end!"

Golda giggles, oval gray eyes suddenly notice me standing off to the side and betray a maturity beyond her adolescent years as she scans me up and down. "Who's he? Another special project?"

"– Ahp!"Meir quickly interrupts Golda. "This is my friend, Laeth; he's here as my guest for the show." He steals a glance at me, eyes widening when he notices me staring right back.

Golda's vague question answered something I've been asking myself ever since Meir took an interest in me two years ago: what makes me so special? Turns out, I'm not. Before I can probe any further, Golda grabs Meir's hand with her right and mine with the left to pull us both through the threshold and into what can only be described as a speakeasy theater. At the opposite end from where we stand is a stage on a raised dais partially concealed by red velvet and gold-trimmed curtains. On the Persian carpet floor sit round tables with dripping candles and gemstone chandeliers floating from magnetic repulsion. Behind the white light-shelved bar with Techni-colored elixirs, a dark woman disregarding our entrance chews on a toothpick behind the sidebar as she cleans a mug with a white rag. Standing in a circle at one of the center tables is a group of four conversing in low, tense whispers despite there being no one else in the chamber. There's a broadsword of a man with an all-gray military buzz cut leading the discussion, sausage arms threatening to tear his burgundy polo at the seams. Clockwise to him stands a slender woman beyond all our years hunched over a cane made of stalactite emeralds. She's garbed in a sort of black beaded 'abaya that drapes over her head like a mattress sheet would, making it difficult to see her com-pletely. There's another blond-haired kid around Golda's age in the same pajamas. By the way he fixates on the titan, I figure this man must be their father. Not sure if Golda calling Meir "uncle" should be taken literally or not because if that were always the case, I'd have hundreds. The final figure turns before I get a chance to observe her, a peculiar trail of pixelated sunbird feathers gently flows from her back as she crosses the room away from us to some place behind the stage curtains.

"Just say hello and take a seat," Meir whispers when we're paces from the group.

That's completely fine with me. "Ladies and gentlemen," Meir announces in Hebrew, "we're honored you've granted us a seat for this matinee and sincerely apologize for our tardiness."

The clock in my lens informs me we're one minute past the hour. Unfor-tunately, my gaze meets the old crone's hollow beaded, prompting her to huff. "Hello," I say trying my best to ignore the goosebumps. Meir hisses and tugs me over to sit at the table across from them.

He approaches the patriarch, shaking his hand with a formality that leads me to believe they're not actually family. They whisper lower than I can hear, but the man shifts his footing to catch me staring over. Thankfully at that moment the overhead chandeliers blink on and off in three rapid succession before fading to black, indicating the show's about to start. While everyone takes their seats, the bartender comes around to each table taking orders. When she gets to mine, a sapphire amulet hamsa tattooed on her wrist catches my eye as she clicks a stylus over an ancient tablet.

"What'll it be?" she first asks Meir in Hebrew.

"Boulevardier," he says focusing on the stage, "and don't heavy hand the Campari this time, hm?"

She confirms with a tip of her derby cap and cocks her head to me, hazel eyes glimmering like the dunes of Jericho. "And for you?"

"Whatever's lightest on tap," I gamble a prediction by answering in Arabic. Familiarity stiffens her posture, but her attention darts from Meir to the patriarch before settling back on me.

Her mouth opens then shuts. "OK," she says quickly in English to dismiss herself.

The curtains rise to begin the play. It's one I know precious little about called *Bar Kokhba*, named after the "hero" of Judea who liberated the Temple Mount in Jerusalem from Roman control after the Imperial Senate decreed its destruction for a shrine to Jupiter in the second century. Drones flitter in place above the stage to project an uncanny landscape of broken stone rubble battlements with distant Roman catapults slinging boulders on fire toward the oppressed Jewish forces under siege. Valiant trumpets and chest-thumping war drums envelop the room with gusto. From stage right comes the protagonist like an angel from heaven surrounded by his kin as slave-knights, Simon Bar Kokhba. The soldiers remind me of the Neturei Karta. It's easy to forget that behind the pixelated chiseled jaw and veneer of hard leather armor is a gelatinous machine with limited AI capabilities. I'm so engrossed in the story unfolding despite my large gaps in Hebrew that I don't even notice the bartender serving my drink.

The next I find my awareness, it's an hour into the play due to a commotion coming from the family beside us. Synthetic blood splatters the walls and pools on stage, dripping onto the Persian rugs below. They're questioning whether this is too much gore for the children, but the father insists. The Roman governor antagonist, Turnus Rufus the Evil, shakes his obese-ringed fists at a sheepish general as he laments the inadequacies of his legions. The monologue pauses mid-sentence along with the orchestra, erupting a silence that sobers me from the action over to the family in question. The children stand beside their father who encourages them toward the stage. The little girl skips excitedly while the boy drags his feet to position themselves beside a caricature of a man. Their father raises a remote, springing the marionettes to life to run behind the curtains.

Drones hidden behind stage lights whir into action, changing the landscape to sunrise dust trails outside the walls of Aelia Capitolina with Solomon's Temple in the background.

From stage left, a squad of Roman scouts search for Bar Kokhba's encampment, wondering aloud if the heathens will show. The ordained savior himself appears from stage right, confronting his adversaries in open combat with slave knights of his own in tow. The girl in striped pajamas casually walks up to the Jewish hero of old and strips Bar Kokhba of his sword, pausing the scene once more. The mannequin returns to a blank gelled slate then turns to walk off stage. The boy protests a moment over the stolen lead role but eventually concedes to the spear and shield of some nameless soldier. Before the scene resumes, the two fidget with their bracelets until every weapon except theirs glows with the blue hue of harmonic vibrations buffering the edges from inflicting any real harm. The little girl reads from a script scrolling through her lenses as she passionately waves her sword at the Romans, denouncing their attempts at erasure. Behind Golda, soldiers with the same faces grunt and beat their shields in approval, reverence; the willingness to die for an idea. Mid-speech she charges forward out of the script, slicing a Roman legionnaire through the neck, twisting to rip the jugular exposing broken trachea cartilage. Flecks of blood blush the girl's pale cheeks, mouth grimacing with strain.

The boy in striped pajamas recoils a few paces back, his genetically modified features a mask of shock that no doubt resembles my own. With a sudden burst of energy, Golda swings her heavenly blade at another Roman scout making the drones fast-forward the background scenery while androids rush to change positions. Incongruous lights and high-pitched music wind forward; spitting me out of my drug-induced suspended disbelief back into a sober reality. The father pushes out of his seat cupping his hands to his mouth.

"Honor our legacy, David!" He continues to shout encouragement to his son over the racket, but when the boy doesn't move to attack the Romans, his father shakes a giant fist. He threatens: "Do it, or so help me God, there will be no *bar mitzvah*!"

Meir chuckles at that, but a shrill prepubescent shriek pierces through the theater as David charges forward with his spear, penetrating the enemy through the sternum. He stumbles backward on his butt, scrambling away from his fallen adversary while Golda and the rest of her soldiers massacre those left. Amid the empyrean carnage, David's screams can't be heard, but his horror is more clearly defined for me than the rest. He can only find enough courage to find his feet and run off stage, where his father soon follows.

An intermission follows that drags out long enough for the grandmother to depart the way her family went, grumbling something disdainful about coddled children and ill fortune. For reasons beyond me, Meir's refusing to hear me whisper his name so I can ask just what the hell we're doing here. Instead he fixates on the chandelier prisms until a door slams open from behind the curtains. The father returns to center stage and calls to Meir. That's when he turns to me with a coltish smile as he pats my thigh.

"Time for what we really came for," he says standing to his feet.

"Apologies for that embarrassment," the father says to Meir when we reach him at the massacre, congealed blood sticking to the soles of our boots. He doesn't even glance in my direction, as though I don't exist. "As compensation for ending the show early, we've added an extra half hour to the timers." He reaches into his pockets to retrieve two magnetic keys, placing them over Meir's outstretched hand.

"Think nothing of it," Meir says, "but go easy on David, eh? If I remember your first time, a turd left your trousers when you bent over for your first kill."

The man takes offense by the way his shrapnel brows rise, but after a pause, knee-slapping bellows of laughter. "Ahh – true enough, true enough; but I did do it, didn't I? Followed it through till the end!" He composes himself after a few hearty chuckles and clasps forearms with Meir. "But enough of this. Come: let me take you to your rooms."

Behind the backdrop veil, spare heads and android limbs dumped together in laundry baskets clutter a long maroon hallway of doors the lobbyist guides us down. An aseptic smell that reminds me of hospitals sets me on edge, tells my gut not to trust this place. We stop at a pair of rustic ranch doors opposite one another, and the man turns to Meir.

"Hour and a half," he says. "Oh, and try not to make such a mess this time; Fatima's psyche can only take so much. Good help's hard to come by, y'know?" Our host looks through me with indifference, almost as if by accident. "Leave the room and wander too far – doesn't matter if you're his – I'll blow your fucking head off." Webbed veins flex from forearm to bicep while he lets the threat hang in the air. He nods to Meir one last time, then taps a key fob to the adjacent door, heavy footsteps departing up a metal staircase.

"Cheap bastard probably set the timers before he came down to get us," Meir mutters. He tosses me one of the magnetic keys, glowing with renewed anticipation. "Ready?"

"For what?"

He's already slipping through a crack in his door, but turns back to poke his face through the slit. "That's the best part, my friend," he says before shutting it, "it's whatever you want it to be."

Casting aside my building frustrations from being leashed and dragged around all day, I push through my door to enter a fifteen-meter oblong chamber saturated with white tile floors and padded eggshell walls. In front of me, jetting out of the floor like a curved silver nail is some type of control panel facing the expanse of the room. The only other thing here with me is a blank-slated automaton slumped on a chair on the opposite wall. I approach the control panel humming to life when I tap the rectangular screen, projecting an interactive menu with countless tabs ranging from light brightness and color to furniture, weapons, and a variety of landscapes mainly involving battlefields but some cozy locations too like a cafe in Barcelona or a cabin in the woods. Curious about this, I select a table and chair from the menu, prompting the floor in front of the inactive robot to open up. A lift with the items I've chosen places them neatly between me and the automaton then hisses back down for the floor to zipper shut after it. Clicking a tab labeled Gladium, an extensive list of prominent names throughout human history floods my reticles; false identities divided by period and country waiting to be cast onto the gelatinous mannequins from Saddam Hussein to Madonna, Einstein, Tupac Shakur, any of the Dalai Lama incarnations or Nietzsche. It's interesting that any prominent Zionist figures I can think of have been censored from the list. There's an entire folder subcategory set aside for porn stars. Feeling overwhelmed by options, I click the randomized button over renowned Palestinians, and a resuscitating jolt spasms throughout the automaton. Sitting before me is none other than Yasser Arafat dressed in a wide-lapelled suit, head loosely wrapped in a kufiyah. Whatever high is left in me evaporates through sweat like a hot flash.

"Uhm," I struggle with what to say to the elder. "Hello?"

The stiff mannerisms fit what I've seen in interviews by the way he snivels his toad-like nose, and crosses his legs with the same downward point but when he opens his mouth to answer, nothing comes out. He continues speaking until he folds his hands on his lap, waiting for an answer to a question I haven't heard. Fiddling around with the settings, I realize there's not an option to control speech and audio. I wonder if some of the others might come with preset scripts like their acting counterparts, but after selecting over a dozen personalities, I've come up short. Clicking buttons I don't fully understand in my growing frustration, I find myself standing in the heavenly room with one wall sectional covered in hanging neon dildos of various sizes, beaded whips, and tentacled vibrators. To my right, spread Excalibur blades and grim reaper scythes, bone saw chains, and spiked medieval tools I wouldn't know the first thing what to do with. George Habash stares up at me shape-shifting into his newly acquired green eyes. He sits poised as a younger suited version of the man memorialized on the Net; head full of raven hair, dimpled arrogant smirk challenging the gods themselves. I don't dare untether myself from the console, wrapping my arms around it as I lean forward to vomit Moscow mules.

When I compose myself, I beg: "Hello?"

His mouth moves without a voice.

I'm fed up with this game and wipe the identity slate clean from the dais before walking over to take a seat across the blank mannequin hunched hand over knee as though thinking; praying, maybe. Together we wait surrounded by tools of lust and war for the timer in some hidden place to simply run out.

When there's a knock at the door, my stomach's cramping from hunger. Realizing I haven't eaten all day is becoming a bad habit. I pull open the door to see Meir with the two fat security guards from earlier behind him. His clothes are clean, but his porcelain face is marred with mud and blood not properly washed away. The flamboyant energy I've seen all day is replaced by lethargic bloodshot eyes and a grumpy attitude.

"You look like shit," I say.

"Shut up," he mumbles wearily. "Come on. Let's get out of here."

Back in the night on the Magic Carpet Express, Meir takes up half the backseat sprawled out like a dead fish. He raises a limp arm to input our destination on the dividing screen keyboard. I recognize the address the car relays back over the loudspeakers as his condominium. Forehead against window, I witness a castle called Parliament twinkle like an earthbound star in the stratosphere. No point in wishing upon it when it's already granted, knowing most must suffer under their own capitalist machinations.

"Hey." I shove Meir's thigh to interrupt his rest. "I was thinking: why not grab some food by the sea? I'm starving."

"Thinking's your problem," he grumbles low. "What's the point? It's too dark to see the water anyway. We'll order room service and go tomorrow for breakfast if it's that important to you."

The word "tomorrow" strikes a chord from somewhere deep inside me, stirring a consciousness slumbering within my psyche. An ancient memory recently acquired; a forgotten purpose and calling. A muffled little voice inside my head telling me I've gotta get out of here. Tomorrow, Aylul will herald the next *intifada* in Ayn Yassin. Tomorrow, Jabriel becomes a *shahid*. Tomorrow, many people will die unless I can do something about it. But, what? With what limited resources at my disposal? My hands clam, palms sweat, lightheaded, weightless. How do I do this?

When we climb out of the taxi inside the hotel elevator lift, it backs out onto the street before the doors shut, activating the glowing red light. Meir sleepily punches in our floor and room number, prompting our ascent up the tower. We stand on opposite ends facing one another. In my overanalyzed search for an all-encompassing answer to the hundred unasked questions I have for this man, the simplest among them conquers all.

"Why did you bring me here?"

Arms crossed, eyes closed, a guttural chuckle escapes Meir's maw. "You know, ever since I saw you that day outside Ayn Yassin with that overgrown Asian and pompadour cousin of yours, I knew. Said to myself, 'Now there's a guy who's always too little, too late.' And in the two long years we've known each other, Laeth, you've never once disappointed. Bravo, truly."

"How could you kill one of your own?"

Meir huffs, annoyed by another misfire. "Same reason the Knesset secretly sanctioned your cousin's little uprising."

The shocking news roils through every fiber of my bones; preordained plans within plans within plans. I shiver from the goosebump-frigid cold of being stuck inside this coffin with a vampire. I knew what this was the moment I received his summons, but never would have anticipated the Zionists permitting a large-scale attack on their own. The cauterized wound Aylul left me starts to itch, but I ignore the impulse as the elevator goes sideways. "You're an asshole for chipping me, but I still don't understand. Aylul removed it, so how'd you find out?"

He's losing his patience with me by the time the doors open to his flat, ocular astral lights of a city alive beneath our feet twinkle like stars through the high-rise windows. He claps thrice offbeat, and the fireplace sparks, crackles, and whirls into blaze-casting shadows on the edges of the room. Meir takes a seat facing away from the heat and laces his fingers together, staring up at me with a cocky smirk.

The realization sinks in with Sundus' father at the bottom of the pit. "Wissam Tayyib," I whisper the name of Al Mubarizun's benefactor. Some primal instinct tells me to run for the elevator, but I take my stand. Striding over to the fire behind him, I search for anything from within the flames, but the only question remaining is the very same one I've been asking since the day I was born. "Why me?"

"You're giving me a hangover," Meir bemoans. There's a stretch of silence that follows so long that I begin to wonder if he's fallen asleep. Then: "I've got my own question. You could have reported your lens feed to any of the countless reporters broadcasting that protest. With some honest investigation – if such a thing exists – it's possible they'd have found me behind the mask. But you didn't. Not then, inside Al Khalil's mines or outside Huwara's bazaar. Even after you discovered the plant, it took you 'til now to say anything. You did what you do best: nothing at all. Why?"

"Wouldn't have made a difference liberating Palestine from you colonizers."

"Don't talk like one of them," he snaps, "no matter how much you wish it, you're not and that's precisely why I choose those like you."

Staring into the fire barely formed images of things I can't quite imagine dancing in a void between the flickers of flames. The heat's fierce on my face, but tears are burning. "I wanted a place to call home."

"Yes," Meir rasps in ecstasy, "and who could blame you for wanting an end to what's essentially already lost?"

There. For a brief moment, I catch something that can never be forgotten. An admittance of weakness like a viral infection that spreads: *essentially*. It takes hold of my heart and cherry blossom-blooms, curling, wrapping like a present. "I think I know one person who would."

Meir kicks his feet up on the coffee table, leaning back in the leather armchair with a pleasant sigh. "Their opinion will be of no consequence by the time we're finished having breakfast by the sea."

The bloodstained prophecy hangs in the air between us. Gold flame reflections off the sheath of the *saif* hanging over the mantle glimmer-shimmer. "Maybe," I whisper Aylul's word in the stupor of revelation.

He stands suddenly, noticing my attention on the sword. "Beautiful, isn't she? Got her off a warlord in Gaza, you wouldn't believe what the British Museum's willing to pay –"

Agency compels me to grasp the leather-bound hilt and wrest the saif free from its cage, turn, and thrust eighty-one steel blade centimeters through his sternum; piercing, tearing, ripping through spinal cartilage, and out the other side of Meir's back.

١٠

The microchip processor clatters to the floor before every single light in Meir's condo begins to flash like a heartbeat. The captain sags back, mouth twisted from shock and pain. He slides off the blade slick with blood as I hold against the friction, crumpling at my feet like a dying spider. His guttural death-rattle whimper-wheezes, coming in short bursts. Whatever amphetamines are left in my system buffers me numb enough from the horror to continue what needs to be done. Or maybe not even....

An inhuman voice crackles over the loudspeakers:

"Emergency alert, emergency alert: this system has detected a significant change in your vital signs, *M e i r   C o h e n* , and will notify the proper authorities in *t h i r t y   s e c o n d s* . If this is a mistake or hardware malfunction, please input your security pin now. Emergency alert, emergency alert –"

Shit. No time to search this place for the code, and I'll get about as far as the asphalt if I run. With no time to lose, I fall to my hands and knees beside the blood-soaked tentacle processor and carefully pluck it between my fingers. Switching my grip on the sword, I use the tip of the blade to search for the cauterized wound on my back.

"– and will notify the proper authorities in *f i f t e e n   s e c o n d s .*"

Too late to consider *ifs*. Applying just enough pressure to pierce the skin, I slice down the scar a few centimeters. Pressing the chip against the opening, the tentacles come alive, wriggling, grasping to reach inside. One breath, two breaths, three breaths. I jam the unit in and cry from invasive agony. The searing pain is fleeting but long enough to make me wonder what in all gods' names I just did to Meir.

"*Emergency   alert,   emergency   alert –*" the AI starts but doesn't continue the repetition.

No; can't bring myself to look over at him. If I do, there's no chance I'm leaving this place. It takes telling myself a few times to get moving before I stand wobbly, breath rough, and ragged. The lights remain on and the fire still rages and the gambit's paid off for now. Taking the sword with me, I cross the living room area through the hallway and into the porcelain bathroom; there's a first aid kit I remember seeing in the cabinet earlier. Some vertigo-sense of the universe converging leaves my knees weak as I wrap the wound across my torso between both pits with icy gauze. Buttoning my top back up, I notice there's gore smeared on the webbed skin between my thumb and index finger. Avoiding the mirror to wash it off, I watch Meir's soap bubble blood swirl down the drain.

All I can do is stride out of the hallway as the grandfather clock strikes midnight and keep my eyes on the elevator door at the opposite end of the hallway. Halfway there, the fuzzy crumpled shadow of Meir's dead body enters my periphery, so I walk a little taller to only see what's ahead. Once inside the elevator, I punch a series of buttons to have my truck waiting for me by the time the door dings open at street level. I climb back into the leather interior home of my beloved Warlock and place the sword on the passenger's seat. My hands tremble on the steering wheel until I press down into a white-knuckled grip. When the corrugated glass lifts high enough to squeeze through, it's time to test the redline.

Like a gas-burned needle threading against the metropolis tapestry loom, I burst out of downtown Tel Aviv due east to where I'm meant to be. The ever-elusive question of just what the fuck I'm supposed to do once I'm there captivates my attention while I drive past domed government buildings and eclectic lines of people waiting for their chance to get inside neon-lit clubs. My surroundings begin to stretch into obscure blurred colors as astral city skylines become two-star towns then green-beige-brown, no-speed-limit countryside. Japanese jazz saxophones blare through my speakers to repel intrusive thoughts of blood back from where I came from and where I'm going. I slam on the breaks in the middle of the freeway when I crest a dune hill overlooking the infertile fields of panopticon reeducation camps stretching beyond the southern horizon. They stand in this frigid winter night, a shadowed collection of stone gods. Will-'o-wisp military vehicle headlights surveil their parameters like sacrificial offerings blinking in and out of existence. It's the first time since killing Meir that I feel the need to stop, but there's no time left to bear witness.

The first checkpoint I hit is a two-manned sack of sandbags about an hour outside Ayn Yassin. Throwing my jacket over the sword, I slow the truck to a stop in front of a thin wooden lever. One of the scarab-scaled youths, a chubby boy with a unibrow thicker than his biceps, comes yawning up to the truck like I've just ruined his entire shift.

"What are you doing out past curfew?"

Shit. This must be the Knesset's work at play. I'm sorry, Teta. "Yeah, sorry, I'm doing construction work in Tel Aviv but got a call that my grandmother might not make it past the night." Half-truisms always hurt the most. It's not that difficult to feign emotional distress and have my eyes water just a bit as I hand over my documentation. "Please, I need to see her."

He flips through the paperwork too fast to be reading anything. No doubt he's weighing whether denying me passage is worth dragging this out, consequently pulling him further away from what's most important: his dreams. "Fine, but don't expect the others to be so giving."

"Thank you," I say between grit teeth.

Every one of the thirteen checkpoints along the way was, in fact, just as indifferent about letting me through in lieu of returning to their rest or card games. On the dusk outskirts between Ramallah and Ayn Yassin, a possible solution occurs to me, and I swerve left down Cid's street instead of proceeding straight home. Considering Meir dangled just enough intel on his role in Al Mubarizun to coerce me, it's likely Cid made Jabriel's armaments himself. Not sure how I'm supposed to convince him to help me disarm it, but it's the closest thing to a plan that I've got.

At four in the morning Muzayin Street is absent of people, wind howling a few octaves higher than distant packs of wild dogs scavenging in the morning-night. Most of the street lights don't work, and those that do flicker fluorescent. Without the sweet cacophony of midday business and falafel sidecars, the empty mechanic shops look more abandoned than closed. My tires slowly crunch along Cid's gravel lot until I park right outside the front door. Not allowing time to scheme with doubt, I exit the vehicle into the bitter cold and knock hard at his steel gate three times, and wait. Nothing. Huffing frustration to warm my hands, I circle the perimeter with some little hope to see a bedroom light on or the HoloVision blaring sappy Turkish soap operas but everything around me is weirdly still; not just quiet, but absent. In my haste, I hadn't noticed that their cars weren't in the driveway. My one last wish takes me to the junkyard in the back, but I know I'm wasting time scanning these hallways of twisted steel and broken machinery on the way to his shed. Three knocks and I'm gone. My boot knocks against a bottle on the ground, glass shattering like an atomic weapon. I activate the night vision mode on my lenses to see the whiskey I had brought for Cid as a peace offering before Huwara. Well, then, fair enough.

There are a few cars ahead of me at the checkpoint outside Ayn Yassin. Each spends twenty minutes arguing with Lieutenant Haya before she turns them around whether they're residents or not. I wonder if she's simply carrying out orders or knows the deeper reasons for this curfew. Is she preparing for some violent inevitability or will killing my people, whether they're militants or not, come as a total shock to her psyche? I'm not sure even when I roll the truck to stop beside her. Her blonde hair flows against regulation in crimps down to her shoulders like a lion's mane. I can recognize puffy insomniac eyes anywhere because game recognizes game. It's odd that she's out here so late shivering in a camouflage down jacket instead of one of her subordinates.

"Yo," I try to sound casual, "what're you doing up so late?" Rolling down the window, faint stale smells of burning rubber tires and tear gas from earlier protests taint the air. Ah, to be almost home.

She scoffs through her nose. "I could ask you the same thing."

"Meir." His name tastes bitter on my lips, but it's all I have to say to have her understand the reason behind this abnormality. Then again, I ask myself why I need an excuse to be anywhere. Looking around, the only other soldier is the rough silhouette of a man inside the officer's cabin. My right hand shifts to the sword grip under my jacket just in case; I can get the gun from the glove compartment after. "Look, I know there's a curfew and all, but Hassan called with news that Teta's not doing so hot. That damn heart of hers started acting up again."

"Oh, no," she sounds sincere, clasping her hands over her chest. "Is she going to be okay?"

"I'm not sure..." Does she know? "He's taken her to the hospital, and they're waiting for an available bed. I know you're not supposed to, but I have to see her. Please?"

"Of course," Haya says without suspense. She walks off to lift the lever, but stops mid-stride, then backtracks to my window. "Listen, I'm sure this isn't the best time, but since they're only waiting; do ya wanna...share a cup of coffee with me?"

"What – like – now?"

"Yeah," she says, swiping a thumb across her nostril to catch snot from the cold. "Those doctors love to take their time, who knows, ya might need it."

With the digital clock still ticking in my corner view, I look ahead beyond the gates to Ayn Yassin still slumbering and back at Haya. "Okay."

I park the truck off to the shoulder and let her lead me to the officer's cabin. It's a concrete shed that betrays the inner beauty of sleek vinyl wood floors and porcelain tile walls. Across the room, next to a gas oven fire with his feet up on a chair sits Private Horam, the ape that harassed Leila and me on our way to the Compound. He's resting like so many of the soldiers I came across at the other checkpoints, arms crossed behind his shaved sausage neck as he's dozing peacefully beside the warmth. Glass screen Excel sheet projections glow on plywood desks, Technicolor hologram news anchors bicker incessantly about funding the space program in the corner at low volume. Haya grabs a stack of papers on her walk over to Private Horum, rolling them up tight to slap like a bat across the back of his head.

"Who dares?!" he screams, whipping around quick enough to see Lieutenant Haya and the vitriol drains from his face.

"Go guard the entrance outside," she says firmly. "You're not supposed to be here anyway."

Horum salutes, noticing me a few paces away, shooting his superior officer a raised eyebrow as if asking, "But he is?" When she doesn't entertain it, he stomps off outside, shoulder-checking me on the way out.

"So," Haya says once the door shuts, "what'd Meir get you into today?" She walks over with a tired limp to a station littered with cables and wires, pushing them aside to place a single-burner stovetop and ibrik on the table.

If there's anything I've learned from living in the Middle East, it's that the easiest lie is withholding information. "We went to Tel Aviv for some sightseeing."

"Hm," she says weakly, distracted by some distant thought.

Not caring to elaborate, the conversation fizzles to a chipping click backdrop of me biting my nails. When the coffee's done brewing, she hands me a steaming mug and offers a seat next to her at a roundtable. She retrieves a half-eaten box of halvah I bought her the other day. It occurs to me then that Haya and I have never sat together like this before. Our entire relationship is based on passing pleasantries. Now that we're here there's only one question repeating in my mind: what does she know? "How're things with you?" I venture instead.

"Can't complain," she sighs wistfully. "It's just these curfews that always set me on edge; nothing good ever follows. I wish…" she trails off, shaking her head. "Never mind, it's stupid."

"Aw c'mon, what is it?" So she's not aware of Aylul's plans. Good.

"Must sound naive," she excuses herself, "childish, even: but I wish we could ignore the past sometimes, you know? Set aside our mistakes – our anger, our pain – and maybe someday…just coexist as…people? God, that sounds even cheesier out loud."

I don't laugh along with her nervous chuckle. If I wasn't so certain she'd arrest me on the spot, I'd consider warning her of what's coming to Ayn Yassin so she could save herself. My heart sinks deep in empathy having heard the sentiment, but I know now it's just some pretty poisonous dream born from confused tyrants. I focus on Haya's military montage of colored badges and insignias detailing her achievements in a language I don't understand. "Maybe someday," I mutter, blow on the caramelized steam, and sip.

The remainder of my time with Lieutenant Haya is spent making idle conversation about how crazy it is that we're supposed to get snow in September while I finish my drink as quickly as I can. When we're back outside, I thank her kindly for her hospitality and climb back into the truck. She closes my door for me, leaning into the open window.

"Keep your eyes open today, hm?" Scratching her head, she looks like she's about to say something but changes her mind. "Give Teta my best."

"Will do," I lie with a smile and turn the ignition.

Even when I'm through the gate and down the road, her silhouette lingers in the rearview mirror at the checkpoint watching me leave. If this all goes sideways, this is the last we'll see of each other again and even if it doesn't, it's the last we'll meet as... as what? As friends? I can't convince myself of that, though standing on opposite sides of the line will still be a hard pill to swallow. But that's later. Now that I've reached my destination, my head's left spinning with unknown variables and worst-case scenarios. I don't know when Jabriel plans on carrying out his attack on Ma'al Luz. I don't know how to persuade him of another way. I don't know the locations of the other tunnels; hell, I don't even know how many of them there are. The only thing I'm certain of is Aylul's squad waiting twenty meters underground beneath my old man's shop, so that's where I'll go. Shifting into performance mode, I test the redline, speeding through the empty streets under the starless radiance of a crescent moon.

Ayn Yassin's changed under two years of occupation more than I pretended not to notice. Skulking behind streetlight shadows, the buildings are a hodgepodge mismatch of limestone tradition and vogue tinted glass. High-rise slums and luxury bungalows alike speckle amber with inner light. The elementary school I used to attend now functions as a clinic barely standing, a dilapidated, makeshift mess with neon red plus signs for Zionist fighter pilots to ignore. Hell, we even have a Starbucks. Adding more lead to my foot, I push through what remains of my hometown and hurdle towards an endured eventuality.

Parking my truck outside the front of the shop, I hesitate going inside once my feet hit the gravel lot. Turning back to face Teta's persimmon farm, I can't help but doubt what little I've planned because it means not fleeing through the tunnels. A voice like ego whispers full commitment to my cause. There's no turning back.

Hassan must have cleaned up after I left for Tel Aviv because the store looks immaculate with freshly mopped floors and fully stocked shelves. Once this is over, that man's getting a raise. Crossing an aisle of canvas bags filled with baharat-spiced seeds and instant dinners I grab a pack of cigarettes from behind the counter and light up on my way down to the basement. The walk-in freezer is still open from the last time I was here with Aylul, but the dogged hatch is closed over the hole inside. Now that I'm here, I'm not sure how much good this will do. Jabriel will signal the next intifada, but when? Rerouting their commander may not delay things long enough even if I do manage to stop him. And if all goes well, what then? No, no. Stop. One step at a time. Striding over to the hatch, I strain to spin the wheel to a grinding metal lock.

"Laeth?"

The muffled voice scares me into a high-pitched shriek, blood pressure skyrockets to make my stomach cramp. I wipe heated sweat off my brow with a sleeve, leaning my face closer to the hatch. "H-hello?"

There's a tense, frictive silence. Then: "Is anyone with you?"

"Aylul?" I ask close enough for my lips to brush the metal.

"Is anyone with you?" This time, their question seethes with suspicion.

They're probing for the possibility that I've told Meir about the operation. The accusation hurts, but it's far from unjustified. "It's just me," I assure them.

"Then what do you think you're doing?"

"I..." don't know, if I'm honest. "Why are you here? Are Uri and Sakine with you?"

"Down below with the others," they reply. "I won't ask again: what are you doing?"

"Warning you," I attempt what I know is futile. "Mossad knows about the *intifada*. I'm not sure what they're planning, but call it off now before Jabriel –"

"We're well aware of the curfew in place," they interrupt. "Think what you will, but we aren't daft enough to consider this a coincidence. It matters little; we've planned for such contingencies. The five thousand waiting beneath Ayn Yassin all know the price of their lives, Laeth. Do you?"

Five thousand. I can't fathom such a weight on my shoulders. "No," I admit, "but I think I'm finally discovering who I'm meant to be."

A barely audible sigh follows. "Okay. And that is?"

There's a profound pause pregnant with endless possibilities. "You know," I start, "Teta invited me over for *kousa* and *warak dawali* last Tuesday. I should've known better considering what a pain in the ass it is to cook." I delay, anxious and afraid of their reaction to the hard right turn.

They don't respond at first but eventually take the bait. "And?"

"Little did I know that she had heard from Ibrahim that Leila's car hasn't been around the shop lately. So there I was, knocking on her door at six o'clock sharp because *kousa* and *warak dawali* is –"

"– Fucking delicious –"

"– Right? And as soon as I walked in, I saw Farah Hamdan sitting on the couch. Do you remember? She's the girl who –"

"– Sundus knocked out for getting too handsy with you at the Olive Tree that one night, how could I forget?" Their muffled laughter at the memory reaches me like a distorted symphony.

"Two hours of the most awkward shit I've ever experienced, but a small price to pay for dinner and *knafeh*."

Aylul whistles from below. "*Knafeh* too? Teta meant business."

"Yeah, she wasn't too happy with me the day after." It's not hard to recall the slap on the neck. "Gave me the whole 'you're at an age' talk; said I should stop playing games and settle down, give romance – the future – a chance, and all that. Mind you, this is in front of half the block."

Aylul chuckles sweetly. "Maybe you should," they encourage, "it really is a wonderful thing."

"Yeah," I say, feeling our time come to an end, "maybe I will." There's a part of me that begs to ask about Jabriel, but I can't ask them to betray their own people.

"Laeth?"

I press a hand flat against the hatch, leaning my forehead on the cold metal. "Hm?"

"I love you, cousin, but unlock the goddamn door. It can't contain us. We'll cut our way through if we have to. "

Fearing as much, my throat burns with the tears I swallow back. "I love you too."

Repeatedly reminding myself that this isn't goodbye becomes the only employable method to peel me away from their presence. Crossing the room to rummage through the side storage closet, I start pulling the propane tanks from inventory. There's enough to place ten paces or so apart leading upstairs and ending at the cash register. It makes me think I should check my bedroom, but there's nothing up there worth wasting what time I don't know I have. Running downstairs for the last of the propane, I close the freezer door without looking back. I grab a five-gallon can of gasoline and drag it upside down as I retrace my steps. The final tank gets placed right above where I guesstimate the freezer should be and I dump a quarter of the canister on that spot. Walking backwards to the front door, I try to think of what my mother and father would say but it's been so long since we've last spoken. I come up short between pride and flip-flop-throwing resentment for burning his legacy to ashes, but once I empty the can, what I know to be true is staring right at me amid all the insecurities: I am their legacy. Who they are is who I am is who they will be in five or five hundred.

For as much as I want to stay with the fire, watching how quickly it spreads after I throw a wick-burning lighter at the gasoline has me running for the truck. Not sure how long it takes for a burning building to collapse, but I suppose it doesn't matter since Ayn Yassin's fire department consists of citizen volunteers and a handful of portable extinguishers. By the time someone reports it and they roll out of bed, it'll be too late. Thousands of rubble-ruin kilos on top of the hatch should be enough to force Aylul's redirection, taking their forces somewhere further away from Teta and Hassan. This is all I can do for now.

When I finish a three-point turn, a deep atomic quake of several propane tanks catches propulsion-fire shakes produce off the shelves; breaking, smashing, shattering, and burning. Tapping a bead on my wrist as I pull out onto the open road, I welcome the distraction of translucent windows scrolling through my contacts as I search for my parents' number. Something's not right the moment I start the call; a dial tone doesn't beep but extends, holding the single note endlessly. Dropping it, I check my network settings: connectivity severed. They've blacked out Ayn Yassin. Chewing on the inside of my cheek, I reach into the glove compartment grabbing my medication, forgetting it's empty. Frustration builds, and I punch the steering wheel until my knuckles hurt. Throwing the pill bottle aside, I find Leila's number knowing it's in vain. There's nothing but the consistent sound of a heartbeat flat line on the other end of the receiver.

The not-yet-risen but inevitable sun casts clouded shades of light blue, waking tweeting birds, calling on roosters to crow. Eerily, I haven't seen a single squadron of IOF patrolling the area as I drive toward Ma'al Luz. When I parallel park outside of the hotel housing over three thousand souls all waiting for their number to be called for a home once ours, reconstructed into a purpose for them... I'm not sure where to go from here. Ambitious vendors set up their stands early for another day of hustling falafel and manakish on the courtyard lawn in front of the angelic ovum building. Sharp-suit businessmen with briefcases flitter about them in pockets playing charades to pierce through a language barrier. Fidgeting in my seat, I decide to grab the gun and tuck it into my waistband. Slinging the strapped *saif* over my shoulder and onto my back, I wear my leather jacket over it and throw up the hood.

Walking on a path lined with every flag in the United Nations, I cross the grassy palm courtyard and find a bench to sit on, facing the only public entrance. From here, it'll be easier to see Jabriel approaching and intercept him before he's able to get inside. Stiff as a board, a couple near me strolling arm in arm. I scan the passing pasty faces of Americans and their Birthright whores, luring them further into captivity. They don't even notice I'm here; wonder if it has anything to do with wearing Meir's clothes. At some point in the next few hours, someone's going to go looking for him. It won't be long after checking security cams that they'll come after me, and I'll be branded a fugitive. Hopefully by then, the battle will have started and I'll be under Aylul's protection with Jabriel beside me.

Under the penumbra crest of the rising sun a dark plume of smoke in the shop's direction lifts into the atmosphere. Distant sirens blockaded at the nearest checkpoint echo as Sheikh Omar begins the *adhan* over the mosque loudspeakers. I breathe fresh air in through my nostrils and close my eyes to bask in the warming light. I can convince Jabriel to stop the bombing. Aylul will forgive me for foiling their plan because we're family. Together we'll find an alternative and endure. I repeat these desires over and over until they become blind faith in myself: I can do this. I can do this.

When I open my eyes, a bald man with sharp elfish features in a trench coat walks by me a few paces away, heading toward the front door. This whole time I worried I wouldn't recognize Jabriel, only having met once years ago, but as I scan a face that can't possibly be his, I notice a gap – a notch – between the lower eyelids. A mask! Jolting to my feet I stand immobile wondering what to do next.

"Jabriel!" I scream at the top of my lungs. The man whips around to face me, and I know it to be true.

Seeing through a person he doesn't seem to know, Jabriel doesn't wait to find out and sprints toward the entrance.

Chasing him not twenty paces away, he reaches the door before me and scrambles past the metal detectors, generating alarms to wail. I shove through private security, confused dependency on their military counterparts, leaving them useless. Pushing, I find Jabriel standing still in an oval crystal-chandelier lobby. All around him, hundreds of small cogs in the Zionist machine eye the boy with suspicion, moving around him like a hive. Jabriel tilts his head up, observing a digital blinder-shade window flip from weather forecasts to a painting of a girl in an olive orchard. When he hears me stop just a few steps behind, he lifts his arms back to shed his trenchcoat skin. He turns to face me, naked malnourished torso stapled and stitched with tubes of liquid ivory bubble-flowing through explosive packs embedded under his skin, running chest to navel through the small of his back like vivisecting umbilical cords. In the grips of divine tranquility, he stands before me a sutured monster. Cid...what have you done?

The rushing guards screech to a fearful halt behind me.

"Jabriel," I say, holding out my hand for him to take. Jabriel searches my face, eyes behind the mask widening in recognition.

"What are you doing here?"

A woman's scream alerts the crowd surrounding us. Curious mutters become pointing fingers and howls of horror, acknowledging that there is no fleeing from this bioweapon. Some still try, but then Jabriel shouts:

"Anybody moves and I'll fucking do it!"

It amazes me that they cling to a zero-sum game by freezing rather than taking the odds by continuing to run. Granted, I can't judge; I can't feel my legs under the gravity of the situation. Warm, humiliating piss soaks through my briefs and jeans, running down my thighs. A baby cries from neglect on the second-floor balcony.

"Jabriel..." I shudder, teeth chattering in a temperature-controlled room.

No, no, no... says a voice inside my head....

"Come...come with me. B-back to Aylul, come on..with me..there's been a change of plans."

Jabriel ignores the obvious lie. His eyes scan the faces of every man, woman, and child staring back at him. There! For a moment! A glisten! In his eyes! Is it doubt?!

"T-they're –" speak to his humanity, "they're not the enemy, Jabriel. The government is the enemy. The IOF are the enemy. Knesset are the enemy. These –" I spread my hands out all around me but their faces are blurred from my tears. "These are innocent people. D-don't do this, brother."

Jabriel rips the silicon mask off his head and throws it at my feet.

...*this isn't right*... the voice in my head continues...

I expect some zombification; hollow eyes, gray-drained skin; something more psychotic than what is below his neck, but Jabriel stands a man alive. He's grown into a thick chestnut beard, wooly locks flowing down between his shoulders. There's stoicism to him now; brow slightly furrowed, teeth grit. Fists clutched at his sides, he radiates heartbreak.

"Am I not as they are?"

...*I'm going to....*

Sharing the same quiet despair with every armed man and woman in the lobby, we fumble for our weapons. Jabriel presses his fingers into his palms, releasing the chemical catalyst into his bloodstream.

Of all the absurd things to do, I grip the pommel of the *saif* over my shoulder. Slicing my neck as I rip the sword free from its scabbard, there's only time left to point the blade in his direction.

Within the space between seconds I was completely afraid but now I am finally free.

Epilogue

itter winter winds sever through flesh and bone standing at this high an altitude. Switching between personal reports in one eye and government accounts in the other, it's not until my lungs burn that I realize I've been holding my breath. Thousands of Palestinian men, women, and children are dead or dying in overwhelmed hospitals between Ayn Yassin and Ramallah from what international news organizations are calling the largest loss of life in one day since the Gaza Exodus. Clearly they haven't witnessed the organ-reaping panopticon fields just fifty kilometers east. Of those who perished, nearly five hundred were my Mubarizun with another thousand captured.

Once the dust settled, Jabriel's sacrifice killed more Zionist enemies than Hamas or Fatah combined in over four decades. Four hundred sixty-seven men, five hundred ninety-nine women, and...

...and eighty-six children. Self-soothing notions I've repeated to get myself out of bed these past two years taste stale and trite. I'm wavering too long inside endless gray philosophy like the fool I mourn did too often.

We never believed we'd hold Ayn Yassin for long – a week at most – just long enough to garner some leverage; some global attention in exchange for prisoner-slaves. Our greatest defeat comes from the loss of having a voice in the narrative. The public opinion of people with no stake in the matter swayed from calling us freedom fighters to terrorists for the tenth time since our inception so for now, we'll be hunted rabid. Vivid flashbacks to the quarter-kilometer crater where my main forces once stood underground at the southern checkpoint haunt me; screams bargaining with God, limbs, defecating stench. Most simply evaporated under the pressure. Who could have predicted the crypto-Nazis would shoot a prototype Rod from God? Wissam Tayyib, I'm sure. Lesson learned the hard way: there's no wrath like heaven's.

Armored with masks of invisibility, I stare up at the overcast sky through to the enemy of the sun, knowing they can see me with their satellites among the stars. I sense Uri tense behind me for good reason as I step too close to the rooftop ledge. He's angry with me for bringing us here; too much risk, he said, one a reckless kid might take. He's right, of course: the impulsiveness isn't suited for a commander of freedom fighters, but I had to say goodbye. I'm only human, after all. And Zion wouldn't dare.

Eight hundred meters below The Royale rooftop, hundreds of thousands march the streets of Ramallah as a fist-raised sea of black-clad ceremony. Stretching from end to end of the neon greenstone metropolis, they carry caskets above their heads with colorized hologram portraits of loved ones lost, their bearers chanting, weeping, screaming in symphony. They follow the head, a martyr's funeral procession centering around two empty onyx coffins draped in neatly folded Palestinian flags. Elevated upon open palms, wailing passionate prayers and war chants of their Palestinian brothers and sisters as they honor two *shaheed*: Jabriel Zakaria Salibi and Laeth Muhammad Awad. The martyrs flow toward Ayn Yassin to the houses of their immediate families as tradition dictates. They will be deflected at the checkpoint now that the town's closed. There will be violence.

Staring at his pixelated portrait reminds me of the man who saved me all those years ago. My failure for not doing the same. His parents were detained at the airport for daring to return for their son's funeral. I don't think of his betrayal burning down his father's shop, but the redirection he provided from the death jettisoning from space.

My mind drifts to cardamom coffee outside Ibrahim's stand while Teta – God rest her soul – hassles him over having children with Sundus; the first time he took me to hear Rumi in an underground bar; pizza box gaming on the shag rug floor, sunbathing on rooftop lawn chairs and metaphysical discussions about our place in the universe. Tears stain my cheeks, but I chuckle to myself thinking about what he'd have to say about his funeral: he'd hate every bit of it. Probably scrunch his face like he'd eaten something sour and brush it off as an irony of impossible nightmares. Thousands chant his name in death until their voices are hoarse with reverence and gratitude for a sacrifice he never cared to make in life. A sudden gust of September's first snow knocks me off balance, vertigo sliding the world upside down as I teeter-slip off the ledge. Then two tender, warm hands clasp over mine, pulling me back to balance and everything's alright.

"Gotcha," Diwa declares.

"Oopsie-daisy," croons Cid.

It's a miracle they were able to notice my fall since I'm technically invisible. No, they had to have been fixated, waiting for my next move. Cid releases his grip, but Diwa doesn't let go. Together we watch the funeral procession march as an organic black arrow without end, piercing through urban sprawl to the dehydrated steppe dunes between Ayn Yassin. We stand as a family, bidding silent farewells like prayers to the dead for long enough to shed some burden.

"What's next, Aylul?" Cid asks beside me.

That's right; there's still more to be done. Thousands of Mubarizun split between here and Galilee waiting for my orders and armless millions more who share in our struggle to decolonize this place. Turn the colonizers' dystopia into indigenous sublimity. Those panopticon fields...they're the key. I step forward knowing my dearly beloved hides in golden-spired shadows, finding him without the need for visual confirmation. He's already one step behind me as I walk over to the north-facing side of the skyscraper, unholstering the only pistol I've got left. It's just a matte black .22, small and ineffective at any great distance. Pointing the gun in the direction I know to be true, I command all who cannot possibly hear me: "We regroup in Jenin. Then we'll see about Bayt Lahm."

Yes, I remember now: allies behind enemy lines.

Bountiful option-paths left to explore.

One for every Palestinian alive.

Curl my finger like a question mark around the cold hard trigger and squeeze.

Perhaps my struggle doesn't lead to victory, but I swear upon our ancestors we won't die in defeat.

THAER HUSIEN is a Palestinian educator living on Turtle Island. He is a co-founder of The Posterity Alliance, a Returned Peace Corps Volunteer based in the Republic of Georgia, a Fulbright scholar in Amman, Jordan, and holds an MFA in Creative Writing from American University in Washington D.C. Short stories can be read in *The Written Resistance, Litro Magazine, Sonora Review, Rusted Radishes,* and *Emrys Journal* with selected work in *Poetry Wales*.

TITLES OF INTEREST FROM DARAJA PRESS

Palestine Wail
Yahia Lababidi

Using both poetry and prose, Yahia Lababidi reflects on how we are neither our corrupt governments, nor our compromised media. Rather, we are partners in humanity, members of one human family. Lababidi, an Arab-American writer of Palestinian background, has crafted a poignant collection which serves as a tribute to the Palestinian people, their struggles, and their resilience in the face of ongoing genocide and ethnic cleansing.

ISBN 978-1-998309-11-5 • 116 pages

Oh, Sorry! Rituals of Forgiveness, Crises and Social Struggles in Postmodern Capitalism
Panagiotis Doulos, Edith González Cruz, and Milena Rodríguez Aza

As the world grapples with its many injustices, the performance of public atonement has become increasingly prevalent. Apologies are issued in solemn ceremonies, often acknowledging collective guilt for historical atrocities. Despite the solemnity, there is a growing scepticism surrounding the sincerity of these apologies. The authors unveil the complex interplay between public apologies, social justice and popular mobilisations.

ISBN 978-1-990263-93-4 • 205 pages

Anticapitalist Economy in Rojava: The Contradictions of Revolution in the Kurdish Struggles
Azize Aslan

This book looks at the anti-capitalist economy and the organization of social relations in the context of the revolution and autonomy of Rojava (Kurdistan-Syria). It questions both the limitations and the historical problems of the phenomenon of revolution, and the conflicts and contradictions that emerge in this process.

ISBN 978-1-990263-71-2 • 150 pages

Domains of politics and modes of rule: Political structures of the neocolonial state in Africa
Michael Neocosmos

This is a brief attempt to orient the study of the neocolonial state in Africa through an assessment of the manner in which it rules its people. Imported Western ideas about human rights overlook the huge assumption that the right to have rights is conferred upon citizens. In uncivil societies and 'traditional' societies, that assumed right to rights is not observed by the state.

ISBN 978-1-990263-77-4• 44 pages • Also in French

Order from **darajapress.com**

Daraja Press

www.ingramcontent.com/pod-product-compliance
Lightning Source LLC
Chambersburg PA
CBHW071436260626
47170CB00008B/2739